THE
BRIGHTON
EFFECT

Regina,
Thank you for the
beautiful inspiration!
xoxo, Colleen

...and I mean everything, becomes centered around that...

One simple word: No. Before that, our eight-year marriage was built on one respect...

the darkness loss after loss. The only thing that can set you free is the truth. It's good...

...as sacred as our wedding vows, and maybe even more so because it came after the loss...

...were one hundred percent honest with one another, that would be enough. That would...

...through another miscarriage. Until, finally, that tragic false hope we'd share...

...after how honest, could bridge the hollow gaping hole where my heart used to be. The...

...attempts to reach me. To save me. To restore me to the woman he'd fallen in love with. Eve...

..."And you fall in love with him?" Dr. Paul asked...

...enough. Through the darkness that caused me to...

...I lifted my eyebrows and glared at...

...if I fall in love with a man. I...

...a nasty habit. I count myself...

...respect. He sat back in...

THE
BRIGHTON
EFFECT

THE
Truth About Love
DUET
BOOK TWO

USA TODAY BESTSELLING AUTHOR
C.M. ALBERT

THE BRIGHTON EFFECT
The Truth About Love Duet, Book Two

Copyright © 2021 by C.M. Albert | FlowerWork Press

Genre: Contemporary Romance/Women's Fiction

Cover Design: Cover Me Darling, LLC
Cover Photographer: Regina Wamba
Editing: Dot and Dash, LLC
Proofreading: Lynn Mullan and Denise McGhee
Print Interior Formatting: Alt 19 Creative

DEDICATION

For Heather, my emotional support person during the writing of this duet. You're even better than Canada.

THE BRIGHTON EFFECT
Playlist

These songs spoke to my heart while writing the conclusion of this emotionally difficult duet. I bolded the songs that really make me smile and think of Olivia, Brighton, and Ryan's untraditional love story. Don't even get me started on "Just Breathe."

"Afterglow"—INXS

"Be Your Man"—Rhys Lewis

"Best I Can"—American Authors & Seeb

"Best of You"—Andy Grammer (with Elle King)

"Between Me and the End of the World"—Adam Hambrick

"Bleeding Love"—Leona Lewis

"Chances Are"—Vonda Shepard & Robert Downey Jr.

"Control"—Zoe Wees

"Don't Let Me Go"—Tyler James Bellinger

"Falling"—Harry Styles

"Feeling Good"—Michael Bublé

"Flicker"—Niall Horan

"Here Comes the Sun"—*Glee* Cast

"Holy"—Justin Bieber (Feat. Chance the Rapper)

"Hurting"—Kygo & Rhys Lewis

"I'm Yours"—Alessia Cara

"It's About Us"—Alex & Sierra (Interlude)

"Just Breathe"—Pearl Jam (Live at *Austin City Limits*)

"Let Me Take You There"—Plain White T's

"Love Me Like You Do"—Alex Goot (feat. Sam Tsui)

"Mad at You"—Noah Cyrus & Gallant

"Me Because of You"—HRVY

"Not Over You"—Will Champlin

"Remedy"—Adele

"Ruin"—Shawn Mendes

"Shine On"—Sawyer Fredericks

"Stay with Me"—Sam Smith

"Sun Comes Out"—Decco & Leo Stannard

"Sunshine"—Schuyler Fisk

"Surrender"—Natalie Taylor

"Survivin'"—Bastille

"Tell Your Heart to Beat Again"—Danny Gokey

"Today's Not Yesterday"—Shane Filan

"Up"—Olly Murs (feat. Demi Lovato)

"We'll Be Fine"—Luz (acoustic)

"When I'm With You"—Westlife

"You're Just My Luck"—Adam Ezra

THE BRIGHTON EFFECT

THE
Truth About Love
DUET
BOOK TWO

Brighton Kerrington

Olivia North was everything I always wanted. From the moment I laid eyes on her, I knew nothing would stop me from having her. Not even her husband, Ryan. *In the end, I got her.* Maybe it wasn't all to myself, but Olivia was worth every sacrifice I made to be with her.

What started as a chance to help Olivia heal from the loss of her babies, ended up changing us all forever. Because there wasn't anything Ryan and I wouldn't do to make her happy—including sharing her love. Forgiveness and healing are strange bedfellows, but when it comes to love, *nothing is off limits.*

But everything comes at a cost, and there are key moments that end up changing our lives forever—altering the trajectory we were once on. Before all is said and done, the three of us end up paying more than we ever bargained for. Could our unorthodox love survive the hands of fate, or was it all just *the beginning of the end?*

"sometimes
the first step to
getting it right
is to own the
possibility that
we had it all
wrong before.
that is what will
separate you from
so many.
because we live in
a world where there
is a certain shame
associated with
admitting being
wrong. everyone wants
to be right, if only
in their mind."

—JM STORM

nd I mean everything, becomes centered around radi...

One simple word: No. Before that, our eight-year marriage was built on love, respect...

the darkness loss after loss, the only thing that can set you free is the Truth. It's your...

as sacred as our wedding vows, and maybe even more so because it was all... the lies...

were one hundred percent honest with one another, that would be enough. That would...

...ile—through another miscarriage... Until, finally, that fragile, false hope could shatter...

...tter how honest, could bridge the hollow, gaping hole where my heart used to be? The...

...mpts to reach me. To save me. To restore me to the woman he'd fallen in love with. Even...

..."And you fell in love with him?" Dr. Paul asked. I knew...

...rough. Through the darkness that caused me to...

...I lifted my eyes forward, glanced at...

...if I fell in love with a woman...

...a nasty habit I found myself...

...expect. If you talk it...

...r. Riley O...

...el you from...

...d you your say in th...

...I wanted with my fri...

...taking, in fact...

...and prep...

...a pleas...

...elevate. Th...

...was no...

...or. Here's what I...

PROLOGUE
Olivia

THE FUNNY THING about a lie is that instead of making you feel better, the truth starts to eat at your soul, demanding you to look in the mirror and face it. Until you do, everything in your life, and I mean everything, becomes centered around that lie—and what made you speak the poisonous words to begin with.

For me? It was nothing less than bone-splintering fear.

The lie? One simple word: *no*.

Before that, our eight-year marriage was built on love, respect, and most of all—honesty. When your relationship was born out of grief and slides even deeper into the darkness, loss after loss, the only thing that *can* set you free is the truth. It's your lifeline. Your only ray of hope.

Which was why we'd created a truth pact, Ryan and me. It was as sacred as our wedding vows, and maybe even more so because it came after our first miscarriage. How do you bear such grief? How do you go on? We naively thought if we were one hundred percent honest with one another, that would be enough. That it would solve all our misery, like a crutch through the thick pain and muck of heartbreak.

It worked for a few years—through another miscarriage. Until, finally, that fragile, false hope we'd shackled around honesty shattered after the loss of our daughter. Stillborn. The truth was, no words, no matter how honest, could bridge the hollow, gaping hole where my heart used to be. The loss of Laelynn obliterated me, until I became so broken my husband was desperate in his attempts to reach me. To save me. To restore me to the woman he'd fallen in love with. Even if it meant sharing me. But when Brighton Kerrington entered our lives, the truth suddenly became a whole lot more complicated.

"And you fell in love with him?" Dr. Paul asked, reviewing my chart.

"I did," I answered honestly. Because after that one lie burned hot across my tongue, I knew the only way out was through. Through the darkness that caused me to lie to begin with, betraying myself and all our marriage stood for.

"And do you still love him?"

"I've never stopped."

"How does Ryan feel about this?"

I lifted an eyebrow and glanced at my therapist. "How would Mrs. Paul feel if you fell in love with another woman?"

"Touché," he said. "However, *Mr. O'Brien* would be pretty shocked if I fell in love with any woman, I'd have to say."

His warm smile helped me relax. "Point taken."

"Why don't we stick to *your* marriage?"

I nodded, picking at the cuticle on my thumb. It was a nasty habit I found myself leaning on when I was uncomfortable. Which was often these days.

"Back to my question. How is Ryan handling all of this?"

"As well as you could expect. He went back to work and is finding excuses to be away from home more."

"Do you think he's avoiding you because he knows you lied?"

"I don't think he knows," I said quietly. "Not for sure."

"Really, Olivia? You don't think he suspects at all?"

I thought back to the subtle ways he'd changed over the past few weeks. How distant he felt, and how our lovemaking had gone from the best it'd ever been to almost nonexistent. It felt as if all the progress we'd made over the summer was disappearing just as quickly as the warm temperature that would soon give way to the bitter cold of winter.

"What would be the worst thing that would happen if you told him the truth?"

Dr. Paul was Ryan's idea to begin with. Four months ago, I'd wanted nothing to do with him. Now, he was my biggest ally and staunchest supporter to heal and get things right this time. I'd failed so epically in handling my grief after losing my babies. In fact, I still had work to do there. But we were tackling one fissure at a time. Because you can't address the foundation when the upper floor is in flames.

My job was to put out the fire and pray that the damage wasn't irreparable. Then address the unstable foundation my life was built on these days. I felt like at any moment, everything would come crashing down again, plunging me back into darkness.

"That he would leave me. That he would stop loving me."

The words crawled over my skin like death itself. For all our troubles, Ryan was my soulmate. There were no two ways about it. Losing Ryan would be like cutting off my oxygen. I wouldn't make it long without him. I wouldn't *want* to.

The only problem was—Brighton was now wedged into my heart, too. It was so strong and palpable that I no longer felt complete without them *both*.

I know "they" say you should be complete all on your own. Here's what I say: SCREW THAT SHIT.

Am I a complete and happy human being without a man? Well, sure. But who really wants to be alone? Not me. The only problem? Now that I'd felt the warmth of Brighton being in my life, it was impossible not to want them both. That's not something I've been able to share in those exact words with Ryan. Partly because he's been stuffing down his own pain for so long that I was afraid one more "truth" might send him overboard. But mostly it was because I highly doubted his idea of happiness involved having an open marriage. The term itself left an icky taste in my mouth, but at the end of the day, that's all it would boil down to. And Ryan deserved better.

Brighton did, too.

"You need to tell him the truth, Olivia. Your real healing won't begin until you do. Though, I have to say, I'm proud of how much you've opened up since we first started working together."

"Yeah, sorry about that. I was in a place."

"Oh, I remember," he said and chuckled. "While I don't agree with Ryan's methodologies, you do seem happier and more capable of handling whatever comes your way. Including telling Ryan the truth and dealing with the fallout from that. You're stronger than you give yourself credit for."

Was I? I wish I had the confidence in myself that Dr. Paul now had. They say the truth shall set you free. I guess we were about to find out.

nd I mean everything, becomes centered around that one...

One simple word: No. Before that, our eight-year marriage was built on two...

the darkness loss after loss. The only thing that can set you free is the truth. It's...

as sacred as our wedding vows, and maybe even more so because it came after the loss...

were one hundred percent honest with one another, that would be enough. That would...

ile—through another miscarriage. Until, finally, that fragile...hope we'd sh...

atter how honest, could bridge the hollow gaping hole where my heart used to be. T...

mpts to reach me. To save me. To restore me to the woman he'd fallen in love with. Even...

...ted. And you fell in love with him? Dr. Paul ask...

...rough. Through the darkness that caused me to c...

...I lifted an eyebrow and glanced at...

...if I fell in love with a woman I...

...nasty half I turned myself...

...spect. He would be to be...

...you... Katie B...

...and you breathe...

...you gave way to th...

...it seemed with my to...

...baby, so he had...

...and pro...

...us, pleas...

...ele into. Th...

...was now...

...on. Here's what I...

CHAPTER ONE

Olivia

I T WAS HARD to heal when I was spending most of my days finishing a job with the man I needed just as badly as my husband. It was torture for us both. I'd been upfront with Brighton about my lie, which only made me feel that much worse about my betrayal with Ryan. But I didn't want him to accidentally hear from Brighton that we'd slept together alone—without him.

The fight we'd had was no excuse, nor was the way Ryan yelled at me or slammed his hand against the door where I stood, shattering the tiny glass windowpane. He wasn't generally a physical man, and I was confident he would never hurt me. But these were not normal circumstances, and no one expected the jealousy that came with sharing me. You would've thought we'd have seen that one coming, but Ryan was a confident man by nature. Then again, he'd never had to share any part of me before Brighton.

The intimacy he'd handled well. It's when I fell in love that things got tricky.

"Almost done?" Brighton asked, rounding the corner. His blond hair was getting a little longer on top, and he had to run his hand through it to get it out of his eyes.

There was just something about the man—the way he filled a room the moment he entered, commanding attention. It was like trying not to look directly at the sun when someone says, "Look how beautiful that sunset is!" It's damn near impossible. Not only had I looked at the sun, but I'd reached for it, trying to hold the whole damn thing in my arms before it slipped away.

I tucked the last napkin under the place setting and stood back. "I think so. I just have a few more pieces to unload and a mirror to hang in the living room that I couldn't do alone. Do you have a minute to help?"

"Sure," he said, wiping his forehead with his mint-green T-shirt.

I snuck a quick glance, longing for a part of him I had no business having anymore. But you can hardly share every part of your body, heart, and soul with another human being and just expect it to go away overnight. No more could I purge Brighton from my system than the babies I'd miscarried. I felt lost and hollow without each of them.

I focused on the task at hand, holding the ladder as Brighton checked the markings with his level, then screwed the anchors into the wall. I remembered the feel of every hard plane of his body, and my insides reacted when his calf flexed from the strain of standing on the ladder and positioning the heavy mirror into place. Brighton was raw, sexual power built from hard work on a jobsite every day—and my body still responded every time we were close.

But it was more than that.

I missed everything about him. Our soul-baring, late-night talks in the yard. The fun evenings we shared with Ryan by the firepit. Watching the easy way they played basketball, more like best friends in a bromance than two men craving the same woman. How easily he'd fallen into step with our lives this past summer—bringing out the playful side we'd somehow lost over the past few years.

But every day since the lie, Ryan found excuses to distance himself from the jobsite and from his friend. Then it turned into longer days at the university once he'd gone back, finding every reason under the sun not to be home alone with me.

Maybe he did know. My stomach revolted at the thought of telling Ryan later.

"Excuse me," I said, grateful that Brighton was done and off the ladder already. I ran to the downstairs bathroom and threw up my lunch.

Brighton knocked at the door not even two minutes later. I was too weak to answer. I knew I wasn't taking good enough care of myself. My stress was causing me to lose weight I couldn't spare to part with.

"Liv?" His voice was laced with compassion I didn't deserve. When I didn't answer, he opened the door. "What happened?"

I moaned as I rested my cheek against the cool porcelain. "I can't," I said before tears started pooling.

"Are you going to get sick again? Do I need to call Ryan?"

"No!" I said a little too forcefully. I didn't even know if he was home from work yet.

"What's going on?" He bent over and scooped me into his arms as if I weighed nothing. He carried me to the conversation nook off the kitchen and set me down gently onto the large, L-shaped couch. Then he went into the kitchen, where I could hear him rummaging around in the refrigerator. A few minutes later, he sat down next to me, casually wrapping his arm across the back of the sofa as he handed me a bottle of water.

"Are you sick?"

I shook my head. "It's stress. The same thing used to happen to me in high school. Dr. Paul thinks it's because I need to tell Ryan about—well, you know."

"You're ready to do that?" He looked relieved. I hated that I'd ever asked him to hold the lie with me.

"I'll never be ready."

He hugged me closer with the arm that was on the back of the couch. "Ryan loves you more than anything. There's no way he won't forgive you. It was one time."

"It's not the sex that's going to destroy him."

"Right. The truth pact."

"He will never trust me again," I sobbed. I couldn't even blame him because I'd done the one thing we vowed never to do. My body shook against Brighton's, and shame heated my cheeks. Because, even while grieving my epic betrayal, I still wanted nothing more than to curl into this man. Have him love away my pain again.

"Then he'd be a fool," Brighton said. "You guys have been through so much together. You've been tested more than a couple should be. I was worried that throwing me into the mix was just going to make things harder. He was so sure it would be what you needed."

"And it was," I said, sitting up and looking into his pale green eyes. "It was exactly what I needed to start feeling alive again. You have no idea how empty I felt before I met you."

I finally took a sip from the water bottle, the cold liquid burning my raw throat. "I feel so selfish for saying that, especially because of what it cost you. And Ryan."

"I'm glad I could be there for you, Olivia. But we always knew there was going to be an expiration date on what we had. The open house is Friday. Ryan's made it clear that the three of us are over. And I need to get back to my life in Watertown. There's no room left for me here."

That only made me cry harder. I'd gotten so spoiled over the summer, getting to see him and Ryan nearly every day. To have him just disappear—I wasn't sure my heart could handle the absolute grief his absence would bring. Not on top of everything else.

"What if it didn't have to end? What if you didn't have to walk away from this?"

"Liv—there's no way Ryan would ever consider something like that. I can't let my heart go there. Besides, you need to focus on making things right with him now that you're in therapy. Just promise me something?"

"Anything," I said quietly. "It's the least I can do."

"Talk to him before the house sells. I'll stay until it does. If you need me for anything after you talk to him, I'm just a yard away. I mean it," he said, his eyes darkening. It was because of the fight that'd happened with Ryan the afternoon I made love to Brighton alone. Here in this house. It was Brighton who listened to me that day. Comforted me. Then he'd loved away any doubts I had left about whether I could really let him go. And yet, I wasn't brave enough to do anything about it.

I nodded. I didn't want Brighton to worry about me. I didn't have a right to that part of his heart. But I had no clue how to say goodbye to the man who had changed our lives and opened my heart after feeling dead inside for so long.

"Promise me something, too?"

"Anything. It's the least I can do."

I ached to reach out and touch those dimples. Run my hand through his thick, blond hair. Feel his full lips on mine one last time. But that isn't what I asked from him. "Promise you won't leave without saying goodbye?"

This time, he gathered me into both arms and held on tight. I sank against him, drowning under his scent and the comfort of being close to him again after so many weeks.

"I had a feeling this is where I'd find you," I heard from the kitchen entrance.

My body stiffened as I pulled away from Brighton and turned. I met my husband's accusing eyes. "We were finishing the staging today, Ryan. This isn't what you think it is."

"Where have I heard that before?" The death stare he shot Brighton was full of silent accusations. Whole stories were passed between them in that one, intense gaze.

When he looked back at me, his brows furrowed in frustration. I knew that look; I'd screwed something up. "I see you were too busy to remember the alumni fundraiser tonight. I have to leave in twenty minutes, and you're supposed to be dressed in cocktail attire by now."

He ran his eyes over my body, and it felt as if he was reading every sordid secret it held. "Clearly you won't be ready in time."

"I can be ready. Just give me fifteen minutes." I stood, putting some distance between Brighton and me. "Can I finish up the last items tomorrow?"

He was still glaring at Ryan, and I hated seeing anything but affection pass between them. But I knew what it was like to let fear and pain turn into anger. Ryan and I had been living in that limbo for years before Brighton moved into his Uncle Isaiah's house at the beginning of the summer to renovate it.

"Sure, Liv," he said, purposefully using Ryan's pet name for me. There was a time not that long ago when Ryan told him he'd earned the right to call me that. I highly doubted that intimate offer was still on the table after all we'd been through.

I just wanted to go home and take a hot, fast shower—not manage a pissing contest between two testosterone-fueled men.

"When does the house go on the market?" Ryan asked, straightening the cuffs on his tuxedo. He was devastatingly handsome in it, the black a dashing compliment to his dark good looks and closely shaved beard.

"I was just telling Liv that the open house is on Friday. I hope you'll both still come."

"Wouldn't miss it. Would we, *Liv*?" He held his hand out for me, the first time in weeks he'd instigated touch. "Coming?"

I let him lead me from the kitchen and across the yards to our perfect house, with the white picket fence and our sweet puppy, Stitch, who was jumping excitedly at the gate, waiting for our return. I glanced back at the Kerrington estate one last time before following Ryan inside. Brighton was standing at the door, his body just a shadow against the light that surrounded him.

d I mean everything, becomes centered around that on...

One simple word: No. Before that, our eight-year marriage was built on love, respect...

the darkness, loss after loss. The only thing that can set you free is the truth. It's...

s sacred as our wedding vows, and maybe even more so because it came after the loss...

re one hundred percent honest with one another, that would be enough. That would...

le—through another miscarriage. Until, finally, that fragile false hope and that...

tter how honest, could bridge the hollow gaping hole where my heart used to be. The...

pts to reach me. To save me. To restore me to the woman he'd fallen in love with. Even...

...ted. "And you fell in love with him?" Dr. Paul ask...

...through. Through the darkness that carried me to the...

...I drifted on my grief's end and grasped at...

...if he fell in love with a woman I...

...nursing babe. I burst myself...

...much. It wasn't back then with...

...sure. "Really, Beth...

...your mouth...

...did you give way to the...

...and sagged nothing to...

...baby. In fact, I...

...and jump...

...vulnerate. That...

...her was not...

...Here's what I sar...

CHAPTER TWO

Ryan

I KNEW EXACTLY WHERE Olivia was the moment I got home and didn't find her getting ready. She'd known about the fundraiser for a year because it was always on the same day. Disappointment flooded through me, but if there was one thing I'd learned over the years, it was that Olivia couldn't be controlled—not that I had any desire to clip her wings. She was always the wild to my holy, as she liked to say. Though, with the anger and sadness that lived inside me these days, I didn't feel like the holy part of any equation.

After walking into Kerrington's house and finding them alone there—with my *wife* in his arms no less—it was a slap in the face as far as I was concerned. I was still stewing when, fifteen minutes later, Olivia was dressed and ready to go. That alone spoke volumes about how far we'd come. Back in May, she wouldn't have had the energy or desire to come to an event like this—no matter how important it was for my career. At least she was trying. But I wasn't ready to forgive her. I could hardly look at her without images of her and Brighton being alone together haunting every crevice of my mind.

The fundraiser turned out being as droll and boring as ever, but the appetizers were impeccable, and everyone who needed to see me there did. Olivia even offered to drive us home so I could have a few beers. We were ready to leave when Kimber Shanahan and her husband stopped us.

"Ryan!" she said, air-kissing me on both cheeks.

Someone had been dipping into too much free champagne.

"Olivia," she said curtly before turning back to me. "We're so glad to have you back after your summer off. Did you get everything you wanted accomplished?"

Everyone knew why I'd taken the time off. After burying our daughter last November, Liv and I desperately needed the time alone to grieve and heal. But Kimber treated it as if we'd been vacationing in the Poconos. I looked at my wife, thinking not of our progress, but of Kerrington.

"I don't know, hon. Did we?"

I wished I could take back my assholish response the moment Liv's face paled, but I was hurting. Seeing her and Kerrington comforting each other today hadn't helped.

"It was exactly what we needed," she said with a tight smile. "Now, if you'll excuse us. We were just heading home. It's been a long day."

"Oh, I bet!" Kimber said. She turned to her husband. "Olivia has been working intimately with a contractor to flip that old, green house over on West Liberty this summer."

"That must've been quite the job overhauling that old dump," he said, pulling a cigar from the inside pocket of his tuxedo.

"It's quite spectacular, actually. And it's gray now," Olivia said calmly.

"Roycroft Pewter," I retorted. She knew I didn't give two shits about paint colors. That was her and Kerrington's "thing." When I thought about the dark plum paint they'd used for his front door—and his obsession with tulips of the same shade for my wife—anger burned beneath the surface of my skin, making my heart rate soar.

"I hear the open house is Friday," Kimber said, glancing coyly from under thick, black lashes, despite her husband being *right there*. "Maybe we'll swing by and check it out. We've been looking for a bigger place."

Oh, hell no. The only thing worse than having my wife's lover living beside us would be to have Kimber and her weaselly husband there instead. I'd buy the damn thing myself before letting that happen.

Olivia's face was still pale as we said our goodbyes, but she never said a word as we drove away. The university was close to our house in the city, so it was an uncomfortable but short ride home. The first thing she did was go straight upstairs and strip out of her silver, beaded Mac Duggal, dropping the lacy ballgown to the floor like it was an old pair of dirty jeans. After she padded to the shower, I picked up the dress and hung it back in her closet. Then I plopped onto our bed, pinching the bridge of my nose.

I knew Liv was still hurting. I wasn't a complete bastard. My heart ached for how hard it must've been to get through an evening like this, even after all her progress this summer. We hadn't been around the entire faculty since Laelynn died, so people naturally wanted to offer their condolences. I watched as the light she'd worn to the event slowly faded from her eyes until all that was left to carry her up our creaky stairs when we returned home was an empty shell wrapped in despair.

When she got like this, there was no letting me in. So, I fixed myself a drink and sat on the back patio while Stitch relieved himself, then pounced on small frogs in the cool evening air. The plum-colored tulips had long since surrendered, but Olivia had spent an entire weekend replacing them with pompon dahlias of the same color. My backyard still screamed of Kerrington's presence. Even though he was no longer living under our roof, his imprint was everywhere. I would never understand why, but for some reason, it caused an ache deep in my chest. I couldn't pass by his bedroom and not remember the freedom and release we all shared there. I knew it would hurt, but I headed there now, not knowing exactly what I was looking for or needing. He'd been my friend first. Even though he was just a yard away, it felt as if he'd been torn from my life completely, the distance was so vast between us now. It would take just one word from me to tamp the tension between us so we could be friends again. But until I knew for sure whether Liv was lying to me—and I felt in my bones that she was—that wasn't going to happen.

Maybe I needed to have a conversation with him instead of Olivia. If she wasn't ready to tell me the truth, maybe he would—man to man.

I looked around the large, first-floor guestroom and immediately felt a visceral kick to my gut, my chest tightening. This is where we'd unraveled Olivia's grief, loving her until she was so raw and vulnerable again, she had nowhere left to hide. God, I'd been stupid to think we could walk away from something like that with no repercussions. As much as

I hated to admit it, the jerk was still in my heart. How could he not be in Liv's, too?

I was on my way out the door when a piece of paper caught my eye from the top of the desk. I picked it up and unfolded it, not sure if I was going to like what I saw. The last time something like this happened, I'd found proof of my wife's feelings as she bled her love all over the rendering that she'd sketched of him. There wasn't a doubt in my mind that she loved him then—and she confirmed it when I confronted her. Because that's what we did. We told the truth.

That is, until she decided not to. Until she chose to deliberately lie straight to my face when I asked her point-blank if she'd fucked him when I wasn't there.

No.

Funny how one simple word could decimate a marriage so wholly, so quickly. I saw the way the guilt ate at her since then. Knew she was finally talking to her therapist. I hoped one day she'd start talking to me again, too. Because this in-between business was torture.

I looked down at the paper and realized the letter was addressed to me.

Ryan,

> *We've been through some stuff, haven't we? Remember when you sat me down at the Crown and Feather and asked me to help you? What was the one thing we promised? Honesty above all else. I'm sorry if I ended up hurting you. I never meant to. Just like I never meant to fall in love with Olivia. You have to believe me.*

On days when you're mad at me, or at her, just remember that we weren't the ones who started this. But even now, I don't regret it. Because you were right.

When Olivia's happy, there is nothing more beautiful in the world. I will always love her, just as I will you. (As a friend, dude, so relax.) As funny as it sounds, this summer was the happiest I've ever been. I don't want to fight anymore. I don't want you to hate me, either. I know it hurts to see me around, and I wish I could change that. I guess it'll just take time. I hope someday I can have you both in my life again, somehow. For now, go easy on her. She's trying, and we all made mistakes.

She loves you more than anything in the world. You know that, so don't push her away. Forgive her. Keep being the rock she needs. She's come a long way since I first met her. You have, too. Though you could stand to lose the scowl. (Just sayin'.)

I'll leave you with my favorite quote from a remarkable human named Stephanie Johnson. "At all times, people are doing one of two things. They're either showing love, or they're crying out for it."

Get clear which you're doing, what you need from Olivia, and what she needs from you. Then be there for each other. And love, damn it.

If our kids have taught us anything, it's that life is too fucking short. Don't waste another day of it holding on to anger.

Take care,
Brighton

I didn't even realize the tears were falling until one splashed onto his note and smeared the blue ink. I made my way upstairs because I knew exactly what Liv was doing tonight. She was crying out.

And somewhere along the way, I'd forgotten how to listen.

...I mean everything, becomes centered around that one

One simple word: No. Before that, our eight-year marriage was built on love, respect...

...the darkness, loss after loss, the only thing that can set you free is the truth. It's you...

...sacred as our wedding vows, and maybe even more so because it came after the loss...

...were one hundred percent honest with one another, that would be enough. That would...

...—through another miscarriage. Until, finally, that fragile, false hope used to...

...matter how honest, could bridge the hollow, gaping hole where my heart used to be. T...

...attempts to reach me. To save me. To restore me to the woman he'd fallen in love with. Even...

..."And you fell in love with him?" Dr. Paul asked...

...through. Through the darkness that caused me to lie...

...I lifted an eyebrow and glanced at...

...of I fell in love with a woman I...

...nasty habit, I went...

...He sat back in...

...Kathy. Dr...

...all gone from the...

...you got used to the...

...wanted nothing to...

...In fact...

...and perh...

...plung...

...Then...

...was now...

...Here's what I sa...

CHAPTER THREE
Olivia

I NEVER HEARD RYAN enter the bathroom. The glass shower walls were fogged all around me, and I was sitting on the tiled floor, my head against the wall, as hot water streamed over me, scalding away all the hurt and pain I was releasing. I was clutching my stomach, as I often did, remembering the feel of my babies inside of me. I could no longer tell the difference between my tears and the water streaming over the long tendrils of my hair, now plastered to my face and chest.

"Jesus, Liv."

Ryan stepped inside the shower in his tuxedo and sat on the floor with me, pulling me into his arms. Then he did what I'd been needing for weeks. He held me. He rocked me while I cried in his arms. He kissed the top of my head. He told me we would be okay.

When he lifted my chin, his eyes stripped me more naked than my body already was. I clutched his white dress shirt in my hands as I searched his familiar brown eyes. What happened to us? Where did we go so horribly wrong?

Torrents of tears freely fell down my cheeks as I whispered the dark words of truth holding my heart hostage. "Ryan, I need to tell you something."

"Livy," he said slowly, his voice breaking, "we don't have to do this right now. I know tonight was hard enough. I'm sorry I was such an ass instead of helping you through it."

"I have to," I said, my eyes pleading with his. "It's breaking me, Ryan. If I don't, there won't be anything left of me—of the Olivia you fell in love with."

He brushed my lips softly, his beard dragging across the delicate skin of my cheek as he pulled me against his body, holding on for dear life. His hand cupped the back of my head as the water streamed hot over us. Ryan's crisp tuxedo shirt was now soggy beneath my fingertips. I needed to remember every moment, because there would always be a before and after from this devastation. And I wanted to remember the feeling of my husband holding me, loving me still.

I whispered quietly in his ear, so softly I wasn't sure he would hear me. "I'm sorry, Ry. I'm so sorry."

His body racked against mine, and I knew I'd broken him.

I wrapped my arms around the barrel of his chest, sinking farther into him. "When you asked me if I'd slept with him—"

"Don't," he begged. "It's been a long night."

"I need you to know."

"Do you really think I don't?" he rasped. He pulled back so I could see the tears pooling in his eyes. Then he ran his hand over the front of my face, his fingertips resting on my lips.

"You asked me for the truth, so I need to give it to you. I swear to god, I've never lied to you before. Not once in our marriage."

"But you did that day, didn't you?"

I nodded, my breathing getting shallower with each inhalation. "We were alone together. Without you," I cried out, my voice breaking. "Oh, god. I'm so sorry, Ryan."

My body shook as I descended into a full anxiety attack. My body heaved, as if trying desperately to corral my splintered heart.

Ryan turned me around, so my back was to his chest. He wrapped me in his arms and rested his chin on my shoulder. "Take a deep breath, Livy," he said, his voice thick with the emotion he wasn't letting himself unpack yet so he could focus on me.

"The worst is behind us. Find something to focus on. Tell me what you see."

He was helping me ground, to come down from my panic attack. "The loofah," I said, my chest rising and falling as I took short, quick gasps of air.

"What do you smell?"

"You," I said, resting my head against the hard muscles of his chest as I fought to stay present.

"What do you feel?"

"The wet fabric of your dress shirt against my skin."

"What do you hear?"

"The water running through our old pipes. Your breath against my ear."

He kissed it then, and the tenderness nearly broke me. I whimpered, but my breath was evening out. He put his fingers on my chin and turned my head so he could find my lips with his warm, sensual mouth.

His love crashed over me, and I turned into him. Into his kiss.

"What do you taste?"

"You," I said. "Your love."

He lifted me in his arms, turning off the water before leaving the shower, dripping wet. He grabbed one of our large, monogrammed towels and carried me to our bed. He stood me up, wrapping the gigantic body towel around me as he dried my skin. When I climbed into bed, he tucked the comforter around me and ran his hand over my wet hair, glancing at me with a love I was sure I didn't deserve.

"I'm going to change, then get in bed with you. Is that okay?"

I nodded. "Sorry about your tux."

"It's just clothes, Liv."

Ryan shrugged out of his dress shirt on his way to the bathroom. The muscles in his back flexed as he yanked the wet material from his skin. I longed to reach out and touch every ridge of his body, to familiarize myself with it again.

He lowered his pants over the round curve of his backside, strong and muscular from working out. Even at forty, his body was a work of art. I hated that I'd shut him down so many times over the past few years, at times turning our intimacy into a baby-making endeavor instead of a union of love.

When Ryan finally crawled into bed, he slid his large SU T-shirt over my head. I sunk back against the pillow, my heart ravaged from my admission. He still hadn't addressed it, but I had to make sure we were going to be okay. That we could somehow get through this.

"Talk to me," I said.

"I wish you'd just told me the truth that day." He stared up at our ceiling as if invisible answers were written there. "Why didn't you?"

He wouldn't look at me, his jaw set hard as he waited for an answer.

"I don't know. I was so upset and ashamed, and you were mad. Things were so tense between us after our fight. I just needed time to think. To process everything. I should've said that, but you kept pushing for an answer I wasn't ready to give. I was scared, I guess. So, I panicked. It was stupid, but I couldn't answer truthfully when I was still in shock myself."

"Did you know you were going to sleep with him when you went over there that day?"

"No," I answered.

"Have you always wanted to sleep with him alone? Without me?"

"No!" I cried out truthfully.

"I know this isn't going to make sense to you, Ry. I didn't mean to fall in love with him, but I did. I'm sorrier than you can ever know for that. But it was harder than you can imagine—to open my heart like that again. Let someone *into* my body that wasn't you, or one of our babies. You asked me to be emotionally raw and vulnerable with you and Brighton. There was no way to do that with a closed heart."

"I'm the first to admit I made a lot of mistakes, too, Liv. But I would *never* lie to you. I wish I could say it didn't hurt so fucking bad. But it does. It gutted me. Then you just walked away. It felt like everything was over. That we were over."

"Ryan, please. No."

"How can I ever trust you again? Trust in what we have?"

"Because even though I love him, I don't love him *more* than you. We have a history that Brighton and I will never have."

"But what if he's meant to be your future? Wouldn't that be easier? Less complicated? You could start fresh with him—if that's what you really wanted."

"I don't!" I insisted.

"Then what? Why did you have to sleep with him?"

I bit my lip, remembering back to that day. It was etched into my heart every bit as real as the letter A that woman had to wear in Ryan's book. "I was so angry with you," I admitted, my breath small with shame.

"For how you acted during our fight. For blowing up at me and hitting the damn door—breaking the glass like that. I was sad and emotionally drained. Brighton was there for me as a friend. We mostly talked, but then, I don't know. I guess I *had* to figure out if it was Brighton I wanted, or if I just missed the three of us being together. I had to know what the intimacy meant for myself."

"Do you want to leave me for him?"

"No."

"*What* then, Liv? What are we supposed to do now?"

"I don't know."

"Have you slept with him since then?"

"No," I promised, shaking my head. "That's the god's honest truth. I will never, ever lie to you again, Ryan."

"I wish I could believe you, but that's going to take some time."

I nodded, wishing he would look at me.

When he finally turned to face me, I couldn't bear the pain reflected at me. He was holding so much inside. I wanted to curl up in a ball and die. I'd done that to him.

"If I could take it back, I would. Sleeping with him alone. Lying. All of it. That's not me. You know me."

"I thought I did."

"You *do*. This isn't fair. I never would have slept with him to begin with! *You* pushed the issue, Ryan. Even though we both had reservations."

"But it didn't stop you, did it?" he said ruthlessly. "Admit it, Liv. You wanted him all along."

I took a deep breath, willing my emotions not to spin out into anxiety all over again.

"You once told me that sex wasn't really about the sex. I had no idea what that even meant then. But I think I do now. My heart was broken for so long because of our miscarriages, and then losing Laelynn changed everything. I couldn't feel *anything* for the longest time. I didn't want to live, really. Not without them. But you didn't give up on me. The intimacy that we felt with Brighton was an opening for us to love again, harder this time. To heal all the pain we'd held inside for so long. It's hard to go through something like that with someone and *not* fall. To not feel. It was about so much more than just our bodies, Ryan, and you know that."

"Yeah, but what you two did—that was *only* about your bodies. And your own selfish needs. Did you once stop to think about me? Think about how it would gut me to know he was inside of you without me? One minute I think I understand how it could've happened. The next, I'm fucking wrecked by it."

"You're right. It was selfish. I don't have any excuse to justify what happened. But it wasn't just about our bodies. Maybe I wish it would've been, because then it wouldn't be as complicated as it is now."

"It's complicated, all right." He put his arm over his eyes and lay back again. He was so close, yet his heart was as distant as it'd ever been. I didn't know how to make it right.

"Maybe we could see a couple's therapist?"

"And say what, Liv? Are you going to talk about our three-some? You think a shrink has a playbook for how to deal with the repercussions of having an open marriage?"

"I do, actually. Dr. Paul has helped me a lot these past few weeks. Maybe we could see a different therapist and work on our communication. Especially because of what happened. We haven't really processed everything. Don't you miss him? At all?"

Ryan took a sharp inhalation but stayed quiet for the longest time. I didn't think he was going to answer me, but then the faintest "yes" came.

"He misses you, too," I said quietly. "He misses *us*. We promised him it wouldn't change anything, but that's exactly what happened. And he's getting the short end of the stick because it's easy to blame everything on him. To shut him out. But it's not his fault. We asked him for this, Ryan. And just so you know, he doesn't know what to do with any of his feelings either. And with him getting ready to sell the house . . . it's just putting more stress on the situation because he feels like he's about to lose us completely. And he loves us both, Ryan."

"What does that even mean? What am I supposed to do with all that?"

"I don't know."

"Do you wish the three of us were still sleeping together?"

"Maybe it's best not to go down that path tonight. It's been a long day and we're both tired. Can we talk about that tomorrow?"

For once, he nodded instead of pushed. Then he wrapped me in his arms and kissed the top of my head. "I figured out how to share your body once, Liv. I don't know if I can figure out how to share your heart."

Within a few minutes, Ryan was asleep, and I lay staring at the ceiling, more confused than ever. This summer we'd opened Pandora's box but had no clue what to do about it now. Did we shove everything back inside and act like it never happened? Try to hide the damn box, and go on with our lives? Or keep it wide open, giving in to a pleasure that both terrified and completed us all at once?

I didn't have an answer. But all night long, my body chose the last option over and over again. I woke up the next morning sad to find it was all just a dream.

d I mean everything, becomes centered around that

One simple word: No. Before that, our eight-year marriage was built on our respect

the darkness loss after loss. the only thing that can set you free is the truth. It's

s sacred as our wedding vows, and maybe even more so because it came after the loss

ere one hundred percent honest with one another. That would be enough. That would

be—through another miscarriage. Until, finally, that fragile false hope would shat

tter how honest, could bridge the hollow, gaping hole where my heart used to be.

pts to reach me. To save me. To restore me to the woman hed fallen in love with. Even

"And you fell in love with him? Dr. Paul asked

rough. Through the darkness that caused me to

I lifted an eyebrow and glanced

if I fell in love with a woman I

nasty habit I found myself

expect. He sat back to

Really. Di

you

you go

CHAPTER FOUR
Brighton

THE REST OF the week was a blur. Olivia finished staging the house and the backyard patio. It was one of the most beautiful homes I'd ever created, and I wasn't ready to let it go. Maybe that was because it wasn't just my creation this time. It was the marriage of mine and Olivia's creativity on every wall, in every room, and in every detail. And it all worked together effortlessly—kind of like us.

It was Friday morning, and I was reviewing paperwork in the kitchen, getting ready for the open house. I was hopeful we'd have an offer over the weekend. After that, I had no clue what I was going to do. I had other projects on the horizon, but I longed for a break to process everything that happened this summer. Though, deep inside, I knew there was no break long enough to purge Olivia and Ryan from my system.

"The house looks amazing."

I turned, surprised to see Ryan standing there.

"Thanks," I said, leaning back to stretch.

"Can we talk?" he asked.

"Sure. Here?"

"Maybe out back?"

We headed to the backyard, sitting under the pergola. The hopeful vines were already climbing its sides, eager to see which would reach the top first. I wished I were going to be around long enough to find out.

"Look, I'm just gonna cut to the chase, okay? I figure we've been through too much to sit here and BS each other."

That was an understatement. "I'd expect nothing less."

He nodded but didn't rush right into whatever was eating at him. I'd give him the space to work out whatever he needed to get off his chest.

"Liv and I talked."

Oh. Shit.

The air was still and quiet around us. Ryan gripped the arm of his chair.

"Give me one reason not to deck you, Kerrington."

"You have every right to."

He looked at me, surprised.

"What? You're not wrong. I deserve it," I said.

"I asked just one thing of you."

"I know. I'm sorry, Ryan."

"Are you, though?"

I was quiet. Did I regret sleeping with Olivia? No. I didn't. As much of a dick as that made me, I'd never regret being with her. "I'm sorry it hurt you."

"At least we're starting to be honest."

"Look, I know it sounds contrite, but I don't want our friendship to end just because Liv and I fucked up."

"Interesting choice of words."

"God! You know what I mean."

"Where *did* you fuck her?"

"I'm not—"

"If you want me to forgive you, I have to know, Kerrington. I don't want any more goddamn secrets between any of us."

I ran a hand over my face and sighed. "Fine. It was in the library."

"In your house or mine?"

"Mine."

Ryan nodded. "Show me."

"What? No. You already know what happened. It's just a room."

"It's not just a room, Kerrington. It's where Olivia broke her vows to me."

"That's not fair."

"You're talking to *me* about fair?" he grunted. "So much for bro code."

"Really, Ryan? This isn't college."

"I asked you not to sleep with her!"

"That was before you shared her with me," I said quietly.

"Get up," he growled.

I stood, squaring off with him. If he needed to hit me to feel better, so be it.

"Show me the goddamn room."

"I don't think you really want to see where—"

"You screwed my wife behind my back?"

I clenched my jaw, crossing my arms over my chest. "What does this prove? What good will it do to know?"

"I went to your library that day, Kerrington! You weren't there. So, where the fuck were you?" he yelled. He shoved my chest, but not hard enough to move my body.

"Fine. Come on."

I was done with this. I had an open house to get ready for. I led him up to the library, then opened the secret door. Ryan stood there with his arms crossed, his jaw clenched tight as I revealed the hidden room.

"You brought her up here so you could screw in private? You sure this wasn't planned out all along?"

"No, you asshole. She was crying after *your* fight. You scared the shit out of her, losing control like that. She was shaken. So, I was trying to distract her—"

"Yeah, I bet."

"By showing her the book I was holding aside for you, jerk."

I walked into the room, my body aching for Olivia all over again. I gripped the stairs as I searched for the book. I finally found where Olivia had stashed it on one of the shelves. I hadn't been back since that afternoon, and the visceral memory of being inside her flooded over me, dropping me to my knees emotionally. I could still smell a faint trace of her citrus perfume and hoped Ryan didn't come any closer.

I stepped out of the small room and shoved the book at Ryan. "My uncle had a lot of first-edition books. This was my favorite in high school. I thought you might've read it, too."

He took *The Razor's Edge* from my hands—I gave him no choice, slamming it against his chest.

"So, you went from grabbing a book for me to sliding inside my wife? How exactly does that happen?"

I pushed past Ryan and headed to the sofa across from the fireplace. He sat on the arm of one of the chairs and stared at me.

"Could you stop being so crude? It's Olivia. I know you're pissed at me, and you have every right to be. I can't justify what happened. But she's your wife. So, stop acting like it's anything but the most important woman in your life. Treat her with the respect she deserves. You want to lash out at me? Fine. Take your best shot. But leave her out of this."

"It takes two. Her guilt is written all over this."

"She's not a cheater, Ryan."

We were quiet for a few minutes, and it was me who finally broke the silence. "I never had a brother, okay? I have four sisters. I have a lot of friends I see every day at work. But the last time I had a real friend was in college." I shoved my hand through my hair, frustrated and uncomfortable. "You and I were friends first. We talked about a lot of personal shit while working on this house together, well before Olivia and I even met. Then we shared something so personal and intimate—something I couldn't have done with anyone else. I don't want this to mess everything up. It's not just about Olivia. I don't want to lose your friendship either, you know."

"Maybe you should've thought of that before sleeping with her behind my back."

"Can't you forgive me?" I asked. "Or is this what it's always going to come to between us now?"

Ryan ran a hand over the book that was on his lap. "Salvation doesn't come easy, Kerrington."

"No. It doesn't."

"How am I supposed to get over the fact that you slept with my wife?" he asked, pinning me with his dark eyes.

"I'd already slept with her, Ryan," I quietly reminded him.

"With me!" he said, exasperated.

"I knew it was a bad idea. I told you it was."

"Yeah, but you also promised you'd distance yourself if feelings got involved. You lied. You stuck around. Kept taking more. Until it wasn't enough, and you just had to have her for yourself. Did you think she'd leave me for you? Is that what you were hoping?"

I stood up, pissed now. "Screw you. If you want to talk without being an asshole, let me know. I have an open house to get ready for. Hopefully, after this weekend, I'll be out of your hair for good."

I turned and stormed from the library, leaving my good friend sitting there, wrestling with the truth of our betrayal, not even twenty feet from where it happened.

I'd messed up. There was no denying that. But the truth was, I still wanted Olivia. Nothing could ever make me stop wanting her. Not even seeing Ryan breaking as I walked down the stairs.

Maybe it was me who was the asshole, after all.

CHAPTER FIVE

Olivia

"WE REALLY DON'T need to go."

I'm not sure if that was more for me or Ryan. He said he was going to talk to Brighton earlier and came back looking frustrated and sad. He'd changed into athletic clothes and went to the garage to work out, so I'd given him the space he seemed to need more of these days.

Now, we were getting ready for the open house. Cars were already arriving, and the party was coming to life. The house looked beautiful at night with outside lights illuminating the front entrance and abundant flowerbeds. The fairy lights we'd strung last week over the pergola twinkled across our yards like morse code—warning me to stay home.

Ryan sighed, and I could tell he wished that was exactly what we could do. But he calmly knotted his tie as he faced the mirror. "No. I think it'll be good closure, for all of us. Plus, you could get some work from this. Everyone's going to love the job you did over there. It'll be good for business."

"I already have my next client lined up, Ryan. I don't need any more than that yet."

"If you really want to get back to work, you need more than one client. As you know, it's all about networking."

"Thanks, but I know how to run my business," I snapped.

"Yeah, I know. I seem to remember being there when you first learned how," he said, arching a brow at me. "You know—in your MBA classes."

Point taken.

"Sorry. I'm just . . ." I wrang my hands together, anxiety swelling in my unsettled stomach. I hadn't been able to eat all day. I was so nervous about being in the same room with both of them again now that the truth hung naked and raw in the air between us.

He gave me a sad smile. "I know. It's going to be a hard night, no matter how we slice it."

"He's going to be leaving soon," I whispered.

He ran a hand over my hair. "I know, baby."

I bit my lip as I looked up at him, searching for any of the compassion I remembered him having for Brighton. "Are *you* ready for that?"

He steeled his jaw, the twitch near his eye giving him away. "It's probably for the best. Every day is a constant reminder, Liv. We all need to move on."

I'd heard those words before. Was asked to move on before I was ready. I wouldn't do it again. But now was not the time to press the issue.

"Let's go," I said instead, taking his hand in mine.

"We could be late."

I knew this was an olive branch. The only way Ryan knew how to bridge us back together. I'd missed him so much these past few weeks—afraid he'd never be able to touch me again after everything that had happened. Relief flooded through me, my heart aching at how hard that must've been for Ryan to reach out for me this way.

I couldn't help the small smile that lifted the corner of my mouth as I stared up at my husband. It wasn't all sunshine and tulips for us yet, but it was a step in the right direction. Even I knew that. I tugged at his tie, letting a genuine smile overtake my face for the first time in weeks. "As long as you don't mess up my makeup."

Being thirty minutes late was a small price to pay for Ryan and me being intimate for the first time in almost a month. I had to admit, I'd missed him terribly. As Ryan slid inside me, I closed my eyes, letting him erase the memory of my betrayal with Brighton from my skin.

THE OPEN HOUSE was in full swing by the time we got there, and I recognized many of the neighbors and guests. Everyone congratulated me on a job well done, but somehow, all I felt was sadness. This house was meant to be flipped, but it was full of personal, intimate memories I was scared to part with. I hated seeing all these strangers in this home.

I looked around for Brighton but couldn't see him anywhere. Ryan took my hand, and we headed toward the kitchen in search of a beer. The room started closing in on me before we even got there. There were too many people, and I was getting hot under all the lights. I tugged at his hand, trying to get his attention.

That's when a family walked by. A small baby was bundled in a blue blanket and tethered to his father's chest in a BabyBjörn. The mother's hand was getting pulled by an overly excited little girl with strawberry blond ringlets. My heart hammered in my chest, but I couldn't look away. The kids were just about the ages ours would've been, had they lived.

My mouth went dry. I tugged at Ryan's hand again. "I can't do this. I have to go."

"What? Why? We just got here."

"Stay then. Tell Brighton I got sick or something."

"Liv, what's going on?" His gaze swiveled, following my line of sight. The mom was pressing a straw into an apple juice box and handing it to her daughter. "Do you know them?"

I shook my head, my eyes landing on the baby's chubby leg hanging from the baby carrier. Little blue socks warmed his tiny toes.

"Did we put socks on Laelynn before we buried her? I can't remember," I said suddenly, my voice cracking. I held his hand tighter as panic gripped at me. I was going to vomit. I could already feel the bile rising.

Ryan led me to the back door, parting guests without apology until he got me outside. He gripped my shoulders, trying to get me to look at him, but I couldn't.

"I think I forgot to put socks on her, Ryan."

"Liv, it's okay."

"It's not okay," I said, my brows furrowed in horror as I looked at my shoes, concentrating on anything other than the party around me. "What if she doesn't have any socks on? I can't be a mother. I couldn't even do that right."

I sank to the hard stone steps, draping my arms over my knees and taking in deep, jagged breaths. A panic attack was imminent, and I wanted to leave before it came.

"She had socks on," he finally said.

I glanced up at him. "Are you sure?"

He nodded. "They were the tiny white ones with the ruffled lace tops. They were supposed to be for her baptism, but Carly said they'd be perfect."

"Perfect?" I asked, horrified. "There's nothing perfect to bury a baby in. What does that even mean?"

"I just meant that my sister was trying her best to help."

I hardly remembered her even being at the funeral. "I didn't know there would be kids here tonight." Maybe because it was a nighttime open house, I assumed it would be for adults only. Families usually came on Saturdays and Sundays. "I can't stay. I thought I'd be okay, but I'm not."

I stood, my legs shaking as I steadied myself against the large stone column. That's when Brighton rounded the corner, heading our way with an attractive brunette on his arm. Her highlighted hair was curled in perfect beach waves and angled over her shoulder in an asymmetrical bob. Her eyes were a bright and vivid green, and they sparkled as they looked up at Brighton with obvious affection.

Just like that—time stopped. My breathing quickened, and the party around me faded. Brighton was the only thing in the center of my line of sight. His eyes were trained on mine, but I couldn't get past the fact that he was here with another woman.

"Kerrington," Ryan said, somewhere off to my side.

"I was just coming to find you. Everything okay?" he asked, scrunching his eyes to really look at me for the first time.

I felt clammy and nauseous. I could not stand here while he introduced me to someone who clearly had feelings for him. I knew it wasn't right. I knew it was beyond hypocritical. But my heart would never be ready to see Brighton with another woman—and that was never clearer than it was right now.

"No," I said, licking my lips. "I'm really sorry, but we can't stay. I'm not feeling well."

"We just wanted to say congrats. The house looks great," Ryan said.

"It's in large part because of their help," he told the woman standing next to him. "This is Ryan Wells and his wife, Olivia. She's the designer I was telling you about."

The designer. Not the woman I'm in love with. But the designer.

"It's so nice to finally meet you both," she said, reaching out her hand. "I'm Paige Morgan."

She was his realtor. I knew I'd recognized her face from somewhere. She was with a well-known boutique group that catered to the wealthiest clients in our area and the greater part of western New York.

Ryan shook her hand, then wrapped his arm around me. "Sorry, Kerrington. Paige. We really have to go."

"I understand. We'll catch up tomorrow?" he asked, his brows furrowed with concern.

I couldn't answer. The parents I'd seen in the kitchen stepped out onto the porch, and their daughter accidentally brushed my leg on her way down the stairs as she ran into the backyard to explore. I watched as Brighton took in the same scene, his eyes falling on the baby boy in the dad's carrier. My heart constricted because I knew what he saw when he looked at that baby.

The blue socks. Sam. The son he would never have.

Brighton's Adam's apple rose and fell, and his jaw clenched almost imperceptibly. But I knew him now. I knew what drove him, and what hurt him.

Ryan didn't wait for me to answer. He linked his fingers through mine and led me home. The loud din of conversation was at our back as we finally shut the door behind us. That's when my tears fell. I kicked off my favorite black loafers and padded to the guest room. I had no energy to make it up the stairs.

White. They were white, Ryan said. I remembered those delicate, lacy socks I'd picked out for her with so much excitement and hope.

I sank onto the thick carpet next to the memory chest that Brighton made for me by hand. It was partly what caused mine and Ryan's fight all those weeks ago. I tucked my legs under me as I opened the lid, grateful that the hinges kept the box open so I could look through its contents. I'd put everything I had from all our pregnancies inside. I needed to make sure Laelynn's socks weren't in there.

Hot tears slid down my cheeks as I held each item. I lifted the soft, pink blanket and pressed it to my cheek.

Ryan sat next to me, pulling my hair off my shoulder so he could see me better. He ran a thumb over my cheek, wiping away the moisture as I lifted a small yellow bow to show him. There were hospital forms and condolence cards at the bottom, along with a box of the most important items. A small clip of hair. Her fetal death certificate.

"It's not fair," I finally said, looking up at him through my tears. Stitch barked from his crate in the other room, hearing that we were home. But all I could see were Ryan's sad, brown eyes as they held mine, the weight of his palm on my back.

"Why would god do this? Why would he take her from us and give them two perfect babies?"

"Liv, you can't think of it that way."

"It's the only way I know how, Ryan. We didn't deserve this. We're good people. We would've been great parents."

"We still can be someday."

"I don't trust my body anymore," I whispered.

I looked down at my breasts. They held milk in them less than a year ago. Almost an entire year had passed since we buried Laelynn. I'd never forget having to expel the useless milk from my breasts in the shower to prevent my glands from getting swollen. It eventually dried out, and I was partially relieved and partially devastated. Unsure if they'd ever hold sustenance again.

The odds were too great that my body could never hold a life to term inside of it, but I didn't say that to Ryan tonight. Instead, I fell onto his lap, the contents of the box scattered all around us on the floor. I stretched my legs out and curled around his bent knees as he ran his hands through my hair.

I thought I'd gotten past this. I thought I was getting better. My body shook as I cried into Ryan's lap, realizing it was never really going to get better.

This was all there was.

CHAPTER SIX

Ryan

OLIVIA FELL BACK into a funk I couldn't drag her out of for the next three days. Luckily, I had Mondays off from work. I puttered around the house while she slept late, tackling some of the easier projects on our never-ending "honey do" list. It kept my hands busy while staying close by in case she needed anything. Stitch followed closely on my heels as if he knew something was off. I wished I could call Dr. Paul for advice, but he wasn't my therapist.

Maybe Olivia was right. Maybe marriage counseling was the answer. I was still angry about her lying to me, even though I was trying hard to forgive her. They'd both been right about one thing—it *had* been my idea. Part of me wanted to hold onto my justifiable anger, but the rational side knew I had to come to peace with what happened if we were going to save our marriage. And if not peace, then at least come to terms with my responsibility as the catalyst.

41

I grunted as I crawled under the laundry room sink and worked on fixing the small leak. I was sure I just needed to tighten the slip nut and maybe wrap the old pipe with a little plumbing tape. I lay on my back, looking up at the ancient piping system. They sure didn't make things like they used to. As I worked on tightening the clamp, I thought of Brighton. It wasn't the first time I wished things could've turned out differently. He's someone I would've felt comfortable talking through stuff like this with—and not just about the leak, but how to make things right with Liv.

I heard a small creak I didn't like and pulled my hand back. I inspected the pipe, and it looked as good as it could for a house that was over a hundred years old, so I went back to tightening the slip nut.

I didn't like how I'd left things with Brighton on Friday. Yeah, I had every right to be pissed about what he'd done with Olivia. But I certainly hadn't intended to *see* where everything went down. I don't know what came over me. But the jealousy burned hot in my core as I stood there staring at him, thinking about him touching her without me.

That was the kicker. The part I was afraid to examine too closely.

Without me.

The truth was, I missed us all being together more than I cared to admit. I wished I could rewind time and reconsider how quickly I'd cut everything off out of fear. Because as weird as it sounded, there was a part of me that loved the way he touched her. Loved the way she opened up with him differently than she was able to with me. Not better, just . . . different.

I wasn't sure how I really felt about everything now. I was torn between being angry and upset to just wanting everything to go back to the way it was—when Brighton was a part of the solution and not the problem.

It wasn't even the physicality that was the issue—he'd been right about that. The emotional intimacy that drew them to one another was what terrified me the most. I knew she loved me. That wasn't even a question. What I didn't know was whether she loved him too much to truly let him go. And if she couldn't? What then?

I didn't have time to ponder the answer because the corroded pipe creaked a little louder, then proceeded to snap. Residual dirty water that was lingering in the P-trap dripped all over my clean, white T-shirt. I held a section of the broken pipe in my hand and cursed. On my way out of the cabinet, I hit my head on the hardwood casing and swore again.

I marched over to Brighton's house and knocked. His truck was in the driveway, and I knew he could help me fix this. I knocked louder. When he still didn't answer, I tested the knob and found it unlocked.

Pushing the door open, I called out, "Kerrington? You home?"

Home. The thought lodged itself in my heart. He hadn't lived here for most of the summer, staying with us instead as the dirty renovations amped up. Still, it now felt like Brighton's home. The thought of anyone else living here churned my stomach and made me feel like I had a bad case of indigestion. I'd have to talk to him about Livy's reaction to the family she'd seen at the open house. Maybe ask if he could be a little picky about who he sold it to. I knew I didn't have a right to ask. But if he loved her like he said he did, he'd do anything to protect her, wouldn't he? And I needed his help doing just that.

I searched the first floor and couldn't find him anywhere, so I headed up to the second floor to the library. It called to me like a siren, my curiosity luring me in farther, deeper into the heart of the home. Kerrington wasn't there, but the door to the small, hidden room was open, taunting me.

I ground my jaw, unable to step toward it, even though I couldn't tear my eyes away. The room was small—not long enough for a man as tall as Brighton to lay down on the cozy reading bench. That meant one of two things—and both options created a poisonous mix of rage and desire within me.

"Ryan?"

I swung around at the sound of Brighton's voice, dropping the corroded pipe.

"What the hell are you doing in here? Did you come to take me out? With a pipe? In the library?"

I snorted. He had no clue the crazy thoughts that were racing through my mind right now. But as I stood there staring at him, the anger slowly ebbed from being directed at him and aimed at all we'd lost. And I didn't know what the hell to do with any of that.

"Nah, I'm no Professor Plum," I joked. "If anyone wants to take you out, I'll leave it in Miss Scarlett's hands. She's more than capable."

"Touché," he said. "But seriously. What's with the pipe?"

"I was trying to fix our laundry room sink. Had a little leak. Now I have a gaping hole where this pipe used to be."

"And you're here because . . . ?"

"I don't know. I thought you could fix it really quick. Surely you have some PVC pipe lying around. Maybe a new P-Trap?"

Brighton folded his arms over his broad chest and lifted a brow. "I'm not your personal handyman, Ryan. Why don't you just call a plumber?"

I started to answer, then stopped. Why *had* I come over here instead of calling a plumber? "Look, can we sit and talk for a minute?"

Brighton eyed the pipe, skeptical. I set it on the nearest table and walked over to the couch. "I'll be careful not to get my dirty shirt anywhere near your fancy pillows."

He sauntered over, but it didn't escape me that his eyes flickered briefly to the hidden room. "Hang on," he said. He walked over and pressed a button inside the small space. The wall immediately began to close, a bookcase swiftly covering up the evidence of my wife's affair.

He joined me in the sitting area, plopping down in one of the comfortable armchairs near the fireplace. His arms draped over the back, his body filling the space with his overwhelming presence. Is this what she'd fallen for? The confidence that radiated off Brighton was brighter than Edward Cullen's chest in the sunlight. He was a man unapologetically used to taking up space, yet never caring that all eyes were on him. I couldn't help but recall the first time I'd met him. How I thought he would be a douchebag with his square, firm jawline, overly bright smile, and shirtless chest flexing as he crossed the yard toward me after a long day of hard work.

"It seems like just yesterday that I met your cocky ass coming across the driveway," I said, my mind racing through reels of memories that included our neighbor since then. Things had changed so fast—and I found myself wishing we could go back to beers on the patio and easy conversation.

"Now look where we are," he said drolly. "A picture of bliss."

"Are you truly sorry about what happened?"

"I already told you this, Ryan. I'm sorry about how it hurt you. Are we doing this again?"

"Liv's not doing so great," I said quietly.

"What do you mean?" He pulled his body forward, so he was now sitting on the chair's edge.

"You saw how she was Friday night."

"Yeah? So? I thought she'd just gotten nauseous again."

"What do you mean 'again'?"

"Uh." He ran his hand over his blond hair. The summer had been kind to him, lightening it from the first time I'd met him and making him look even more like a walking Adonis.

"Kerrington?"

"I'm sure it's nothing. She just—the day of your fundraiser, she was finishing up her punch list over here. And she went a little pale, then got sick in my bathroom. She said she hasn't been eating enough, and the anxiety of everything just got the better of her. You don't think it's something worse, do you?"

"No. It's more emotional than physical. I dragged her to the fundraiser last week, and it was taxing for her to be around all those people asking about Laelynn and how she was doing. Then Friday night—I don't know. I thought she was getting so much better. But she saw a young family at the open house. They had kids who were around the same age ours would've been, and she freaked out a little bit. She's been in bed all weekend. She says she just needs a few days, but she hasn't done this in a long time. Maybe since the car accident this summer."

"Do you think it has something to do with the fact that she opened up to you about what happened with us? That maybe the weight of everything is crushing down on her? When is her next appointment with Dr. Paul?"

It felt weird talking to Brighton with so much concern for the same woman—for *my* wife. Yet, somehow, it also felt right. We both loved her.

"Tomorrow."

"Make sure she goes," Brighton said.

"I plan to. Think I'm going to call in and take a day off to be with her. I'm worried." I glanced down at my dirty shirt, stained from all that was once trapped inside. It was a visual reminder that even though it had broken, at least now it could be fixed. All things could be, eventually.

"Do you ever think of staying here? Instead of selling?" I asked cautiously.

Brighton's head snapped up, his clear green eyes drilling into mine. "Why would you ask me that?"

I shrugged. "I don't know. It just feels like your home now," I said, looking around. "It's hard to imagine another family filling this space."

"I can't, man. I've got nothing to tie me here. It's too hard, you know? Being here next door to you guys. I think it would be best for us to get some distance. Give you the space you need to make things right once and for all. Looks like your journey got waylaid a little on a speed bump named Brighton," he said, chuckling. "This summer might've slowed down your progress, but you guys are well on your way, and it won't stop you from finishing up your trip together."

He shook his head, looking out of one of the large, floor-to-ceiling windows. It had been drizzling all morning. Even though the sun was trying to surface, little rivulets of water covered the windowpanes, leaving sad, little trails as they slid down the glass.

"What if you weren't just a speed bump, Brighton?"

He swallowed, then cracked his knuckles. "I can't do this, Ryan. I can't play these games anymore. You think this was all just fun and games for me? Some sick, twisted fantasy to come between someone's marriage?"

I knew it wasn't. That's not what I'd meant.

"I'm not as strong as I pretend to be. I told you before this started that I wouldn't jeopardize my own heart to save Olivia's. That if feelings got involved, I would leave." Brighton cleared his throat. "You know it's time for me to leave."

My chest tightened, like I had the weight of the world crushing down on it. I clenched my jaw, nauseous at the thought of him not being around. Maybe Olivia was right—I hadn't thought through all the down-road consequences of him leaving yet. I just knew I wasn't ready to say goodbye, and I didn't even *love*, love him the way my wife did.

What the hell had I done to everyone because of my own selfishness?

"Not before I apologize, too," I said low. The surprise on Brighton's face was evident. He closed his eyes, taking in a deep breath as he waited. I knew what needed to be said, once and for all, to start fixing things.

"You were right," I admitted.

"Excuse me?"

"Look, I'm only going to say this once. You were right that I didn't think about you enough in all of this. How it would affect you when all was said and done. I was so worried about Olivia that I was freaking willing to share her with you. I would've done anything to make her happy again, but I didn't stop to really consider the collateral damage it was going to cause along the way."

"And I'm the collateral damage."

"So am I, my friend. So am I. But I never meant for you to be."

Neither of us said a thing. I tried to figure out where we could possibly go from here. What did I want from Brighton? What did I have any right to ask for? And more importantly, I needed to find out what Olivia wanted—what she really *needed*.

I stood up, angry at myself. I needed to make this right somehow.

"Where are you going?" Brighton asked, standing up with me.

"To call a plumber. Then I'm going to have a heart-to-heart with Olivia."

He shook his head. "You're not calling a plumber, Ryan. I was just chopping your balls. I got a kit down in the back of my truck. It'll take me ten minutes to fix. How about I come over when I finish my meeting."

"What meeting?"

"The meeting I was in the middle of with my sister when you barged into my house unannounced."

"You didn't answer," I said lamely.

"I'll be over in a few. Shut the water main off at the street so we don't turn one problem into two."

I nodded, then headed toward the library door.

"Hey, Wells?"

I stopped, gripping the door frame. "Yeah?"

"I forgive you," Brighton said, then cleared his throat. "It was worth it."

I grinned, letting his words sink in. As I left the room, so many confusing emotions flooded over me. But one thing was for certain—it didn't feel right to say goodbye. Not yet. Things felt unfinished.

I turned back around, catching Brighton's eye. "Hey, Kerrington?"

He grinned, shoving his hands into his pockets like he always did. "Yeah?"

"Maybe you weren't just a speed bump. Maybe you were supposed to be our destination."

I don't know why I said that, or if it would just make things worse. But I headed across our yards with more determination to fix things than ever before.

And it would start with the laundry room sink.

CHAPTER SEVEN

Brighton

"**Y**OU NEED TO untangle yourself from all of this," Paige said, looking over the rim of her coffee mug at me. I'd left her on the back patio, waiting all this time, while Ryan and I had our little—I don't know. Whatever the hell that was.

"It's not that easy, Sis," I said, frowning as I plopped into the comfortable rocker that Olivia had hand selected. That was the problem. Everything in this house reminded me of her, and our time together. It was like an addiction I didn't want to walk away from.

"Oh my god," she said, setting her coffee mug down on the small table between our chairs. "Do you *love* her?"

When I didn't answer, she groaned. "Christ, Brighton. You fell in love with a married woman?"

"It's not like I did it on purpose," I said. "And I'd really appreciate it if you kept this bit of news to yourself. I don't need all my sisters on my ass about it."

"You know I keep my word, and I've already promised to keep mum about whatever it is that's going on with you. But what's going to happen now that you're leaving? Did you really think you could just walk away?"

I ground my teeth, looking down at my clasped hands that rested between my knees. I wouldn't go into all the details with Paige. She was my *sister* after all. But I could really use some unbiased advice. Though with the way she was reacting, I wasn't sure that was possible. She seemed to already have an opinion about the whole situation—with just the limited information I'd shared. But she didn't have the whole picture.

"I haven't met anyone like Olivia, ever," I started. "My plan wasn't to get involved with a married woman. We were just friends at first. It's complicated. But, Paige, we've both been through a lot of the same things. She understands the pain I went through after losing Sam."

"Yeah, but why not just keep it friendly? If you join a support group, they'll all understand what you went through after losing your son, too."

"It's different," I growled, gripping my hands tighter together. "It's hard to explain how and why it progressed the way it did. You just have to trust me when I tell you the feelings are real—on both sides."

Paige gasped. "Does her husband know?"

I nodded. I could not possibly tell her any more than that. Or about how he had been an integral part of it all—part of what made the whole situation even more confusing than ever. Or how the two of us worked symbiotically to heal Olivia by loving her. How it actually made sense at first and was working. Until it wasn't.

"And he's okay with it?"

"It's not exactly what you think. It's complicated. That's all I can say."

"And all I can say is—you need to untangle yourself from this. From whatever game it is they're playing. I don't want to see my baby brother get hurt again."

"It's too late for that," I said, lifting my coffee to my lips. It was cold, but it was still coffee, so I finished off the mug.

"What now? Do you still want me to put the house sale on hold? I have three families who are potentially interested in it, Brighton. They won't be for long."

"I just need to make sure Olivia is going to be okay, first. I can't focus on making a decision around the house or deal with negotiating contracts when she's all I can think about."

"But what if she isn't okay in the long run? What then? Are you going to be able to walk away? You can't stay here forever. And I can't keep listing and delisting the house. It looks bad for buyers. They're going to start thinking something is wrong with the place."

"I'm sorry, Paige. Maybe I should've waited a bit longer before listing it."

"Brighton, I'm going to be blunt. There's nothing worth staying for here. This is not going to end well for you."

I set my mug down on the table and stood.

"Where are you going?"

"I have a pipe to fix for my friend. I'll let you know when to put the house back on the market."

"What do I say to buyers?"

"Tell them anything you want. Just don't sell it yet. I need a few more weeks, maybe a month."

"You may as well not list it until after the holidays then. No one is going to buy near Thanksgiving and Christmas.

Not even in this market. And what about your cousins? It's not fair to the estate to let it sit that long."

"I'll cover the mortgage myself, then."

"Brighton! That's thousands of dollars."

"I have it covered, Sis."

She shook her head back and forth, her lips pursed. "It's not just about the money, Brighton. What about your heart? Or do you have that covered, too? Because from where I'm sitting, it doesn't look like you do."

"What's a heart worth having if you aren't willing to risk it all?"

"Said the man right before his heart was crushed."

I grinned at my older sister. She had the best intentions. I knew she did. But I was already, and irrevocably, in way over my head. I knew the right thing to do was to leave now and never look back.

Instead, I headed to my work truck and pulled out the sink repair kit. I'd start with the broken pipe. But sooner or later, the three of us were going to need to have a heart-to-heart about what to do about everything else that had shattered. It might not be as easy to fix as the pipe, but it would be a whole hell of a lot more rewarding.

THE PIPE TOOK longer than we thought to deal with because of the age of the house. We got the main issue fixed, and the sink no longer leaked, but the pipes would all need to be replaced sooner or later. It just came with the territory of owning a historic property.

When I was done, I went to the kitchen to find Ryan. It had gotten dark out, and he was at the stove making what smelled like homemade pasta sauce. A big pot of water boiled on another burner.

"All done?" he asked, barely looking up as he added fresh spices into the pot.

"Yep. All fixed. I didn't know you could cook like this."

Ryan nodded. "My family was big on Sunday dinners, and one of my grandmothers was Italian. I grew up learning how to cook one thing only—pasta. Chicken parm. Lasagna. Ziti. Spaghetti. Ravioli. Gnocchi."

"And homemade sauce, apparently."

"Secret family recipe," he said, grinning. "I was hoping you would join us for dinner."

"Does Liv know I'm here?"

Ryan nodded, stirring the pot. "She'll be down in a few minutes. She had to shower first."

I pulled a chair out from the kitchen table. It was more intimate than their formal dining room and where we ate the most over the summer. "Anything I can do to help?"

"Nah, you've helped enough already with the sink. I appreciate that. I didn't mean to take advantage of you being next door or anything. I just knew it was something you could probably fix easily enough."

"Ryan, let's just call a truce, okay? We've each done and said things I'm sure we wished we could take back. But we can't. We've apologized. Can we put the past where it belongs and try to be friends again?"

Ryan snorted. "You want me to be friends with my wife's secret lover?"

"Look—"

"I'm just joshing, Kerrington. Calm your tits," he said, sounding more like the Ryan I knew. He went over to the fridge and grabbed a longneck for me.

I yanked it from his hand and accepted the bottle opener, flipping the top off. I took a long pull as I looked at Ryan. "I think it's a little soon for secret lover jokes."

"If I can't laugh about it, I'll end up crying, and no one wants to see that." Ryan set the spoon down and took a pull from his own beer. "I was just messing around, though. Let the past be the past."

We clinked the mouths of our beer bottles and settled in for a nice conversation about how things were going now that Ryan was back at the university full time. Based on what he was telling me, I suspected he was using work to avoid all the pain he was bottling up again. In my experience, that was never a good idea. But I kept my mouth closed, not wanting to rock this fragile boat any more than it already was.

Ryan set a stack of plates onto the kitchen island and nodded toward them. "Mind setting the table? Liv should be down any minute, and dinner's about ready."

I pushed my chair back and stood, surprised to see Olivia standing in the doorway. She was freshly showered, but quite frankly, she looked exhausted. She had dark bags under her eyes, and I noticed she'd lost a little weight—which she didn't need to.

"Hey," I said quietly. I wanted to go over and hug her. To erase the damaged look from her eyes.

"Hey," she said back, going to lift the plates herself. "I got it. You sit down and relax. How did the open house go?"

She set a plate in front of me, and I could feel her hips brush my arm as she leaned down to add the cloth napkin and utensils. I wanted to grip her hips and pull her onto my lap, crushing my mouth down onto hers. I wanted to feel her curl up in my arms and take away all the stress of whatever was bothering her. Was it still because of her babies? Or was I now adding to her pain instead of lifting it?

I cleared my throat, unable to concentrate with the smell of vanilla and citrus floating around me. "It went well. We have three serious buyers asking about the house."

"But?" she asked, sensing there was more.

"But I asked my sister to put a hold on the sale for now."

Olivia gasped, dropping the plate she was holding. Shards of ceramic splintered off in every direction as Ryan hurried around the kitchen island to help clean it up.

"Why don't you sit down, Olivia? It's been a long day and a hard weekend. You deserve to relax, too," Ryan said, rubbing her shoulder.

Olivia rolled her eyes at me. "He always goes into hyper-protective mode when I get all mopey and shit."

"Isn't that a good thing?"

"It's a wonderful thing. But I'm confused. Isn't Paige Morgan your realtor?"

"She is. She's also my sister," I said, taking a sip of my beer.

"Your sister," Olivia said, as if putting two and two together. She snort-laughed, but quickly waved it away as she took a seat in the chair next to mine.

"Why are you putting the sale on hold?" Ryan asked. "You just listed it. I thought you'd be excited to get a couple of good offers."

"They weren't offers yet, just interest. Maybe we could sit down after dinner and talk about it some more?"

Ryan looked to Olivia. "I'll let the missus decide. I'm taking tomorrow off, so I'm not in any rush."

"You're taking the day off tomorrow?" Olivia asked, brightening.

"Mmm-hmm. I thought I told you already."

"I'm pretty sure I would've remembered if you had," she teased. "I'd love to catch up after dinner, Brighton. I want to hear more about the house and what's going on there."

Indeed. If only I understood my own impulsive decisions.

CHAPTER EIGHT

Olivia

AFTER WE ATE, Ryan lit a fire in the living room. I tried not to focus on the fact that it was the same room where I'd lied to him not that long ago. About the same man who was now joining us after dinner with a glass of wine in his hand.

"So—"

"Tell me—"

"Sorry. Ladies first," Brighton said, laughing at how we both started talking at the same time to fill the awkward silence.

"I just wanted to hear more about the house," I said, curling up on the couch next to Ryan. I tucked my legs beneath my bottom to get comfy.

"Do you really?" he asked, narrowing his eyes at me. "Ryan said Friday was a little hard for you. I was worried you'd gotten sick again."

"No. I just—I don't know how to explain what happened. Things were so hard last week at the fundraiser with seeing everyone again for the first time. Then, going to the open house with your home all finished and looking like another family could just waltz right in and live there . . . I don't know. It just—triggered something in me, I guess."

"Maybe we should back this up a little bit first," Ryan said, clearing his throat.

"This," he said, waving his wine glass in a triangular motion in the space between the three of us, "is an unusual situation to say the least. I know part of this is my fault, for wanting to keep you and Kerrington so separate. My conversations between him and me were just between us; and our conversations about everything were in private too," he said, looking at Olivia.

"While some things need to stay private, there's a lot that the three of us never discussed properly after our . . . time together. I think if we had, none of this awkward stuff would've happened. We're all adults here. Can we just get on the same page and figure out where to go from here? I think we all need that."

I traced my finger around the rim of my wine glass, surprised by Ryan's words. He'd been so quick and sure to cut things off between all of us. It started because of Ryan and ended because of him, too. But somewhere in the middle of all his decisions lay my heart, battered and confused.

"How did everyone feel initially, right after—you know— everything happened?" Ryan asked.

Even though he was the oldest one in the room, he seemed to have a hard time just saying it like it was. "If we're going to be transparent, let's be transparent, shall we?" I said, taking a sip of my cabernet.

"By all means. That's exactly what I want us to do. I don't think we're going to be able to move on if we don't get everything out in the open."

"I agree," Brighton chimed in. "I feel like a lot was left unspoken after all was said and done."

I licked my lips, looking between the men. I'd learned a lot from Dr. Paul. Being honest and speaking my truth was a priority these days. So, if they wanted to hear my truth, I would give it to them.

"When Ryan approached me about being intimate with you both, with all of us together, I thought he was crazy for suggesting something so absurd. But the truth was, once he did, I couldn't stop thinking about it. It's not a conventional way to try to make things better, and some might say it's the worst way—that we were trying to escape from one set of feelings by replacing them with another. But that isn't what happened for me. And I can only speak for myself."

Ryan rubbed my knee and squeezed it. "I'm listening."

"I think you were actually right, in some weird way. It forced me to stop thinking of only my pain, my grief. It made me step outside my comfort zone and be truly present for the first time in forever. It's hard to explain where your heart and head go sometimes after losing a baby. Somedays I would be here, and then the next moment, I was deep inside myself, struggling to cope again. The smallest thing would set me off—and it didn't always have to be baby related. A commercial. A question. A book. Because it was a Tuesday," I joked.

"But your friendship cracked me wide open, Brighton. You and Ryan and the love you shared with me—it forced me to be vulnerable. To not hide anymore. To let myself be a woman again. God! I can't even tell you how much I enjoyed being in my body again like that. So aware of every sensation. I wasn't Olivia—that woman who lost a baby. I was Olivia—that woman who is desired by two amazing men. The woman whose husband loves her enough to share her instead of losing her completely."

I noticed Brighton adjust in his chair and smiled. Yes, the thought of being with them both together again did that for me, as well. But it was more than that. "It may have started out as sex, but someone important once taught me that sex isn't always about the sex. And while it was amazing being with you both physically, the bigger pleasure was feeling back in *my* body again. I wasn't detaching from my feelings anymore. I was facing them. I reached out to both of you for different reasons when I needed emotional comfort or connection, instead of turning inward like I used to."

I took a deep breath. This was the hardest part, but it needed to be said. Dr. Paul was right. I turned in my seat to look at Ryan. I took his hands in mine, even as they trembled.

"We don't have to do this if you don't want to, Livy," he said quietly.

"Yes, we do. Don't you see? If we don't, we'll just be stuffing our feelings inside again. We *have* to face the hard things, just like we promised to do all those years ago. Somewhere along the way, we stopped wanting to. Maybe so the pain wouldn't be as bad. But instead, I think we made it worse."

Ryan's jaw clenched, and I didn't dare look at Brighton right now. My eyes were fixated on my husband's, our souls meeting in the space between. "I have to be honest, and if I had from the beginning, maybe we wouldn't be where we are today, dealing with the messy aftermath of all this."

"Do you wish we'd never done it?" Ryan asked.

I took a deep breath, glancing over at Brighton. His eyes were a dark and stormy green. He looked like he didn't want to hear my answer either. But I smiled softly before glancing back to Ryan.

"No, I'm glad we did. You and Brighton gave me back the most important gift I could ever ask for—myself. It's not that I wished we'd never done it. It's that I was too afraid to tell you I wasn't ready for it to end."

I let that sink in for a moment.

"You came up with this fantastical plan to help pull me out of the depression I'd been grappling with. I finally invested my heart into the idea of what you were proposing, and went all in. I was vulnerable, and I opened my heart. The problem was it wasn't just with you. It could never be just about the sex, Ryan. You asked me to share my body with another man—and I don't know how to do that without my heart, too."

"I'm so sorry," he croaked out.

"That's just it. You don't need to be. But you also didn't have the right to decide when it was over for all three of us without asking about or considering my feelings, or Brighton's. I wasn't ready for it to end, Ryan. I wasn't."

I was scared to look at him. Afraid he would want to leave me for admitting this ugly truth. I'd fallen in love with another man. It may have started because of Ryan, but I chose to open my body, heart, and soul to make room for someone else. I thought it was to chase away the ghosts that lived there. But it wasn't.

It was to fill the Brighton-sized hole I never knew was there.

...I mean everything, becomes centered around, that...

...simple word: No. Before that, our eight-year marriage was built on love, respect...

...darkness loss after loss, the only thing that can set you free is the truth. It's your...

...sacred as our wedding vows, and maybe even more so because I came after the loss...

...one hundred percent honest with one another, that would be enough. That would...

...through another miscarriage. Until, finally, that fragile false hope would stretch...

...how honest, could bridge the hollow, gaping hole where my heart used to be. The...

...to reach me. To save me. To restore me to the woman he'd fallen in love with. Even...

..."And you fell in love with him?" Dr. Paul asked, never...

...through. Through the darkness that caused me to fall...

...I lifted my cigarette and glanced at...

...if I fell in love with a woman, I...

...a nasty habit I would regret...

...respect. He went back to work...

..."Really? You...

...going, how the...

...would you go, saying you...

...I wanted nothing to...

...back to bed, but I...

...and maybe...

...jump very...

...intimate. The...

...was never...

...own. Here's what I say...

CHAPTER NINE

Ryan

OLIVIA HADN'T WANTED it to end. What did that mean? Did she want Kerrington that badly? Did she want him more? Is that what I'd done? Made her bottle her feelings up and pushed her to hold them all in until they couldn't be contained anymore? Is that why she slept with him alone?

"What are you saying?" I asked. "Truth. I need to hear it all."

She nodded, looking even more beautiful and brave than ever. She may not have been feeling well lately, but honesty brought out her light, I realized. Maybe it hadn't been Brighton this whole time. Maybe it was just the honesty between us that something needed to change. That she needed something new to get excited for. To wake up for each day. We just needed to break out of our rut. Brighton was originally the catalyst. But now he'd become much more than that. My stomach churned at what that meant for our marriage. But

I'd been brave enough to start all of this, so I needed to be brave enough to hear how it really affected my wife.

Olivia glanced back at Brighton. Their eyes locked, and a silent conversation passed between them. There was no denying that nothing had changed for them. In fact, it had only grown stronger. It was something that could no longer be ignored. But, this time, it wasn't up to me to tell us all what to do with that. It would be a joint decision. Split three ways.

"I'm sorry I did that to you. I never meant to hurt you like that. I ended things with Brighton because I thought that's what was best for our marriage. And for the sake of transparency, I was getting jealous. You *had* come out of your shell again. You were the radiant, vivacious woman I'd fallen in love with all over again. I wanted her to myself. But that wasn't fair to you."

"No, it wasn't. Or Brighton," she added.

"I've already apologized to him for that."

She smiled, then tipped my chin. "This isn't a 'let's bash Ryan' conversation. I appreciate that you did that. It had to be hard. I just want to be honest about how I felt after it all happened."

"That's all I want, too," I said.

She nodded, then folded her hands back in her lap. "I am so in love with you, Ry. Falling for Brighton was only the tip of the iceberg. I fell more in love with you, too," she said, her eyes growing misty.

"I fell in love with who the three of us became when we were together. I know that sounds strange, but that's what our indiscretion proved to me. It wasn't the best way to go about it—and I am sorrier than you will ever know for lying. I don't want to leave you for Brighton, though."

"Then what do you want?" I asked hoarsely. I wasn't sure I was ready for the answer, but I knew we would never heal if we didn't go through the pain of this honesty together.

"In an ideal world? I would have you both. The way it was when we were all together. I'd never felt more free or happy in my entire life. I know it's not possible, but I wish that we hadn't stopped being together. I wish you'd let us explore it for a little while longer. To see where the feelings could take us."

I swallowed. I was relieved that she didn't want our marriage to end, but how could I answer what her heart called for and not decimate my own?

"Ryan, you look like you've seen a ghost," she said, laughing. "Brighton, can you get him some water?"

"Sure," he said, heading to the kitchen.

"I didn't mean we have to go back to the way it was. But you asked me to be honest. And that's the god's honest truth. I wasn't ready for it to end when it did. But it did. So now we need to figure out how to work through all these feelings that are still here, left behind, suspended in midair. Because me stuffing them away clearly did not work," she said, grimacing. "I never meant to hurt you or lie to you. I was trying to protect us both until I felt strong enough to tell you all of this. I was afraid, Ryan."

"Afraid of what?" I gratefully accepted the glass of water from Kerrington's outstretched hand.

"I was terrified that if I told you the truth, that if I asked you to keep our bedroom and our hearts open to Brighton, that you would think badly of me. That you would judge me for now wanting another man in bed with us. Or worse, that it would make you want to leave me."

I set the water down and pulled Liv onto my lap like I'd wanted to do all evening. "Oh, Livy. Don't you know by now I would do anything to make you happy?"

A tear slid down her cheek and I brushed it away, her skin soft beneath the pad of my thumb.

"But I can't be happy unless *we* are happy. And I wouldn't want to do anything that would push you away, or make you love me less."

"Baby girl, there is nothing on this earth that would cause me to love you less. Even lying. Deep down, I knew why you did what you did. It doesn't make it right, though. And I never want it to happen again. But I never stopped loving you. I hurt because I loved you *too much* still."

She lowered her head and our breaths mingled between our lips. My heart pounded in my chest, and I'd never felt closer to her. She still loved Brighton. But her love didn't feel any less for me. That knowledge sunk my heart even deeper, and I closed the space between us, drawing her lips to mine. The same electricity passed between us that always did, and I felt like I could finally breathe again. She was mine, and would always be, no matter what the future held for the three of us.

I heard Kerrington clear his throat behind us. I slid my hands in Olivia's hair and kissed her even deeper, sticking my middle finger up at him behind her head. I heard him chuckle and was happier than I'd been in a long time.

Liv pulled back and blushed, her cheeks turning an adorable shade of pink.

"Since I think he's feeling a little left out, where does all of this leave Kerrington?"

Liv chewed on her lower lip. "Where does it leave any of us?"

Brighton stood up and crossed the room, pulling up an ottoman and sitting in front of us so we could talk easier.

"We've all made mistakes," he said. "We all invested a little more than any of us realized we would when this started. Though, to be fair . . ."

"Yeah, yeah," I grumbled. "You and Liv both tried to warn me."

Kerrington laughed, and the room felt instantly lighter. Damn Brighton Effect.

"Ryan and I talked earlier, Olivia. We've hashed out some of our stuff. It was nice to hear him admit that he didn't think enough about where this would leave me when all was said and done."

"Where does it leave you?" she asked him.

I wanted to kick myself for putting her in this position to be so vulnerable. I could see the longing etched on her face just as clearly as the worry.

"I don't know. I told my sister to put the house sale on hold until I could make sure you were okay. Until we could figure all this out."

Olivia grimaced. "On Friday, I got so jealous when I saw you walking toward us with her because I didn't know that's who she was at the time. She's so beautiful, and I was shocked that you would bring a woman to an open house you knew I was going to be at, even if we had asked you to move on. I know it's not fair—like, at all. But my heart sank thinking of you moving on so fast."

"Is that why you *really* sprinted out of there?" Brighton teased. "You were so distraught at the idea of me being with another woman that you nearly fainted?"

Oliva swatted at his leg, laughing.

"It put things into perspective, that's all. That, in combi-nation with seeing that sweet, little family. It was too much for me to handle. I started thinking of all the things we'd miss out on with our babies. I let myself get consumed with the grief of what could never be again—only this time, it wasn't just *our* future and *our* babies. It was also the idea of never seeing *you* again. The fear of having your heart be permanently with someone else. Which I know is unfair. You deserve to start over. To have a wife. To fall in love and get married with someone who can—"

"Liv," Kerrington said as he leaned forward to cup Olivia's face in his hands. He glanced toward me and I nodded. I knew he loved her. He didn't need to say it. We would work out what that all meant later. But the longer I tried to deny it, the more it ended up hurting us.

Maybe accepting it was enough to finally set us all free.

CHAPTER TEN

Brighton

LIV WOULDN'T STOP rambling about what she thought was best for me. So, I did the one thing I knew would get her to shut up. I dropped my mouth to hers and feasted on the delicious taste of her full lips. I swiped my tongue along her mouth, parting it for the first time since we'd been alone together. I hadn't dared allow myself to touch her like this since then. To cave. To crave. To lose myself all over again.

A moan swelled from deep inside Olivia, and it only made me want to taste her more. I pulled her to a stand and deepened the kiss. Her hands went to my chest as she finally kissed me back with equal passion and longing.

Then, just as abruptly, she pulled away. She turned to Ryan, mortified at what she'd just done. "Ryan—I didn't mean to—"

"Liv, it's okay," he said, standing too.

"It is?"

She looked back and forth between us. What she didn't realize was that he'd given me tacit permission in that one simple look that passed between us. Just as easily as Liv and I were able to communicate on a deeper level with our eyes, so were me and Ryan. We just seemed to know what the other was thinking. Maybe that's why it worked so easily with the three of us in the bedroom. Or maybe it was because of our time there. But the two of us had gotten used to communicating silently for Olivia's benefit. And we'd gotten exceptionally good at it.

Ryan turned her face toward him, and I could see the years of love and devotion as he stared deep into her eyes. "I don't know what this means, or where we go from here. But you said yourself you wished this never ended. Kerrington told me he's still in love with you—"

Liv glanced quickly at me and I nodded. "He knows."

She bit her lower lip, tears forming.

"I will never stop loving you, Olivia. What we do with all this, I have no clue. We can figure all that out tomorrow," I said.

"What about tonight? I thought we were laying everything out on the table and clearing the air."

"Sometimes, you get to a point where words are no longer necessary," Ryan said, glancing up at me. He leaned forward and gently swiped his tongue over Olivia's full, swollen lips. "Wouldn't you agree, Kerrington?"

I finally dropped my hands to Olivia's hips as I'd wanted to all night and tugged her closer. I loved the way her breath hitched when she realized what was happening. That we were both ready to love her again, openly, with no road map. With just the promise to explore, and to continue healing. All of us. Together.

"Words are overrated," I growled in her ear. While Ryan dominated her mouth, causing Olivia to moan into his kiss, I dropped my mouth to her neck. She leaned into my embrace, her hand searching for mine at her side.

"This one thing needs to be said first." The little flutter in Olivia's throat made me want to hurry. "I'm willing to sacrifice anything to be here with you. I told Ryan once that I'd bail if my heart ever got invested. That I wouldn't risk my own pain to heal yours."

She groaned, pressing her head back against my chest as I kissed along her collarbone, my fingers gently tracing the flutter.

"I was wrong. I didn't know it then, but I do now. I would give anything," I said, pulling her hips even closer. "I love you, Olivia. As long as your heart is open, and Ryan is willing, I'm not ready to leave you yet. I don't know if I'll ever be ready."

I kissed the tears from Olivia's cheeks and lifted her into my arms. I glanced over at Ryan, understanding and need pulsing between us. "Where do we go from here?"

"Let's start with our room," he said, leading the way.

That night, Ryan and Olivia physically and emotionally opened their literal marriage bed to me for the first time. Only now, it wasn't to heal like it was before. And it wasn't just for the sexual release, either. There was a silent understanding that whatever we were creating from this point forward, it was born and forged in love.

Between the three of us.

I WOKE TO Olivia's hand sliding under the covers and caressing my thigh. I buried my face in her hair, not wanting to leave our happy, little cocoon. Sunshine outlined the curtains in their master bedroom, letting me know we'd slept in later than normal.

"Good morning," she whispered, not wanting to wake Ryan.

I ran my finger down the center of her face to her bottom lip. I couldn't believe how quickly things had changed and that I finally had her in my arms again. Especially after the way things ended. She drew my finger into her mouth, never breaking eye contact. I groaned, pulling her closer to my warm body. A bed got toasty with three people sleeping in it.

"Are you two at it again?" Ryan groaned from the other side of the bed. "I can't keep up with you crazy kids."

I burst out laughing, but it died on my lips when Olivia's hand wrapped around me, playfully waking me all the way up.

"Come on, old man. It's been what?" I checked the bedside clock. "Four hours since we fell asleep?"

Ryan chuckled. "Old man, my ass," he said, his hand wrapping around Olivia's waist as he kissed her good morning. "I could get used to this."

"But what would the neighbors think?" I teased.

"Well, technically, you're still our only neighbor. So, I think they'd be okay with it. In fact, I think that arrangement would work out rather well, don't you?"

Olivia's hand stilled, and I pulled back to look over her shoulder at Ryan. "What are you saying?"

"I'm saying shut up and give my wife the proper good morning kiss she deserves. Then I'm saying, let's get some pancakes together. Then I'm saying, let's maybe figure out our day and take it one step at a time. How does that sound?"

Olivia purred in response, her hand continuing to say good morning in the most delicious and intimate way. I groaned as I pressed into her touch, and Ryan chuckled, pulling Olivia's hair aside to brush his lips along her shoulders. Then he disappeared under the covers, and all thoughts about what he was or wasn't saying didn't seem to matter as much anymore. The three of us tangled fluidly, effortlessly. It was unspoken, and not understood by my simple mind. But it worked. And it worked well. In fact, we were lucky Olivia's therapy appointment wasn't until three because we missed breakfast completely, skipping right to brunch.

Olivia made her famous pancakes, and they were worth the wait. It was unsettling, but also comfortable, sitting at their breakfast table once again. Especially without all the tension this time around. I just hoped it would last. I tried not to worry too much about a label, but to be grateful that I was with the people I loved the most—which was more than I could say at this time yesterday. Even though I had no idea what our future held, I was happy.

"You look like you have an awful lot racing through that cute head of yours," Olivia teased. Ryan was cleaning up the dishes since Olivia made breakfast, and he insisted he had it covered.

"Sorry. I can't help but be a little shell-shocked that Ryan is okay with all this again. Don't get me wrong, I'm here for it. I just hope he doesn't regret it later. And I have no clue what any of this means long term."

"I don't think any of us do," she said earnestly. "But I'm willing to find out. Are you?"

I glanced over at Ryan, who was loading the dishwasher. The fact that the three of us were a picture of domestic bliss this morning after a raucous night of lovemaking didn't escape me. I chuckled. "I don't want to wake up and find out this was all just a dream. I don't want to lose this again."

"Let's not worry about losing it before it's even really begun, okay? I'll talk to my therapist about everything today. See what he thinks."

I gaped at her. "You're going to tell Dr. Paul about us?"

"He already knows. I can't very well heal if I'm being dishonest now, can I?"

She said it lightheartedly, but I knew how hard it must be to open herself up to him. Especially since she was so against it at first.

I took her hand in mine. "I'm really proud of you, Liv. Do you know that?"

A huge grin lit up her face, and I couldn't help but reciprocate. "So, one day at a time. What does today hold?" I asked Ryan.

He came over to the table, a dishtowel slung over his shoulder. He put his hand on the back of Olivia's chair. "Well, I gotta drop Liv off at three. I was going to jog while she was at her appointment since it's near the lake. I decided I'm gonna run another half marathon next spring, so I've got to start logging the miles every chance I can get. Wanna come?"

I had a million things to do now that I'd asked Paige to take the house off the market. I had already planned to take some time off from work, so staying a few extra months wouldn't be detrimental there. I wouldn't worry yet what came after that. I was really going to have to embrace this one-day-at-a-time shit.

"Sure. Let me go shower and grab some running clothes, and I'll meet you back here in a few."

I kissed the top of Liv's head before heading home with a huge, shit-eating grin on my face. What could I say? I'd just spent the night with the woman of my dreams, and one of my best friends. It should have been weird, but it really wasn't. Somehow, Ryan and I had broken through the macho bullshit and laid it all on the table. That's when I realized I didn't want to lose him just as much as I didn't want to lose her. I didn't know what that meant yet, but it was settling in my marrow, asking me to live with it for a while before figuring it all out.

One day at a time.

Yeah, I could get used to this setup.

...nd I mean everything, becomes centered around radi...

One simple word: No. Before that, our eight-year marriage was built on love, respe...

the darkness, loss after loss. The only thing that can set you free is the truth. Its g...

as sacred as our wedding vows, and maybe even more so because... To...e after the l...

...ile—through another miscarriage... Until, finally, that fragile, false hope ...d sho...

...tter how honest, could bridge the hollow, gaping hole where my heart used to b...

...mpts to reach me. To save me. To restore me to the woman he'd fallen in love with. Eve...

...ted, "And you fell in love with him?" Dr. Paul ask...

...rough. Through the darkness that caused me to l...

...I lifted an eyebrow and glanced a...

...if I fell in love with a woma...

...a nasty half, I heard mys...

...xpect. He sent back to som...

...ve you." Katey D...

...d you ever...

...ld give you any to t...

...I wanted nothing to...

...babies. In fact...

...and pra...

...in plac...

...timate. The...

...n was sw...

...my. Here's what I'v...

CHAPTER ELEVEN

Ryan

OLIVIA WAS AT her appointment with Dr. Paul, so Kerrington and I set off on a run around the lake and the university where I worked. I'd taken the day off for personal reasons, but it didn't stop my students from calling out and saying hello as we jogged by. We settled into a nice, easy pace. The waves crashed hard against the stones that lined the shore. The water was rough today, which meant a storm was probably coming soon. Upstate New York didn't care that it was only October.

"So, you sure you're really okay with all this?" Brighton finally asked after three miles in. I knew it was on his mind all morning. It was on mine too.

"I'm not gonna act like this isn't weird. I keep fluctuating between self-preservation and begging god to show me a sign to let me know if we're doing the right thing. I honestly don't know where any of this is headed, but it didn't feel right to let you go either. I just don't want to end up hurting you again. That's my biggest concern."

"Your biggest concern should be Olivia."

"Shut the fuck up," I said, laughing. "You know damn well she is. Don't think just because you're back in our bed that you're moving up the food chain or anything. Liv is, and always will be, my number one priority."

"I'm starting to feel like second fiddle," Kerrington joked.

"Dude, I hate to break it to you, but you are."

He bumped my shoulder then took off in a hard sprint. I increased my pace to catch up with him, but he was a lot faster than I expected and I damn near got winded. I slowed to a light jog and took some deep breaths. I couldn't get a good lungful of air because of the cold snap coming in. I cursed under my breath, knowing I'd never hear the end of this from Kerrington.

As I slowed to a walk, my phone vibrated in my pocket. Since Liv was at her therapist and the only other person I cared about was smoking my ass running ahead of me, I let it go and didn't pick up. I put my fingers to my pulse and measured my heart rate. When it returned to normal, I sprinted to catch up. I finally had Brighton in my line of sight when my phone vibrated again. I hollered for him to stop and yanked the phone from my pocket.

Brighton looped back and was about to make some wise-ass comment but then stopped when he saw my face.

"It's Dr. Paul," I mouthed silently.

"Is everything okay?" I asked Liv's therapist. "What? When? The hospital?"

Dr. Paul explained what happened to Olivia and told us to meet him in the ER. I thanked him, then hung up.

"What is it?" Kerrington asked, his worry mirroring what I could only imagine was written on my face.

"It's Olivia. We need to get to the hospital."

IT WAS EASIER to run to the campus and ask a student for a lift than it was to get a cab, so that's exactly what we did. It was a small town, and the hospital was close. But a car was still faster than Kerrington and I could run.

The undergrad dropped us off at the Emergency Room exit in record time and I ran in, trying to find someone in charge. Dr. Paul rounded the corner and rushed over.

"Tell me everything," I said. "Christ, she was fine when we dropped her off."

"Well, we were in the middle of our session, and everything seemed fine. But then she started looking a little pallid. I asked her if she was okay, but it was like she couldn't fully hear me. I told her to put her head down between her knees and take a few deep breaths. She did, then sat back up and said she was fine, just embarrassed. The next thing I knew, she slumped right over and fell to the floor in a heap. I tried to revive her and rolled her to her side just in case. My receptionist got me a blanket to cover Olivia with while she was coming to.

"I gave her some water when she was finally ready to sit up. But she looked too weak to stand yet. I was worried her blood pressure dropped too fast, which can cause you to pass out. So, I insisted on calling an ambulance and getting her checked out."

"Fuck," I said in disbelief. She seemed fine last night and this morning. "Thanks for being there for her, Doc. And staying till we got here. You did the right thing."

"Of course. She's back with a doctor now. I'm sure they'll come get you any moment," he said.

Dr. Paul turned his attention to Brighton, and I knew in an instant that Olivia had used at least part of her session to update him on our status.

"So, you're the infamous Brighton Kerrington," he said.

"I'm not sure how to respond to that," he admitted, laughing.

"My goal is to see Olivia be the healthiest she can be, in all areas of her life. It's nice to finally put a name and face together for someone so important in her life."

"In both our lives," I said, glancing over at Kerrington. "Thanks so much for taking such good care of Liv for us today."

"Of course," he said, before shaking our hands and saying goodbye.

"Guess we wait," Brighton said.

We found the waiting room and sat patiently. Eventually, a nurse came looking for Olivia's family. "Is one of you Mr. Wells?"

"That's me," I said, standing. "Is Olivia doing okay?"

"She'll be all right. She's a little shaken from her ordeal but we're giving her IV fluids to help get her back in shape."

"Can I see her now?" I asked.

"Sure. You'll have to wait here, though," she told Brighton.

When I saw the crestfallen look on his face, I turned to the nurse. "He's family. I'd like him to come back with me."

She hesitated.

"Trust me. Olivia will want to see him, too. I'll catch hell if she doesn't."

She nodded, then turned to lead us down the hall to the soft squishing noise of her blue Crocs.

When I finally saw her, my heart literally skipped a beat, causing my pulse to flutter erratically in my throat. It brought back the deep hopelessness I felt during Laelynn's delivery and when Liv had been hit by a car over the summer while running. This was her second hospital visit in less than six months, and I didn't like the trend.

Liv was now lying in an elevated bed with an IV hooked up to her arm. The astringent smell in the room burned my nose, and the steady beeps from all the monitors were disarming. The doctor standing at her bedside was talking too quietly to hear, and only when he moved did I notice the tears streaming down her cheeks. Was it worse than the nurse let on?

The doctor squeezed her shoulder before making room for us. "You're in good hands now," he said to Olivia, more jovially than I expected, considering the terrible shape she seemed to be in. "I'll let your wife fill you in on what happened. If you have any questions about her post-visit care, a nurse will go over everything with you. She should be able to go home today after she's had enough fluids. So long as she promises to eat more and take her medicine," he said pointedly to Olivia.

She nodded, then reached out for me. I didn't even hear the door close before I leaned over and wrapped my arms around her.

"What happened?" I asked, pulling back to get a better look at her. That's when I realized she didn't really look okay.

There were dark circles under her eyes that I hadn't noticed this morning. Had we kept her up too long last night? Pushed her too hard between the both of us? God. I was a monster.

"Stop!" she said, giving herself some wiggle room. "Take that look off your face. I know you think this is somehow your fault—and I suppose it is, but it really isn't. Sit, and let me explain," she said, patting the side of the hospital bed. "Both of you."

We each took up residence, one on each side of Olivia. To hell with what the nurses thought if they walked in on us. Liv was our priority. "Tell us what happened."

She squeezed my hand. "Well, you know I've lost some weight and haven't really been feeling good recently, right? I just chalked it up to the stress I've been feeling lately, because this used to happen all the time in college, too."

"See! It *is* my fault," I grumbled, feeling awful.

Brighton smacked my arm. "Let her finish."

I shot him the evil eye but nodded for Olivia to go on.

"The doctor said I've lost over ten pounds, which isn't insignificant, considering my normal body weight. He said I'm anemic and need more Vitamin D. But there's something else," she said, twisting the hospital sheet in her hand.

"What's wrong? It's not cancer, is it?" Brighton asked.

It was my turn to smack his arm. "Shut the hell up with that cancer bullshit." I turned toward Liv. "Please tell us it's not cancer."

She smiled. "No, it's not cancer."

"But something else is wrong?"

"Not exactly."

"Stop being evasive, woman. What is it?"

"You guys—I'm pregnant."

CHAPTER TWELVE

Olivia

THE ROOM WAS dead silent as I waited for their reaction.

"Holy shit! Are you serious?!" Ryan stood and paced the small room, his hands going to his messy brown hair. He'd been out running with Brighton when I was admitted, so his hair was wild and untamed. He came back over to the bed and held my face in both hands, staring deep into my eyes.

"Truth?" he asked, his face pained.

I bit my lip and nodded. I was still getting used to the news myself. "Truth," I promised.

"Oh my god!" Ryan screamed. He jumped up and down and hollered so loud a nurse came running in.

"Is everything okay?" she asked.

"I'm going to be a dad!" Ryan shouted again.

"Well, congratulations, sir. But if you could just be a little less loud in your enthusiasm. Not everyone in the ER is here for joyous reasons, you know."

"Oh, right," Ryan said, putting his finger to his lips as she left the room.

I glanced over at Brighton, who was surprisingly quiet. "I think you both need to sit," I said to Ryan.

"How come?" he asked, oblivious.

He sank to the bed and looked between us, and I saw in his gaze the exact moment when the reality of our situation washed over him. "Oh, god. You don't know if it's mine, do you?"

"Ours," she corrected. "And no. I don't. Not really. The doctor thinks I'm about two and a half to three months pregnant. That would put conception date right around the time—"

"We were all intimate the first time around," Brighton answered.

"Yes," I said, sighing. This should be the happiest day of our lives. Instead, it was crowded with fear, confusion, and guilt. It was one thing to think we all could lead a cozy, polyamorous lifestyle in secret. It was another thing altogether to bring a baby into the mix. The truth was, I wasn't even sure my body could hold this pregnancy, let alone to worry about whether my husband or Brighton was the father.

"We don't really know the exact timing because I haven't been getting my periods consistently since Laelynn was born. The doctor told me to schedule an appointment with my regular OB/GYN so she could do more testing and determine a more accurate due date. That might help us back into conception timing a little better."

"Fuck," Ryan said, sitting on the bed beside me.

"Can you find out for sure which one of us is the father? Before the baby's born?" Brighton asked.

"I don't know. It's obviously not something that's ever been an issue for me before," I answered. "I believe there is such a thing as an in vitro DNA test, though. I can ask my doctor how soon we could have a paternity test, if we decide to have one done."

Brighton's head jerked up. "Why wouldn't we want to know? Don't you want to make sure it's your husband's baby? What if it's mine, Olivia? God. What if it's mine?"

I shook my head. "I can't worry about whose baby it is right now. What matters is whether I'm healthy enough to even carry it. I was having an extreme case of nausea and morning sickness, which is why I lost so much weight. In turn, I'm a little dehydrated, anemic, and am severely lacking Vitamin D with all the isolation I've been putting myself through."

"Liv, you can't blame yourself. You didn't know."

I rolled my eyes. It was completely my fault, but I wasn't arguing with Ryan today. Today, my heart was oddly at peace, no matter who the father turned out to be. It would crush Ryan's heart, though, if after all this time and all these losses I finally got pregnant, and it wasn't even his. What were the odds of that happening? I was on the pill, for god's sake. It was one of the main reasons we hadn't been as careful as we should've been.

"I have lost three babies," I said morosely. I looked back and forth between my two loves. "If I can carry this baby to term, it will be a miracle. I will never care who specifically brought this baby into the world. I love you both. This baby will be a miracle either way. So . . . you guys are going to have to come to some sort of grip with this. Because I'm not ever going to be sad about this baby growing inside of me."

Brighton picked up my hand as tears slipped down my cheeks.

"Of course not, Liv. It *is* a miracle. It's just a shock, is all. We have even more to consider now," he said practically. "If the baby's not mine, it changes things."

"It doesn't," I insisted. "We just promised to see where all this goes. That doesn't change just because we accidentally created a baby together. Regardless of who the biological father is, this baby was born from a love that was sparked by all three of us. Without that, this baby would not exist."

"We have a lot to think about," Ryan agreed. "It doesn't all need to be decided today, though. For now, nothing needs to change—except for getting you healthy. That's going to be our number one goal. Right, Kerrington?"

Brighton rested his head on my stomach and began to cry quietly. There was nothing I could say or do to change the circumstances we found ourselves in. I ran my fingers through his thick, blond hair and comforted him the best I could. Ryan was holding my other hand, and we stared at each other over Brighton. No words were spoken, but I'd been with him long enough to know when he was terrified.

"It'll be okay. It'll all work out like it's supposed to," I whispered to no one in particular.

Maybe it was simply a prayer.

THERE ARE KEY moments that define and change your life forever—altering the trajectory you were once on. Seeing Olivia for the first time was one of those for me. The day I met Ryan hadn't been an accident. I'd started the renovations on my uncle's home a few weeks before that. I would never forget my third day on the jobsite, when I first laid eyes on Olivia.

I was in the backyard chucking an old sink into the bright blue dumpster we used on all our construction sites. Maybe it was by chance that I looked up that morning, or maybe it was fate. Who knows? It had been drizzling, and a movement in the sunroom of the house next door caught my eye. I could barely make out the ghost of a woman's silhouette leaning against the glass windowpanes. Her body shook as tears transformed her posture, breaking me to the core as I watched her. I'd only ever seen a few people cry like that in my lifetime: My parents when my youngest sister died of cancer at seventeen, Caroline and her parents when we lost Sam so unexpectedly, and me.

I knew when grief was etched into someone's bones, just as they were mine.

I'd seen the husband coming and going a time or two, so I knew the couple was on the younger side. That's when I first became drawn to Olivia like a magnet, constantly curious about who she was and what made her so sad. I'd caught glimpses of her through the windows of her home, often looking despondent. She didn't move with the ease and grace of a woman her age. She moved with the weight of the pain she was carrying while hiding in the shadows of her home.

Something about her made me want to meet her and get to know who she really was. The only problem was, I never saw her leave. It was always Ryan hopping in his SUV for groceries and dragging out the garbage cans to the curb. He was an athlete, and I watched him jog away from their home several times, a look on his face too serious for a man who was about to release some major endorphins. One afternoon I noticed Olivia's silhouette in the sunroom again, watching as Ryan headed off for another run. When he was out of sight, she slid down the wall of glass windows until she was sitting on the floor sobbing. When I looked back thirty minutes later, she was still there, her head resting on her folded arms, her body shaking in the silence that surrounded her.

By the time I finally got to see Olivia in flesh and blood, she'd somehow become a familiar fixture in my mind, taking up more real estate than I cared to admit. I was tearing down interior walls on the first floor that day when I heard the neighbor's SUV start up. By the time I made it to the front window, it was already pulling out of the driveway. I caught a glimpse of blond hair in the passenger seat as the car rounded the corner. She was getting out of the house for once. I didn't know why, but a smile spread across my face, and I turned on some music as I continued ripping out drywall. Images of her soft, blond hair slipped in and out of my consciousness all afternoon.

It had been a long, labor-intensive day by the time Ryan and Olivia returned. I was pounding down a glass of ice water when I heard Ryan slam the trunk of his car. As I glanced out the window, I noticed that Olivia was already in their backyard. I couldn't see her face from where I stood though, because she was leaning over and playing with a puppy.

Ryan was juggling a cardboard box as I bounded down the front steps, not even bothering to throw a shirt on I was in such a hurry to finally see her. That was all I'd wanted. Just one glimpse of the mystery woman next door to put a face with all the stories that were racing through my mind.

"Hey, man. This your house?" I asked Ryan.

"Yeah," he said, setting the box onto the hood of his SUV and making his way over.

He was older than I was; I could tell by the lines that crinkled near his eyes when he smiled. He was almost as tall as me, and in decently good shape. Ryan's beard caught my eye right away since I never wore more than a day's worth of scruff. It was neatly trimmed, matching the color of his whiskey-colored eyes. He seemed kind and affable, a smile stretching across his face as he extended his hand to me.

"Brighton," I said by way of introduction.

"Ryan," he said and grinned. He shook my hand just as firmly as I clasped his. "You doing some work over there?"

"Oh, yeah. It was my uncle's place. The family's doing some renovations this summer. Probably putting it on the market in the fall. Thing sat here empty for way too long."

"We were wondering if anyone was gonna fix the place up."

I tried to focus on what he was saying, but it was Olivia who had captured my attention. I caught a glimpse of her profile and inhaled sharply. She was too far away to see the small details on her face that I would come to appreciate when we finally got to know one another, but I could see the perfection from where I stood, dumbfounded.

Olivia was the most beautiful woman I'd ever laid eyes on.

"Always wondered what it looked like in there after being vacant so long," Ryan hinted, pulling my attention away from his wife.

"Wanna come take a look?" I asked, using the T-shirt I'd slung over my shoulder to wipe my sweaty brow.

"We'd love to sometime, but you look like you've put in a long day. And we just got back home with a new puppy, so I should probably go give my wife a hand."

"Nice," I said. But my attention wasn't on the shaggy, brown dog. It was on the leggy, mysterious blond. It wasn't just her killer figure that caught my eye, though. Her smile captured my heart as I watched her. Liv was in their backyard, holding onto a small rope toy and teasing the puppy as it jumped to capture it with his mouth.

Time slowed like it does in the movies. Liv's face was flush with pleasure, her cheeks a dewy pink as she tossed her head back in laughter with her long, blond hair tumbling in gentle waves down her back. With her face now exposed, I caught sight of a set of adorable dimples bookending the fullest, most kissable lips I'd ever seen.

When Ryan gently cleared his throat, I finally tore my eyes away. "What a cute dog," was all I could manage to say. I suspected he was aware of how captivated I was by his wife. It was hard not to be. Olivia was the epitome of the sexy-cute girl next door. Except she was all grown up and even more beautiful as a woman.

I drank in her energy, unsure when I would have a chance to see her again. Ryan was one lucky SOB.

"It's gonna take some getting used to," he said, interrupting my thoughts. "Just swing by sometime when you have a free minute to show us around. We'd love to hear your plans. We got lucky when we moved in here. The whole place had been restored immaculately. We didn't have to do a thing to it—thank god."

I couldn't help but laugh. "That's what I'm hoping your new neighbors will say someday."

"You're welcome to come check out our place if you want. Whoever renovated it paid an insane amount of attention to the littlest details. It's what made Liv fall in love with it."

"Liv?" My heart fluttered hearing her name for the first time. What the hell was happening to me?

"My wife," Ryan said a little sharply.

I shook my head. I needed to pull my head out of my ass before Ryan could tell what I was really thinking: Now that I'd seen her, it wasn't enough. I knew, beyond a shadow of a doubt, that I had to meet her in person.

"Yeah," I said absently, my mind still engineering how to make that possible. "Well, I better head out. It's been a long day and I could use a beer about now."

"Nice meeting you. Good luck with the reno."

"Thanks." I yanked the gray shirt from my shoulder and shrugged it over my head before climbing into my pickup truck. I needed fresh air, so I rolled down the window before cranking some Tom Petty as I pulled away.

I knew it would be a mistake to meet Olivia in person. I was already drawn to her in ways I didn't understand. But god help me, I knew nothing would keep me from squelching that curiosity.

I waved at Ryan before making a right turn at the corner, risking one last glance at Liv on my way out of the neighborhood.

It was hard to believe that was less than four months ago.

That was the day I knew my life would change forever. I just never suspected it would alter it as drastically as it had.

I'd always dreamed of meeting a sweet girl, getting married, and settling down in Watertown near my family. And hopefully, god willing, having more kids of my own someday. I worked hard to build my business after graduating from Duke, and I was damn proud of all my accomplishments. But nothing, and I mean *nothing*, compared to the feeling I had when Olivia told me and Ryan that she was pregnant.

She may have mistaken my tears for worry as I folded over onto her stomach and kissed it, resting my head there. But they were happy tears. Tears that came from the depths of my soul as I recognized it for what it was: another life-altering, trajectory-changing moment centered around Olivia. There was no denying our fates were meant to be entwined. No matter how messy it got with Ryan and me both loving her, I knew in that moment I would never walk away from either of them.

For some, it may have sounded like a scandal in the making: A married woman. A three-way affair. A shocking, unexpected pregnancy. But for me, it was my life. It was a pregnancy born out of love when the three of us had fused our hearts and bodies together so raw and openly in those early days. We were all searching for something in that bedroom the first time. Without even realizing it, we were each other's answers all along—just not how we ever imagined it.

We were able to take Olivia home from the hospital that night. There was no question whether I was staying over this time. Ryan helped his wife up the stairs as I filled a glass of water for her. He was helping her out of her clothes and into the shower when I entered the room. I set the glass onto the table next to Olivia's side of the bed. Though, technically, I guess it was my side now since Olivia liked to snuggle between us.

Ryan cocked his head for me to join them. I quickly undressed, eager to peel away the running clothes I'd been wearing all day.

Four months ago, I saw Olivia for the first time. Tonight, I was seeing her with our baby inside her for the first time. And she was even more beautiful, knowing she was carrying it for one of us. I slid into the shower behind Ryan and let the water wash over us.

We washed the day away from Olivia's aching body, worshipping it the way she deserved. Her hands folded over her belly at one point, and she glanced down at it in awe. After losing weight from the morning sickness, her stomach was flatter than ever. But soon, it would expand as our baby grew inside of her.

I couldn't explain why, but I felt an overwhelming need to be buried deep inside of Olivia. It was like a driving, primitive force to be as close to her as I could possibly be in this moment of such deep love for her.

"I need you. All of you," I whispered.

She nodded, letting me lift her from the shower and carry her to our bed. I didn't waste time drying us off, and I was pressed deep inside of her before Ryan even turned the shower off. Liv clung to me as I unleashed every emotion I was storing in my body's memory of her. Each thrust had me calling out her name as if it would bind us together forever.

"Fuck!" I cried out. Her body trembled around mine as I pinned her with my hips and we both came. She pulled my head down and kissed me thoroughly as she rode out the aftershocks. We'd come a long way from sharing secrets in the backyard in the middle of the night. Everything had changed, and there was no more hiding the feelings developing between any of us.

"I love you, Liv. More than I've ever loved anyone."

She ran her fingers through my wet hair, even as droplets fell to her shoulders, getting her pillow wetter. It didn't matter. All that mattered was she was really, finally, mine in some small way. Ryan would be the only man to ever truly have her as his wife on paper. But, somehow, I knew she would always be the only woman to hold that title in my heart.

CHAPTER FOURTEEN

Brighton

"**PLEASE TELL ME** you aren't serious." Paige gaped at me from across the table at the Crown and Feather tavern. It was the same bar where Ryan first dropped the bomb on me that he wanted me to join him and Olivia in bed. I supposed to my sister, the news I just dropped on her felt just as heavy, but she had no idea.

"Brighton, I think you need to think this through a little while longer. This is crazy."

"Is it though?"

Her phone rang, interrupting us. She rolled her eyes. "Yes, it is," she hissed before answering in her sweeter, more professional tone reserved for clients.

The food arrived while she was talking, the savory scent of beef and gravy making my stomach rumble. I didn't wait for Paige to finish her call to dig in. If it were anyone else, I would have. I liked the steady noises that created the atmosphere in here. I'd been several times since working on my uncle's place and left full and content every time. The owner, Alan, often stopped by our table to shoot the breeze and ask how the house was coming along. He'd raised his family on West Liberty Street once upon a time, so it was fun hearing how much things had changed, or not, over the years.

My sister finally hung up and immediately shot daggers at me. "That was another potential buyer, Brighton. For Uncle Isaiah's house. The woman and her husband want to make an all-cash offer today—even though I told her it wasn't back on the market quite yet. They have three small children. It would be a family home again. I can't think of anything better than that, can you?"

"Why didn't you just tell them it was no longer for sale? I literally just told you I was buying it myself. I wasn't kidding, Paige."

"Why would I do that, Brighton? You're all over the place. You only asked me to put it on hold a few days ago. And even though you *think* you want to buy it for yourself, it's a bad idea. We can't afford to turn away an offer like this while you play house with the neighbor's wife. What happens when she grows bored of you and you're stuck living next door? Are you really willing to uproot your entire life for someone you've known for only a few short months? I'm sorry, but you need to get your shit together."

I set my fork down slowly and wiped my mouth with the cloth napkin that was on my lap. "Paige, you're my sister, which is why I'm not going to go off on you right now. You may think you're wiser, simply because you're older, but you have no idea what my life has been like, or why I'm making the decisions I am right now."

"Then tell me!"

"That's what I was *trying* to do before you interrupted our lunch with a business call."

She sighed, picking up her fork to poke at her tavern salad. "You don't get what it's like to work in this business at all. I can't just ignore a phone call. It's how you lose customers."

"Are you happy though? I mean, really happy? Every time I see you, you're glued to your phone, at your clients' beck and call 24–7. Have you ever asked yourself what you're doing it all for?"

"What it's for is to pay the bills, Brighton. It's so the boys can take the ice hockey lessons they want. It's so Vic can retire from the force before he's sixty-two. Some of us didn't luck out and become millionaires before they were thirty."

I sat back and folded my arms over my chest. I simply was not doing this today with Paige. I loved her dearly, but I had more important things to do, and I wanted to get home to Olivia.

"For the record, it wasn't luck. I worked my ass off to get where I am. But you know what? I'd rather be happy than have all the money in the goddamn world. And guess what? I've never been happier than I am when I'm with her. Ryan, too, for that matter. It would be nice if you could be excited for me and be on my side."

"I just don't get it. You're my brother, and I will always love you and be on your side, but I feel like there's something I'm missing. And it's hard to support you when I have no idea what's really going on."

I took a deep breath. She was family. I was about to have a baby. It was about so much more than just a house. I knew if I wanted my family's support, I'd need to come clean about everything sooner or later. I'd chosen an unconventional path for myself over the last few months. And what started out as a fluke request from a new friend quickly grew into a life I never saw coming. But now, there was no way I could walk away from it.

And thanks to Ryan's change of heart, I wouldn't have to.

"I'm gonna tell you straight up—you are not going to like this, and you're not going to understand any of it. But I need you to reserve your criticism and judgment because this is my life we're talking about, and I'm happier than I've ever been. Okay?"

Paige narrowed her gaze, searching my eyes. When she realized I wasn't playing around, she nodded for me to continue. So, I told her everything—well, almost everything. I told her the important pieces she needed to know for her to understand why selling Uncle Isaiah's house to anyone other than me was nonnegotiable.

"It may not be the family home you were envisioning it could be again, but there will be love in it. There is already," I said, thinking of the way Olivia looked as she helped me install the wallpaper in the dining room as we danced to "Here Comes the Sun." Or the care she'd put into hand selecting every drawer pull, every light fixture, and every doorknob to restore its former glory. Even the antler chandelier was growing on me.

It was where she first told me she loved me, without being able to say those exact words out loud. *But, tulips.*

Paige reached across the table for my hand. "I didn't know you were going through all this, Brighton. Or how much you were still grieving for Sam."

"How could you? We hardly see each other anymore."

"I'm sorry about that. I'll try to get better. Vic's on my ass all the time, telling me I'm a workaholic."

"I miss you, too. And the boys. I haven't seen them play in forever. And I want them to get to know my child."

"Oh, Brighton. What if it ends up not being yours?"

"It's already mine, Paige. That's what you're not getting. The three of us—we're a unit now. We'll figure out a way to make this work, one way or another. We already tried walking away from it once—and it damn near destroyed us all."

"Are you sure it's really about more than just the sex? I can see how that could become alluring and addictive."

"It may've started out that way. I'm not going to deny that. I was falling for Olivia before anything ever happened—even though I wouldn't have acted on it because of Ryan. So, yeah. When he goes and offers her up on a silver platter, do you think I could really say no? I'm a nice guy, but I'm not a saint. I thought maybe we would have that one night together, and that maybe it would help purge her from my system."

"Why didn't you walk away then, Brighton? Before it got so complicated?"

"It was already complicated the minute I opened my front door and came face-to-face with her, Paige. You may not get it—being with Vic all these years. But there was always a connection between us, even from that first moment. I couldn't help but fall head over heels for the woman."

I shook my head. Maybe my sister was right. Maybe I was being selfish and should've walked away after that first night we were all intimate together. I'd already known by then that I'd caught feelings for her. But the truth was, I didn't want to. It wasn't just Olivia who had already worked her way into my heart. They both had. And together, they created a soft place for me to land. The first place that had felt like home since losing Sam.

So, yeah. It was about way more than just sex.

"You think she's your soul mate, then?" Paige asked.

"No. I think *they* are."

CHAPTER FIFTEEN

Ryan

OLIVIA WAS NAPPING when the back door opened. "In here," I called out to Brighton. I knew it was him by the sound of his boots hitting the floor as he shook them off and the soft padding of his socks across the hardwoods as he made his way to the guestroom. He found me sitting on the bed, going through Laelynn's things that Olivia kept in the trunk at the end of the bed. The one Brighton made for us.

"Hey," he said, jamming his hands in his pockets. "Where's Liv?"

"Napping. She had a busy morning working with a new client."

A grin slid across his handsome face easily, his green eyes bright with happiness for her. He reclined on the other side of the bed from me, making himself comfortable.

"A new client, huh?"

"Yeah. She's really excited about it. Your renovation lit a fire under her. And when people saw what she'd done at your open house, the calls started coming in. She has a waiting list now."

"That's wonderful!" Brighton said before frowning. "She's not pushing it too hard, though, is she? She's taking the Diclegis like she's supposed to, right?"

I chuckled. "I'm not sure who's going to be the worst Nervous Nellie during this pregnancy out of the three of us."

"Truth."

Brighton glanced down at everything sprawled out over the duvet. My heart constricted as his eyes swept over the fetal death certificate. I knew it would trigger his own painful memories and wished I'd scooped everything back into the memory box sooner. But I needed to feel close to Laelynn. Have a word with her about the new baby.

"The night of the open house, Olivia panicked after seeing a dad there with a baby strapped to his chest in a carrier. It made her think of Sam, because of his tiny blue socks. Then she worried that we'd forgotten to put socks on Laelynn before we buried her. Her mind always circles back to our babies, no matter how much time passes."

I ran my fingers over the soft lock of baby hair that was nestled in a tiny ceramic container with a field of bunnies and wildflowers painted along its sides.

"I wish Laelynn was here with us so she could meet her new brother or sister. Olivia tried to explain it to me once—how she ached for all the things we would be missing out on after Laelynn died. I didn't really get it, though. I thought we could just build memories someday with a new baby—that we wouldn't really be missing out on anything we hadn't experienced yet anyway. We just weren't getting it in the timeframe we originally wanted. But I get it now. The feelings of loss because we'll never get to have them with *her*."

I ran a hand over the side of my face, scratching my beard. "I'm terrified about Liv's pregnancy. But the first thing I thought of was, I bet Laelynn would've been a good big sister."

I didn't mean to get emotional but seeing all her things splayed out like this brought everything I'd shoved deep down inside back to the surface. Tears threatened to spill over, and I didn't even notice when Brighton stood and came around to my side of the bed. He gripped my arms and pulled me up, yanking me to his chest for one of the fiercest, most protective hugs I'd ever received.

I clenched my eyes shut, the pain threatening to break me if I let it out.

"It's okay," Brighton said as he tightened his hold on my upper back. "Dude, you have to let it out. It will never go away if you don't."

The memory of Laelynn's impossibly tiny body nestled inside a coffin not much bigger than a shoe box knifed at my heart, begging me to grieve for it the way I should've the first time. The lining was white silk, matching the tiny white socks and gown she was laid to rest in. My sister, Carly, had been at the funeral to help with all the things Olivia was unable to face, immobilized in her grief. Thank god she was there. It allowed me to focus all my attention on Olivia, who was inconsolable. Maybe that's where it all went wrong. Would things have been different if I'd let myself grieve more, too?

I didn't realize the strangled cry had come from me until Brighton's hand went to the back of my head, holding me as my body spasmed from years of unchecked grief. I felt like I was outside my own body as anguish ripped through me. I could hear him offering quiet words of comfort somewhere in the distance, whispering as he kept me safe. My arms curled around him, holding myself up while leaning into his strength. I'd feel my way through this pain if it fucking killed me. I cried for the two miscarriages we'd had, and for the baby we buried.

I don't know how long I stood like that, my body breaking against Brighton's as I purged every bottled-up emotion I'd carried around for the last few years. He let me ride it out, though, until my body no longer shook in his arms. When he finally pulled back to check on me, I noticed it had grown dark outside. I was embarrassed for letting everything collapse on me like that, but I had to admit, I felt better.

Brighton swiped the pad of his thumb across my cheek to pull away the last of my tears. I couldn't remember the last time I cried, let alone in front of anyone other than Liv. But if anyone knew where I was coming from and wouldn't see it as a weakness, it was Brighton. When I finally had the nerve to look up, to meet his gaze with the unchecked vulnerability that was flooding through me, I was shocked by the depth and knowing in his returned stare. His eyes were a deep, rich green. They were a marriage of strength and compassion. The unspoken thing that often passed between us did again, leaving me breathless and confused as I searched his eyes.

I wasn't sure who leaned in first, but our lips met softly somewhere in the middle, startling me. I gasped, pulling my head back. What in the hell just happened?

Kerrington's eyes were still trained on mine when his forearm came up against the back of my head and he pulled me toward his mouth with an intensity I don't think either of us saw coming. His other arm hooked under my arm and held my shoulder in place as I surrendered to the kiss.

I'm not sure what I was expecting because I'd never kissed a dude before. But it was fireworks, sandstorms, and skydiving all rolled into one. A torrent of emotions flooded through me as his tongue darted out to part my lips, tentatively tasting me for the first time. It didn't feel like I was kissing another man as we cautiously explored this new terrain. It felt like a kiss that brought me home.

Our teeth clattered as we fought for control. If I was going to do this once, I was going to do it right. I fisted his hair and deepened the kiss, surprising the hell out of us both. A deep rumble came from somewhere inside Brighton, making me chuckle against his mouth.

We pulled apart, nipping at each other's lips and pushing off one other, our chests heaving.

We stared each other down.

"What the fuck was that?" I said, running a thumb over my swollen bottom lip.

"It was love, dickhead," Brighton said.

I tried to wrap my head around what just happened, but no words were adequate. I felt scared and confused. But I was also aroused and felt loved.

Most of all, I felt healed.

"Are we telling Liv?" I asked.

Brighton arched a single brow and I laughed. "Right, right. Our truth pact."

He hooked his arm over my shoulder and pulled me in close again. "I love you," he said simply, his green eyes holding mine hostage. Then he playfully bit my nose and headed toward the door.

"Where are you going?" I asked, crossing my arms over my chest as I watched Kerrington walk away.

"I don't know about you, but I'm horny as hell now. I'm going to find Oliva." When he got to the door, he turned back to look at me. "You coming?"

Never in a million years did I think another man would be asking me if I wanted to join him and my wife in bed. Yet, somehow, it was starting to all make sense.

Brighton had become our ohana.

CHAPTER SIXTEEN

Olivia

I WOKE TO RYAN and Brighton acting like two horny schoolboys as they jumped on the bed I'd been napping on. A giggle escaped my lips as arms wrapped around my body and pulled me in close, so I was the middle spoon. Ryan brushed my hair back from my face and brought his lips to mine, searing my insides like he did when we first met. Brighton's hands went to my hips as his mouth crashed over my neck. Ever since I started taking my medicine, my nausea had disappeared. And I was finally reaping some of the pregnancy benefits some women brag about, but I'd never experienced before.

I was hella frisky. All. The. Time.

Luckily, I had two men to lavish attention on me, and they were more intense and passionate than ever. It was as if they were truly moving as one, with some hidden language that was created solely for the purpose of pleasing me. Any doubts I had about whether this could really work vanished quickly in their arms.

Brighton was holding me from behind, my back flat against his chest as he slowly rolled his hips against me. Ryan was busy exploring the front of my body and stroking himself when he leaned in and made a little growly noise.

"Get over here," he said. I opened my eyes, thinking he was talking to me. Then I saw him reach for Brighton's head. He pulled him closer for a slow, sensual kiss over my shoulder that left me reeling as I watched the scene play out before me.

I'm not gonna lie. The sight of their slow, sure strokes as their angular jaws opened wider for one another drove me over the edge fast. I clamped my eyes closed and gripped Ryan's bare chest, screaming as my pleasure spilled over.

"Oh god," I panted as my body shook between them.

Brighton groaned, gripping my hips tighter as he thrust deeply inside me a few lasts times and bellowed out his release, too. Slow, sensual kisses were shared by all as we rode down the high. Then we fell back against the sheets, our chests heaving and spent from the exertion.

"What in the name of all that's holy just happened?" I asked, glancing back and forth between them. They rested on their elbows and looked at me with a playful sexiness in their eyes. Brighton ran his fingers along my face and my hairline, brushing runaway tendrils from my damp forehead while Ryan drew lazy circles on my stomach.

"We decided not to question it," Ryan said, shrugging as he glanced at Brighton. "It just felt natural in the moment."

"Is this something you planned?"

Brighton laughed. "Hardly. But someone smart once told me sex isn't always about the sex. I guess the same goes with a kiss."

My eyes widened as I glanced shyly at my two men. "So, is this going to become like a thing from now on?"

Ryan's expression grew serious as he traced my face with his eyes. "I don't really know, Liv. I was downstairs looking through some of Laelynn's things earlier, and Kerrington helped me through a pretty hard time."

"With his lips?"

"What can I say? They're healing."

He leaned over and tugged playfully on my lower lip with his teeth. My arms broke out in goose bumps and my tummy fluttered all over again.

"So, what are you saying? Brighton's magic lips healed you? From what?" I asked, amused by their playful banter and easy comfort. It was much better than the growling and snarky quips from a few weeks ago.

Ryan grew quiet, his palm warm as he laid it flat against my belly. "I realized you were right about a lot of things, Livy. I needed to come to peace with the feelings I was holding inside over Laelynn. Brighton walked in during a particularly rough moment. I was thinking about what a good big sister she would've made."

I watched as Ryan struggled to share what happened. "One minute, Kerrington was holding me and letting me cry the fuck out of my emotions. The next thing I know, our tongues are down each other's throats."

Ryan laughed it off, but I could see by the tender way he glanced at Brighton that it meant more than that.

Brighton ran his hand along my cheek and turned my head, so I was facing him. "Are you okay with this?"

"I don't know. I—I never thought of Ryan as being bisexual."

He snorted. "That's because I'm not."

"And yet you kissed a boy," I pointed out.

"A man," Brighton quipped.

"I'm not bisexual, Liv. I'm—happily in love with my two best friends. Can't we just leave it at that?"

"If it makes you sleep better at night," I teased.

Ryan picked up a pillow and playfully smacked me with it.

"Oh no you didn't!" I got to my knees and grabbed the feather pillow I'd been lying on and gave Ryan a good thwap across his muscled abdomen.

Brighton tickled my waist from behind and I squirmed, twisting around to smack him with the pillow for good measure, too. That started an all-out pillow fight, and I was breathless and laughing before we all finally fell back onto the bed. When I finally caught my breath, I turned to Ryan.

"Thank you," I whispered.

"For what?"

"For loving me enough to open your heart to the possibility of even more love."

He glanced over at Brighton, and there was no denying that *something* passed between them. I could feel the energy of their silent words just as real as if they'd spoken. That's when I realized what we were building went far beyond anything Brighton and I started. There was a real bond now between the three of us. We would have to delicately navigate how that might change my and Ryan's relationship along the way. Especially with a baby on the way.

"I love you, too," Ryan said, his eyes still trained on Brighton's. Then he slowly rolled over on top of me, his body pressing mine deep into the mattress with familiarity and comfort. He clasped his hands above my head, dropped his mouth to mine, and slid inside of me. I gasped against his mouth as he made love to me, making me soar for the second time that night.

Many hours later, starving, we stumbled into the kitchen in the dark, cooking eggs and making memories as we started adjusting to our new normal—whatever that was. We sat in the sunroom with the fireplace on, snuggled together on the bench swing under a pile of blankets, while we watched snow make its first entrance of the season.

More than anything else that happened that night, this was my favorite memory of all. I would never forget the contentment I felt lying against Brighton's strong chest, with my legs draped over my husband's lap. The huge down comforter kept us all cozy as we stayed up into the wee hours talking, exposing ourselves in an even more intimate way than we had all night.

We laughed. We cried. We poked fun at one another.

Best of all? That night we fell even deeper in love in a way that defied explanation. I knew the world wouldn't approve of the way we'd opened our marriage to Brighton. Six months ago, I would've balked at such a thing myself. But if these past few months taught me anything, it was that nothing happens by accident, and the heart holds far more capacity to love than I ever imagined. Brighton came into our lives for a reason.

Sometimes, the universe just knows what you need before you need it.

...nd I mean everything, becomes centered around that...

One simple word: No. Before that, our eight-year marriage was built on love, respe...

the darkness, loss after loss. the only thing that can set you free is the truth. It's ju...

as sacred as our wedding vows, and maybe even more so because I came after the lo...

were one hundred percent honest with one another, that would be enough. That woul...

ile—through another miscarriage. Until, finally, that trag... false hope and sh...

...after how honest, could bridge the hollow, gaping hole where my heart used to b...

...mpts to reach me. To save me. To restore me to the woman he'd fallen in love with. To...

...ed. "And you fell in love with him?" Dr. Paul ask...

...rough. Through the darkness that caused us to c...

...I lifted an eyebrow and glanced a...

...if I fell in love with a woman...

...a nasty habit I found mys...

...spect. He went back to...

..."Rocky, D...

...you to tell...

...did you go, say to th...

...I wasn't willing to...

...but s...he both...

...and pro...

...a perso...

...tolerate. Th...

...was no...

...Here's what I...

CHAPTER SEVENTEEN

Ryan

"RYAN! WAIT UP," Professor Shanahan called as the elevator doors began to close.

I ground my jaw, not wanting to be trapped in such a tiny space with the likes of Kimber. She'd always been a little over the top and grating, but ever since Laelynn died, it seemed as if she had a personal vendetta to make my life a living hell.

She caught the doors with her hands just as they were about to close. I sighed. There was no graceful way out of this. I pressed the Open button to make things easier. She slid in, her oversize tote bag smacking into me as she turned to face the front.

"Oh, lord. I'm such a mess today," she said, flustered. "Thank you for holding the elevator for me."

I didn't.

"Say, while I have you here, have you talked to that neighbor friend of yours recently? Barker? Boston? I can't quite remember his name. You know, the one who was eating dinner with Olivia that night. At Rudy's?" she said innocently, smoothing a hand over her nearly black hair which had been sprayed into submission.

I inwardly rolled my eyes at how passive-aggressive she was. For someone whose husband was a known philanderer, and had a propensity for grooming his young secretaries, it was pretty ballsy of her to take a drive on the high road.

"I talk to him all the time, Kimber. He's a friend of ours, as you well know."

"Oh, good. Can you pass along my phone number to him then, and maybe a good word? Mr. Shanahan and I are interested in buying the Kerrington home. We were at the open house, and even though there are a ton of cosmetic changes we'd need to make for it to fit our taste, it has lovely bones."

I bit my tongue. She knew damn well that Olivia was the designer who helped Brighton with the renovation. I'd pass along her message with any sincerity when hell froze over. There was no way Kimber and her slimy husband would be neighbors of ours.

"Sure. Though I think he has several interested buyers already. I'm sure there will be a bidding war," I said to deter her. I didn't actually know what the status of the house was. It was the one thing we hadn't discussed, even though the three of us spent nearly all our free time together these days.

I was kinda hoping I could talk Brighton into sticking around long term. It would make our arrangement much easier to justify in the future with a lot less explaining to do if he was simply "our neighbor." I didn't care what anyone else thought, but it also wasn't something we'd be flaunting around town or anything. What we did in the privacy of our own home was no one else's business. Unfortunately, it was also a small town, and I had a visible job that might frown upon an openly polyamorous lifestyle.

The truth was . . . everything was so new to us. We didn't have all the answers about what we would call this arrangement. Or what the rules were now on how and when we could be intimate with one another. And what if Brighton ended up being the father of our baby? Would he be expected to live next door while his baby was under our roof? It was going to get a whole lot messier before we figured everything out.

Speaking of which, I checked my phone for the time and watched impatiently as the floors ticked down. I was running late, and today was Liv's first doctor's appointment. Brighton was driving her to the OB/GYN's office, and I was meeting them there. What I hadn't planned on was one of my straight-A students coming to my office unannounced and letting me know she was considering withdrawing from the program.

The elevator doors slid open, and I waited for Kimber to exit. She turned to face me before I had a chance to make my getaway.

"Ryan, I've been meaning to ask after Olivia. She seemed a little pallid at the fundraiser. Is she doing any better? I thought it might be a little too soon to be out and about after everything that's happened," she said, waving her hands. She dropped her voice an octave, even though no one else was around, and whispered, "You know, after she lost the baby and everything."

I clenched my keys in my hand. There was nothing I hated more than a person who was ugly on the inside. And I was getting tired of Professor Shanahan's backhanded digs veiled as concern.

"Look, I don't mean to be rude, but I'm late for an appointment. And Olivia didn't lose the baby. *We* both did. However, she is a grown-ass, strong-as-hell woman who can decide for herself when she's ready to socialize. So, while I appreciate your concern, it's unsolicited and unnecessary. Perhaps you should keep your eyes closer to your own home than on mine."

I left Kimber opening and closing her mouth like a beached fish gasping for air as she sought an ego-saving comeback. I knew my response was a little much—but, damn, I was tired of her meddling.

I didn't give her another thought as I raced to Olivia's appointment. She and Brighton were already in the waiting room when I walked in, swooping down to plant a full kiss on her sweet lips. She looked radiant, even though she wasn't showing much yet. I couldn't wait to see her stomach fill out again. It was one of my favorite parts of her being pregnant the last time.

When the nurse called Olivia back, Brighton and I both stood to go with her. The woman looked at our little group with confusion.

"I'll just stay here," Brighton said.

"No, you won't," I insisted. "Let's go."

Olivia brushed by the nurse on her way to the scale with a secret smile playing on her lips, leaving the dirty work to me.

"We're all family," I said, as if that explained anything.

"That's fine. I've seen stranger." She jotted Olivia's weight down on her chart and frowned, then ushered us back to the exam rooms, where Liv took a pit stop to pee in a cup and get her blood drawn. After the nurse updated her current prescriptions list and asked a few more questions, she smiled and let us know the doctor would be right in.

Olivia sat nervously on the exam table, picking at her fingernails. I went over and sat with her on the corner of the table, taking her hand in mine. I kissed the back of it and met her eyes. Fear stared back at me.

"It's going to be okay."

"How can you say that and be so sure? It wasn't the first three times. What if it's not again? I can't go through that again, Ryan."

I kissed her forehead. "I know, baby. We'll cross that bridge if we get to it. But I have a good feeling about this."

She put her hand on her belly through the opening of her scratchy blue gown. "I want this so badly."

Before I could answer, the door swung open. "Olivia! I wasn't expecting to see you back so soon." The doctor looked up from her chart and stopped short at the sight of Brighton on one side of Olivia and me on the other. It was a small room and was getting cozier by the second. "And you brought a friend."

Olivia bit her lip. I could see her worrying the cuticle on her nail again.

"Yeah, the pregnancy was a surprise for us, too, Dr. Chavez."

"Ryan," she said, shaking my hand, "congratulations. It's good to see you again." Then she turned to Brighton. "And you are?"

Brighton extended his hand with a warm grin. "Brighton Kerrington. Nice to meet you, Dr. Chavez."

"Let's start at the beginning, shall we?" she said, sitting on her small swivel stool in front of the computer. She started typing as Olivia told her everything she could.

"So, you haven't been getting your periods for a while now? And you don't remember when your last menstrual cycle started? You're making this awfully tough on me, Olivia," she teased. "Luckily, we'll know once we get a look at this little peanut and take some measurements."

Olivia took a deep breath. "There's something else we need to talk to you about."

The doctor looked back and forth between me and Olivia. "Does this happen to have anything to do with your friend here?"

Olivia nodded.

"Olivia, you don't owe me an explanation, but it does help to know what we're dealing with. Especially with your history. Any deviation in details could make a huge difference in the success rate of this pregnancy."

"I know. Which is why I need to let you know that—" Olivia closed her eyes and took a deep breath. Brighton wrapped an arm around her shoulder in support.

"Doctor, we've actively opened our marriage, and Brighton is a part of our family now," I explained. "Olivia was on birth control, so we weren't as safe as we should've been. The truth is, we're not sure who the biological father is. But it doesn't matter who it ends up being because the three of us will be raising it together."

The doctor nodded. "I see," she said. But she didn't look like she "saw" all that clearly.

"A lot has certainly changed since I saw you last. But I appreciate your candor. It *will* help as we move forward. And, of course, you have doctor–patient confidentiality, so nothing leaves this room. Though, as you know, it's a small town, Ryan. People talk. If all of you keep showing up for prenatal appointments, it won't take long for people to put two and two together. Brighton is welcome to be here anytime.

But the three of you may want to consider how to handle these appointments going forward and your level of comfort if people start talking."

I nodded, grateful for the doctor's honest response.

"So, who wants to hear a heartbeat?"

A smile spread across Olivia's face for the first time that afternoon. She lay back and reached for my hand. Brighton stood on the other side of the table, his hand on Olivia's shoulder. The doctor called the nurse back into the room for the exam and placed a fetal doppler on Olivia's stomach. She turned on the sound and rolled the instrument over her stomach, seeking what we were all eager to hear. I wouldn't be able to breathe until I heard a strong heartbeat and got the first peek at our baby on the ultrasound. But first things first.

The muffled sound of the doppler dragging across Olivia's tummy filled the room as we all held our breaths. As soon as we heard the baby's faint heartbeat, Olivia let out a strangled cry, putting her hand over her mouth. Then the heartbeat grew louder, filling the room.

I glanced over at Brighton, who was staring at Olivia's belly, tears in his eyes. He glanced up at me, and I couldn't help but tear up, too, seeing the excitement, fear, and hope there. I leaned over and kissed Olivia's forehead. "There she is," I said quietly.

"Or he," Brighton said, running his hand through Olivia's hair as he looked down at her in awe. "There's a baby in there, Liv."

The nurse joined us at the exam table and smiled at Olivia. "This might be a little cold," she said, squirting some ultrasound gel in her hand. She rubbed it over Olivia's stomach.

The doctor turned on the ultrasound monitor and picked up the transducer.

"Let's see what we're working with."

The fuzzy, gray image of Olivia's uterus came into view. The doctor rolled the wand over her stomach until, finally, the first signs of our little baby came into view. I couldn't have stopped the tears from coming if I tried. They dripped freely down my cheeks as a fully formed baby came into view.

Olivia squeezed my hand and grinned up at me. "There she is!"

"Well, we don't know that quite yet," the doctor joked. "But let's start with what we do know. The first thing you'll see is that the baby is where it's supposed to be in your uterus, Olivia—which is a relief considering one of your miscarriages was because of an ectopic pregnancy. That's not the case with this little fella."

Brighton leaned over and kissed Olivia, taking her other hand as we all listened to the doctor walk through the growth she was seeing and all the things that were going well and were on target, based on how far along she thought the pregnancy was.

"So, you said you were getting sick at the beginning of your pregnancy?"

Olivia nodded. "I didn't know I was pregnant. It was an incredibly stressful time, and I'd just started working again. I wasn't hungry and wasn't taking good care of myself. I found out I was pregnant when I basically fainted at my therapist's office and had to be rushed to the ER."

"Well, according to the urinalysis and blood work, combined with what we're seeing here on the screen, you look to be about twelve weeks along. That puts your due date around the eighth of April. Heartbeat is strong. The baby is measuring right on track size-wise. The good news is that even though you weren't getting enough nutrients, everything was going to the baby. With the anti-nausea medicine you're on now, I expect you to pick up the eating again and encourage you not to worry about your weight with this pregnancy, Olivia. Just enjoy it."

"Oh, I'll have no problem with that. I eat like a horse now between the baby and keeping up with these two."

I nearly choked at Olivia's comment, but the doctor chuckled. "Well, good for you. Do any of you have any questions? Is this potentially your first child, Brighton?"

He cleared his throat, and Olivia squeezed his hand. "No, ma'am. My college girlfriend was pregnant, but we lost our son during delivery."

"Is there a genetic reason we need to worry about?"

Brighton shook his head. "Not that I'm aware of. Umbilical cord."

The doctor made some notes. "And do the three of you *want* to know who the father is? Technology has come a long way in prenatal DNA testing. We no longer need to gather amniotic fluid, making it safer for the baby. We just use a blood sample from Mom and take swabs from the men. Your insurance won't cover the test. But if you're interested in getting one, we can take samples at any time since you're far enough along."

I looked at Olivia, then over at Brighton. We'd discussed this the night we brought Olivia home from the hospital. We decided then that we didn't want to know yet, or possibly ever. This baby was a miracle, pure and simple. Maybe it was for the best that we didn't know. We didn't want to drive a wedge into the complicated relationship that was still beginning to form. And the three of us would love the baby, no matter whose it was.

"You don't have to decide now. There are many quality, at-home mail-in kits you can buy later on. If you decide to find out, just let me know. Also, if you plan on doing any genetic screening, it requires knowing who the father is first. So that's something you may want to consider."

"It wouldn't matter, Dr. Chavez. Nothing would change our decision to keep the baby. For now, we decided not to get a DNA test."

The doctor nodded, but I could tell she disagreed with our course of action. She didn't seem judgmental about it. But with her being Olivia's OB/GYN doctor since our first pregnancy, I knew her concern was more about the overall viability of Olivia's pregnancy.

"We'll need to see you once a month until the last two months of your pregnancy, Olivia. Then we'll have you come in every two weeks. You're still considered a higher-risk pregnancy due to your previous losses. So, I need you to take it as easy as possible. You can do light cardio and easy lifting, but nothing strenuous. If you're working, have someone else do the heavy lifting and installations. Since this isn't your first rodeo, I'm sure you remember what you can eat, and what you should avoid. If you're not on prenatals already, start taking them today. Especially with being anemic—though your numbers do look better than they did during your hospital visit, so keep up the good work.

"Do you have any questions?" she asked, meeting each of our eyes.

"What's the likelihood I'll actually be able to carry this baby to term? After Laelynn, I started doubting my body's ability to ever hold a baby again. I'm really scared with this pregnancy."

"Olivia . . ." Dr. Chavez said, moving closer to the exam table. She wiped off the ultrasound gel and helped Liv sit up after closing her gown. She met Olivia's concerned gaze. "I know you're scared, and it's normal to doubt your body's ability after loss. But you are still young and healthy overall. The baby is doing good right now. Just the fact that you got pregnant while on birth control tells me that this baby is strong. It's a fighter. So, you need to be too. As much as you can, I need you to find healthy ways to release the fear around this baby. Holding stress in the body isn't going to help. Each baby that came before this one had its own story. But this baby does, too. So, try not to borrow fear and project it onto this little one. Give this baby its own chance to tell its story—whatever that may be."

"Thank you, Dr. Chavez," Olivia said, wiping tears that pooled at the corner of her eyes.

"You have a lot of help having two men by your side. Take advantage of it. Find ways to experience joy together and make happy new memories with this pregnancy. Many women go on to have completely healthy babies after miscarriages and stillbirths. Now, that doesn't mean that we won't monitor your pregnancy closer. As your baby grows, it'll be critical to self-monitor movement and activity in there and let us know if there are any changes. I know it might be easier said than done but give yourself permission to be present in *this* pregnancy and try not to compare it to your other ones. You don't want to pass time fretting through each stage." She smiled warmly, patting Olivia's knee before she left. "This is your rainbow baby, Olivia. There's much to celebrate."

Before she and the nurse left the room to let Olivia get dressed, Dr. Chavez printed out a long row of ultrasound pictures and placed them in an envelope. She handed them to Brighton. "Congratulations. I can tell this baby is going to be surrounded by love. You two take good care of Olivia, and I'll see you back in four weeks. Be thinking about whether or not you want to find out the gender," she said, winking.

"I definitely want to find out the gender," Brighton said as the door closed behind the doctor.

"Me, too," I said, grinning.

"Me, three!" Olivia said, sliding off the table. "On that note, the baby and I are really hungry. Ry, would you mind stopping somewhere on the way home to grab us something to eat?"

"Not at all. I'm happy to. Besides, what the baby wants, the baby gets, right? You got anywhere to be this evening, Kerrington?"

"Just dinner plans with my best lady."

"We're really doing this, aren't we?" I said in amazement. "We're having a baby, Livy."

"I was so afraid to believe the doctor at the hospital," she whispered. "But being able to hear its heartbeat today—and to see it healthy in there—it makes everything so much more real. I still remember seeing Laelynn for the first time. But the doctor's right. We need to celebrate every milestone with this baby and stay as positive as we can."

Olivia dressed, and we each took turns giving her long, emotional hugs.

"So, how are we going to celebrate?" Liv asked.

"How about we start with a nice dinner first? Then—I know this is going to sound crazy and impulsive—but what if we got away for the weekend? We have two days off next week, so I have a long weekend. Let's escape the city and go somewhere where no one knows us. Figure some of this stuff out together. What do you say?"

Olivia threw her arms around me. "That sounds like heaven. Where should we go?"

I looked over at Brighton. He had his hand on Liv's lower back and was rubbing it.

"Kerrington and I will take care of everything," I assured her. "Your only job this weekend will be to get pampered."

"I like the sounds of that!" she said. "Now, hand over the pics. I want to see our baby girl again."

"Or boy," Brighton reminded her, handing her the envelope.

We followed Olivia out of the doctor's office and down the long hallway of the boutique medical center. Every doctor you could imagine was under one roof, and they all worked for the same health care conglomeration, making referrals unnecessary and access to other health care providers just a short walk away.

We were all oohing and ahhing over the baby's pictures as we walked toward the parking garage. Which is why we didn't see Kimber before running into her.

Oh hell.

d I mean everything, becomes centered around that one

ne simple word: No. Before that, our eight-year marriage was built on love, respect

e darkness loss after loss, the only thing that can stop you ever is the truth. Its good

s sacred as our wedding vows, and maybe even more so because it came after the loss

re one hundred percent honest with one another. That would be enough. That would

e—through another miscarriage. Until, finally, that fragile, false hope and that

ter how honest, could bridge the hollow, gaping hole where my heart used to

pts to reach me. To save me. To restore me to the woman he'd fallen in love with. Even

ted. And you fell in love with him? Dr. Paul asked

through. Through the darkness that caused me to be

I bobbed an eyebrow and glanced at

of I fell in love with a woman I

a nasty habit. I found myself

ipped. How not to let it work

azure, Walter, No

d you men the

d you go say to the

wanted nothing to

take so far

and ping

CHAPTER EIGHTEEN
Olivia

"RYAN! WHAT A surprise to keep running into you today like this. Olivia," she said, trying to catch a glimpse at what was in my hands. It was obvious from the long strand of folded, black-and-white photos that they were ultrasound images. "Oh, my! I didn't realize you were expecting again so soon, Ryan! Why didn't you tell me earlier?"

"Because we aren't telling anyone yet. I'd appreciate if you didn't either. We want to get a little further along in the pregnancy before sharing the good news."

"Indeed!" She ran two pinched fingers in front of her puckered lips as if zipping them. "Mum's the word! You know you can trust me to keep a secret!"

My stomach churned. Of all people to run into, Kimber was the last person in the world I'd trust with a secret.

"Well, congratulations, Olivia! How exciting. And Brighton!" she said, eyeing our neighbor from head to toe.

"You are just the person I wanted to see. How completely unexpected that you would be with the Wells at such an important appointment."

I ground my teeth, ready to pounce on her like a feral Chihuahua. Ryan took the pictures from my hands and folded them back into the envelope, then draped his arm around my shoulder.

"Well, that's what best friends do, Mrs. Shanahan," Brighton said smoothly. "As the godfather, I plan to be as involved as I can every step of the way. I couldn't be happier for Ryan and Olivia."

I licked my lips and swallowed. My heart ached at the lie Brighton felt we needed to tell to ward off nosy acquaintances and prevent salacious gossip.

"Well, isn't that cozy," she said, glancing right at me. She lifted her shoulders, scrunched her nose, and forced a smile on her caked-on, overly rouged face as if that were the cutest news in the world and she just couldn't stand it. Then she immediately swung her attention back to Brighton. "Did Ryan pass along my message to you?"

Brighton looked at Ryan and shrugged, jamming his hands into his pockets. "Can't say he did, being busy at his wife's doctor's appointment and all. I just ran into them myself coming from my own doctor's appointment."

Smooth. I wasn't sure if I should be concerned with the ease in which these lies kept coming or impressed. Kimber looked flustered, swiftly realizing we were a united front and wouldn't give her a bit of the gossip fodder she was seeking.

Definitely impressed.

"Well, we have good news! Mr. Shanahan and I were at your open house, and after much consideration, we decided we're interested in buying your uncle's property. You did a lot of beautiful work to get started on such a massive renovation. We'd be committed to finishing the job, following the historical preservation guidelines to a T, of course. You can be sure of that!"

Wow. Pretentious much? I couldn't wait to hear Brighton shut this shit down.

"While your interest is certainly a compliment, I'm afraid the property has already sold."

"What?" I said in disbelief at the same time as Kimber. Ryan squeezed my shoulders to remind me not to give anything away in front of his colleague.

"Yep! My sister, Paige, is the real estate agent managing the sale on behalf of our family, and I have it on good authority that the paperwork has already been signed and it's in escrow as we speak."

Kimber's face burned bright red, and she looked like she wanted to rip somebody's head off. I tried not to giggle. Then she blinked and plastered on the fake smile she normally wore. "That's unfortunate. But perhaps it's for the best. This way we can find something more to our taste on the inside, as well. It was nice seeing you again, Ryan. Olivia," she said, barely glancing my way.

As she walked away, doing her best to look unaffected, I couldn't help but feel a little sorry for her. I wouldn't ever understand someone who purposely tried to cut others down. But whatever made her so sour was something she had to live with every day of her life, and that didn't sound so appealing to me. It made me realize how incredibly fortunate I was to have a husband who loved me more than anything in the world. Who loved me so much, in fact, that he was willing to share my heart, knowing that it meant no less love for him.

I looked over at Brighton, and my heart constricted. I never knew I needed a Brighton in my life until he showed up, swinging his hammer, and unnerving me with that half-cocky, half-seductive grin of his. I'd almost lost him. I came this close.

I squeezed my eyes closed. The thought of losing either of my loves made me physically ill. I took a deep breath and fell into Ryan's waiting arms, because I knew it wasn't such a good idea for me to tumble into Brighton's publicly just yet, and I needed someone else's strength to support me.

I looked up at Ryan, my lower lip trembling from the thoughts racing through my head. "I'm sorry. For every day I pushed you away and wouldn't let you give me the support you so desperately wanted to. You were ready to take my grief for me and carry it—even at your own expense. Only I didn't know how to give it to you to share. I don't know if I would've made it without you."

He pushed my hair back from my forehead and kissed it. "Whoa. Where is all this coming from, Liv? Don't let Kimber get in your head."

"It's not about Kimber," I reassured him. "I just can't believe how lucky I am to have so much love in my life. Six months ago, I was pushing everyone away. My friends. My therapist. You." That last one was the hardest to swallow.

"By letting Brighton in, you taught me just how much love a heart can really hold. I was so worried that I wouldn't be able to feel anything when I saw the baby today on the ultrasound. But I did. I don't know why god gave us this blessing right now, the way he did. But my heart finally feels open enough to receive it. And that's because of you."

Ryan leaned down and pressed his lips to mine.

"There's only one problem," I said.

"What's that?"

I turned to Brighton. "We need to figure out what we're going to do now that the house is sold. I can't bear to think of you living so far away in Watertown. I would miss the hell out of you. Not to mention once the baby comes. I don't want you to miss out on any of her milestones."

"Don't you mean *his*?" Brighton flashed me a wicked grin, and I swatted him playfully. "Come on, let's get back to the car. We can talk more about this on our trip this weekend. But you have nothing to worry about, Feisty."

"I don't?"

Brighton shook his head and leaned back on his heels, a shit-eating grin lighting up his face.

"Brighton! What is it?"

"It's me, Liv. I bought the house. It's mine now. Hell—I think it was always meant to be mine. Guess all your hoodoo-voodoo good luck charms really did work."

It felt as if my heart stopped for just a moment. "You bought your uncle's house? Just so you could stay close to me?"

"Well—technically, so I could stay close to both of you."

"You would do something like that? For us? Are you sure— like a thousand percent sure—you want to uproot your entire life and move here? What about your business? And your family? You have family up there."

"Yes, and they're less than two hours away. We can visit them anytime we want. But the family I can't live without is standing right in front of me. Someone wise once told me that you end up creating the family you always needed. Guess that's what I've done." Brighton looked over my shoulder at

Ryan, and that silent language they shared hung heavy in the air between them. He got a little choked up and turned his attention back to me.

"All three of us have lost so much. But we won't be leaving them behind just because we're moving forward. Your two babies, Laelynn, Sam . . . they will always be a part of this odd little family of ours. I learned a long time ago that life is too short not to seize love when it comes knocking at your door. Especially if it's a fancy purple one," he teased.

"I think you mean *plum suede*," Ryan bantered.

Brighton and I couldn't help but laugh. "Yay! We've finally dragged Ryan over to the dark side of knowing paint colors!"

"Smartass," Ryan said, smacking my backside.

"Let's go pack and get this show on the road. As much as I love my new house, I can't wait to travel with you for the first time. And we need to figure out where we're going," Brighton said.

"Or . . ." Ryan said as we walked back to the parking garage, "we could go with the flow—which seems to be working at the moment. Why don't we just drive and see where our hearts take us?"

"I like that idea," I said. "I like it very much."

CHAPTER NINETEEN

Brighton

WHEN WE PULLED into my new driveway, Olivia and I were greeted with a bold "SOLD" sticker placed diagonally across the large, wooden For Sale sign my sister installed at the front of the property before the open house. I squeezed Liv's hand.

"It's hard to believe how much our lives have changed in such a short amount of time," I said, running the pad of my thumb along the ridge of one of her fingers. I rubbed the sides of her engagement ring and wedding band.

"Are you sure it's what you really want?" she asked quietly. "I keep thinking it's all a dream, and I'm going to wake up and find you gone one day."

"I wouldn't do that to you, Liv. Not ever."

She looked down at her wedding rings. "Does it bother you? I feel like you're going to miss out on so much if you settle for being with Ryan and me."

"I'm not settling, Olivia. I love you. Fuck," I said, dragging my hand through my hair as I turned in my seat to face her. "I love both of you so much, can't you see that? Sure, I love you differently than Ryan. But I can't imagine my life without either of you anymore."

"I feel the same," she whispered.

Olivia and I hadn't really had much one-on-one time alone since everything fell back into place. I was grateful that Ryan decided to pick up dinner for us on the way home so Olivia and I could come home and get a head start on packing and finding a pet sitter for Stitch.

"Don't you want to get married someday? We won't ever be able to have that."

I chewed my lip, reading the sadness etched all over her face. I'd never gotten this real about my feelings with Liv or any other woman before. But I knew I needed to put her heart at ease, so she didn't carry this guilt into our future.

"Did you know that I had already seen you before we ever met?"

"No!" she said, surprised.

"The first time was in a rainstorm. The rain had tapered, so I snuck out to the dumpster to throw something out before it started back up again. I saw you in your sunroom, looking like a beautiful, elusive ghost. I couldn't make out your face, but I saw *you*. Even from here I could feel your pain, Olivia."

"I didn't know."

"I saw you a few other times after that, always the same way. I grew curious about who you were and what your story was. I can't explain why I was so drawn to you, but I cared about your well-being before I even met you."

"Brighton," she said, scooching closer to me so she could rest a hand on my thigh.

"When I met you for the first time—and you were no longer this figment of my imagination—I was at a loss for words. I'd never met someone so effusively beautiful in all my life."

"Oh, come on now," she said, giggling.

"I'm serious. You took my breath away. I couldn't stop the pull to you any more than I could stop breathing. But I'd already become friends with Ryan at that point. Do you know how hard it was to know instantly that this was *my person*, and yet I would never be able to have her? To have you."

"Yes, I do," she said. "Because, tulips."

"Tulips," I whispered back.

We sat in silence for a moment as dusk settled in around us. I'd kept the truck running and the heat blasting because it was getting colder every day.

"I don't know when I fell in love with you, exactly. When I knew it, body and soul. It might've been that first day on my front porch. Or the night we lay in your yard and talked about Laelynn and Sam. I knew in my heart I should've told Ryan to fuck off when he came to me about being with you both—because I was already head over heels for you by then. I knew in my heart if I was allowed to touch you, to physically show you what you meant to me, I would never be able to stop. And I was right. But I'm so glad I didn't tell Ryan to fuck off. Because then I wouldn't have known real love.

"I thought I knew what love was with Caroline. But that wasn't love. That was affection based on proximity, and a choice I made because of a baby."

"And here you are, in the same situation again. I know you love me, Brighton. But what if you look back and regret this?

What if you feel like you missed out because you couldn't get married? Or find out you only wanted this because of the baby."

"I promise you, I don't want this just because of the baby." I pulled her nearly into my lap. "I want this because I love you more than anything, or anyone, I've ever given my heart to." I looked her in the eyes, so she knew exactly what I was saying. "I don't throw that around lightly, Olivia. I already tried to walk away from you once. I would've done it so you could be happy with Ryan and move on. My intention was never to come between your marriage."

"I know. It wouldn't have made me happy if you left, though. I was already struggling with the idea of you leaving after the open house."

I slid my hand through her hair to cup the back of her head. Lowering my lips, I brushed them lightly against hers. "Don't you know by now? I can never walk away from you."

"I'd be lost if you did."

My hand tightened in her hair, and I gave in to my desire to kiss her fully. Our mouths crashed against one another's, and it was as if every unspoken fear and every realized desire met somewhere in the middle. We couldn't get enough, and our tongues demanded everything from each other, dragging each other down into a soft, sensual promise of all that was to come.

I wished more than anything that I could take her inside and make love to her. It had been an emotionally exhilarating day seeing our baby on the ultrasound, and it had made me feel so close to Liv. There was a chance that the baby was actually mine. It took my breath away to see a tiny life that I may have created again.

I needed to be as close to Olivia as humanly possible.

"Do you think Ryan will ever let me make love to you?"

"You mean alone again?"

I nodded.

"Yes. I think now that things have changed, he would. But I think we need to talk about it first this weekend, just to make sure we're all on the same page this time. I couldn't stand to hurt either of you. And I'll never lie to Ryan again."

"I want you, Liv. God help me, but I want you to myself again, even if for just one night." I buried my head in her hair and held onto her for the longest time. Her hands found my head, massaging my scalp. Goose bumps raced over my skin, and my desire for her was only growing stronger. She dragged my mouth back to hers and leaned back, pulling me on top of her.

If it was all we could have for now, I would take it. I nearly bruised her mouth I kissed her so deeply, so desperately. I felt like I would never be able to get enough of her.

"Marry me," I whispered hoarsely against her mouth.

"What?" She pulled back.

I sat up, pulling her with me. "I said marry me, Olivia North Wells. I know we can't for *real*. But maybe we could have a simple ceremony, so you know how seriously I'm committed to you, to us, to this. And so I can feel on equal footing with Ryan. It's so hard to know he has you as his wife, when it's the one thing in this world I want but can never truly have."

Olivia ran her finger over her bottom lip. It was swollen from our kisses and her hair was messy from our make-out session. Even the windows were fogged up.

A knock on my window made Olivia and me both jump. I wiped the glass with my sleeve and saw Ryan standing on the other side. I rolled the window down.

"Hey, man."

"I can't leave you two alone for a minute," he joked. But his eyes weren't hard, and his mouth curled softly into a half-smile. "Get your asses out here. I got the Mexican Olivia was craving."

He made his way back to his house through the light snow. Maybe he really was getting more open to the idea that it wasn't always going to be the three of us, and that maybe sometimes Olivia and I might want to be intimate alone.

For some reason, I was more afraid to talk to him about that this weekend than I was to tell him I wanted to marry his wife.

I kissed her nose. "This conversation isn't over. It's something I want us all to talk about this weekend."

As we headed back to their house, I realized Olivia never really answered me when I asked her if she would marry me. Maybe she'd thought I was kidding. Maybe she was scared to consider even emotionally saying those vows to anyone else.

Or maybe I just needed to ask her the right way.

CHAPTER TWENTY

Olivia

I WAS STILL REELING from Brighton's "proposal" as we ate our spicy Mexican from Juan and Don's. When we were done, we called the breeder where we got Stitch and Regina said she'd be more than happy to have him come back for a little weekend visit. So, we packed our bags, hopped into Ryan's SUV, and drove out to Regina's farm to drop Stitch off for his extended playdate. By the time we said our goodbyes, the snow was falling harder, and it was getting late. Luckily, Ryan had already put chains on his wheels for the winter, so we were prepared and ready to go. It had been a long, emotional day, so I wasn't surprised when the gentle lulling of the road and Ryan's heated seats ended up putting me to sleep. When I woke, we were still driving. I stretched as much as I could in the front seat and yawned.

"Welcome back, Sleeping Beauty. Feeling any better?" Ryan asked, glancing over at me. "You passed out in record time."

I blushed sheepishly. "You know how easy I fall asleep on long car rides. Besides, you two and the baby take a lot out of me. Figured I needed to restore my energy before we got to our destination."

"Damn straight," he said, winking at me.

I looked out my window into the inky black night. Snow was still coming down, but I saw the blur of a sign as we drove by. "Pennsylvania, huh? Does that mean you've figured out where we're going, or are we driving through the night?"

I glanced back at Brighton, who was busy on his phone. When he noticed I was awake and staring at him, he leaned forward and gave me a quick kiss. "Patience, Grasshopper."

I rolled my eyes but giggled. I loved the energy when we were all together and happy. It filled my soul with a contentment that I'd never known was possible.

"So, nothing? Not even a tiny hint?" I asked, placing my hand over my belly, and giving it a gentle rub. I fluctuated between terrified and thrilled most days, with the thought of this tiny human being living inside of me. I willed it to hang on, to grow stronger. But I was determined to let myself relax over the long weekend and enjoy our time away.

It was after midnight when we finally pulled off the main road onto an impeccably maintained entrance to an inn of some sort. Pennsylvania was known for its romantic, historic properties, so I was excited to see what the guys had in mind. The road wound its way through dense woods, which I imagined would be beautiful the next day all covered in snow. Black, iron lampposts flickered with real flames along the roadside, making me feel as if we were driving back in time.

I was glad I'd packed a historical romance book at the last minute. I couldn't wait to snuggle up with the guys tomorrow, read a good book all day, and maybe have a hot cup of tea or a bubble bath. This weekend was sounding better and better by the minute, and I was getting antsy as we approached the inn. I could see the warm glow of lights ahead, and a soaring stone entrance.

The Inn at Beaufield Ridge.

I'd never heard of the place but couldn't wait to explore it. As Ryan pulled up to the front, I peeked inside through the tall, floor-to-roof windows that bookended a set of double-hung, massive, mahogany doors with two giant Douglas fir wreaths hanging at the center of each. Inside, a two-story, stone fireplace burned real wood, even though it was well past midnight.

I turned to Ryan and squealed. "This is where we're staying?" I asked, gaping in disbelief.

He placed his hand over mine and smiled. "This is a special celebration, Olivia. We deserve to go a little over the top. It's been a long time coming, hasn't it?"

His eyes grew soft as he looked at me. It sure had.

"Do you think they're going to have any rooms available? It doesn't look like the kind of place where you can just roll up in the middle of the night unannounced."

"Well . . . I might've done a *little* planning while you were sleeping," Brighton said from the backseat. "I know we decided on a spontaneous trip, but with the snow falling, and you needing rest, we didn't want to be driving around aimlessly all night. Paige got married here once upon a time, and I remembered it wasn't too far of a drive. So—I made a few calls, and here we are. I think you're going to love it!"

I sighed. How had I gotten so lucky? "How could I not?"

Ryan and I waited in the warm Jeep while Brighton went to grab our room keys. It wasn't long before we were driving again, this time away from the main inn.

"Didn't they have any rooms?" I asked, disappointed.

"They did."

"Then where are we headed?"

"To our room."

"That's not at the inn?"

"We rented a private cottage," Ryan said, grinning.

"What?"

"They have stand-alone cottages on property that are completely self-sufficient. You can either stay at the inn or in one of these. I thought you might prefer this—for the privacy it offers."

Yeah, it might've been a tad awkward walking through the main lobby with two men. I giggled at what the desk clerk might've thought. She'd be right, of course—which made me smile more as I anticipated our weekend.

It was a short drive to the "cottage," which was accessible by its own private driveway that switchbacked several times before coming to an end at one of the most beautiful homes I'd ever seen. There wasn't another cottage in sight. In fact, the house stood solitary against the pitch-black sky, the entire property surrounded by a mature forest. The house itself was far more modern than the inn, edging closer to Frank Lloyd Wright. So much for the romantic historic inn I'd conjured in my mind.

"Head on in," Ryan said as Brighton opened the door for me. "I'll grab the bags."

Brighton helped me from the car and held my arm as we crossed the icy driveway to the winding front path. It led to a two-story home with flat, modern lines, tall windows, and minimal outdoor effects. I was a little worried that the inside might feel cold based on the sleek entrance that welcomed us.

But I couldn't have been more wrong.

I gasped as Brighton opened the front door. Lights were already on, waiting to greet us. The entrance spilled into an open floor plan with huge, vaulted ceilings. The floors were a weathered gray wood, and the main wall of the kitchen behind the stove was covered in flat stone from floor to ceiling. Cozy living areas defined the spaces and functions of the main room that included the kitchen, an eating area, a living room, and a reading nook. Most of the walls were windows. Despite that, it felt warm and toasty, a gas fireplace heating the space and making the living room even more inviting.

"This is gorgeous!" I walked to the sliding glass doors at the back. Adirondack chairs circled a fire pit and looked comfortable enough to curl up in with a big blanket, some hot chocolate, and my new book. I couldn't see much else, but there seemed to be a little pond or something beyond the patio. I couldn't wait to explore it in the morning and was already planning a romantic weekend back in the spring after the baby was born.

Ryan finished bringing the bags in and made his way to the coatrack, shrugging out of his leather jacket. He kicked off his snowy boots by the door like Brighton and I had and rubbed his hands together to get warm. "Have you looked at any other rooms yet?"

I shook my head, finally spotting a set of floating stairs wrapped around a brick interior support beam. We raced up like kids, eager to see our sleeping quarters. There were three bedrooms. One had built-in bunkbeds that looked like something out of Pottery Barn. They were built right into the wall, leaving a huge, open space for other things like an air hockey table, a huge stack of oversize Jenga blocks, and a wall full of board games, books, and puzzles.

"Ah! The fun room," I said, grinning. "You any good at air hockey, Brighton?"

He snorted. "Only the best."

"Mmm-hmm. We'll find out tomorrow."

He tickled my side and I squealed, fleeing the room in search of the master suite. We passed a large Jack and Jill bathroom and another bedroom—this one with a queen-size bed. At the end of the hall, facing the back of the property, was the master suite. And lord have mercy. My insides clenched when I saw the enormous four-poster bed with crisp white linens. The room was spacious, but the large, dark gray-and-white rug under the bed made it cozier, as did the gas fireplace that matched the one on the first floor. Sliding glass doors with black frames gave way to ample outdoor space with lounge chairs, a gas heater, and a small table with four chairs. I hoped it was warm enough to enjoy some of the outdoor spaces in the morning.

I explored the bathroom, Brighton coming up behind me as we both peeked in. My face flushed at recent memories of sharing a shower with both men. The luxurious shower here would most definitely need to be broken in.

"What are you giggling at?" Brighton asked, wrapping his arms around me.

"Just daydreaming about that shower."

"I hope that daydream includes me," he growled in my ear.

"And me," Ryan said from the doorway. He placed our overnight bags by the closet, pulling out a luggage stand for mine. Ryan sauntered over to where Brighton and I were embracing. "Got room in here for one more?"

"There's always room for you," I said, sighing as he wrapped his arms around my waist. He kissed my collarbone gently, sending goose bumps skating over my body. I purred, leaning back against him, giving Brighton access to the front of my neck. My eyes closed, and all I wanted to do was surrender my heart, soul, and body to them both again.

"Did you lock up downstairs?" I asked.

"Don't worry about a thing, beautiful," Ryan answered. "It's been a long, exciting day. We've got you covered."

Brighton kissed along my throat to my jawline, teasing me with little pecks until his lips found mine. "What do you want tonight, Liv?" he asked huskily. "Do you need some sleep?"

I gripped his hips, moaning as his mouth moved to my ear. "I already took a nap in the car," I reminded them.

"That you did," Ryan said, his hands cupping my breasts from behind and making me lose all coherent thought. "I think it's time to play then."

"The fun room?" I teased.

"Oh, it's definitely going to be the fun room," Brighton said, unzipping my jeans and tugging them over my hips. "But we have more grown-up games in mind."

"I don't know. I kind of had my heart set on Jenga."

But when Brighton dropped to his knees in front of me, and Ryan lifted my sweater over my head, Jenga was the last thing on my mind. My fingers curled into Brighton's hair as I opened for him, leaning against Ryan for support.

"You are so fucking sexy," he whispered to me from behind. His fingers massaged my nipples as he watched Brighton pleasure me. "I could really get used to this."

I turned my head, angling it up and seeking Ryan's mouth. His kiss started slow and sensual, his hand sliding up my throat to cup my jaw. He held me in place, kissing me, until I came undone from another man. Then he picked me up and carried me to the massive bed we'd be sharing for the next four days.

Life didn't get any better than this.

CHAPTER TWENTY-ONE

Ryan

THE WEEKEND FLEW by, filled with laughter, conversation, and many, *many* hours of taking "nap breaks" during the day. In other words, it was heaven. We decided against the hot tub since Olivia was pregnant. But we broke in the shower, the soaker tub, the kitchen counter, and even the air hockey table. I wasn't sure I would be able to walk out of this place in one piece.

On our last night there, we ordered in a full Italian dinner from the inn's restaurant. We had a few glasses of wine—except for Olivia, who was drinking ice water with cucumbers and mint. Then we sat by the fire on the U-shaped, worn-in leather sofa. Olivia curled up all cute-like in a large, chunky-knit blanket with a content smile playing on her lips.

We still had a lot to talk about, and I was eager to get everything out on the table before we got even farther along with the pregnancy. Even though we were trying to go with the flow and be open to what all this meant, it would only get more complicated as time went on. And the baby would be here before we knew it.

"So, what do you guys think? Still want to leave the baby's DNA a mystery?" I asked, sipping my merlot. The wine had a hint of blackberries and vanilla and went down smoother than it had any right to.

Olivia took a deep breath, and I thought she was about to answer when she pressed her lips closed and looked down at her lap.

"Look, maybe we all need to make a new truth pact," I suggested, looking at them both. Brighton was sitting to one side of Olivia, who was nestled in the prime corner spot. And I was on her other side, massaging her feet when I wasn't sipping my wine. "We're going to face a lot of hard times ahead because this is not a conventional situation, to say the least. And we're not always going to be in this honeymoon phase. We need to face the reality that there will be times when one of us gets jealous. When Brighton feels left out because we have obligations as a married couple. Or when the baby comes, and we're all cranky and overtired. There are practical questions we need to start thinking about, too."

"I know," Olivia said and sighed. "I just haven't wanted to face everything yet. I'm still so overwhelmed learning about the baby and picking back up with doctor's appointments again. It's harder than you think. The last time we were doing this, it was for Laelynn. And that didn't turn out the way we wanted. So even though I'm excited, I'm also scared as hell, Ryan. I wake up most nights sweating, dreaming about losing this baby."

"I didn't know that," I said, squeezing her foot in my hands. "This pregnancy was so unexpected. We didn't exactly have time to prepare ourselves for everything we would have to face again."

"Not to mention, I just booked three more jobs over the course of the next few months. They aren't as big as Brighton's, obviously. But I'll have a full-time workload coming up."

"Are you sure that's for the best? Maybe we need to think about having you start to cut back?"

She chewed the corner of her lip while she thought. "No. I think it wouldn't do me any good to have too much time on my hands. Idle hands and all. I think I would just sit around and worry too much about the baby. I don't want to fall into the pit of despair I just pulled myself out of."

"Have you told Dr. Paul yet?" Brighton asked, stretching his arm out on the back of the couch behind her as he crossed an ankle over his knee.

Olivia was seeing him religiously, at least once a week. We took his suggestion about the three of us seeing a counselor together seriously, and our first appointment was the week after next. It'd be nice to have some of these harder decisions ironed out before then so we could all be on the same page and not waste the therapist's time with things we should be able to work out on our own.

"I have."

"What has he said about all this?"

"The same thing he always does. That we need total transparency for this to work."

I nodded. "We expect it in our marriage, so I don't think this should be any different."

Brighton agreed. "Yeah, I never want to hide anything from you again, Ryan. Which brings up a delicate topic."

I ground my jaw, suspecting where this was heading. I'd thought about this same thing many times myself—only I'd never landed on a good, fair answer. It was so easy when it was the three of us. But even I knew if we were going to have an open relationship, I couldn't put rules on when and how they showed affection or saw each other. That wouldn't be a relationship built on trust. And it would always end up leading to feelings of guilt, judgment, jealously, or fear. And they had no place in our marriage.

I ran my hand over the back of my neck, waiting for Brighton to continue. I noticed Liv was awfully quiet. "Go on."

"Are you going to be comfortable if Liv and I want to be alone together?" he asked, his eyes piercing mine with their laser-green focus. Even though he was ten years younger than me, Brighton was one of the most well-rounded, intelligent, well-adjusted men I knew. I think that's why I was so drawn to him myself. He was confident and successful for a reason. And his eyes told me he would not back down from this.

My jaw twitched, and Liv sat up straighter on the couch, squeezing the pillow that was nestled on her lap.

"I don't really know a good answer to this question. Do you want to be alone with him more, Liv?"

I knew it wasn't fair to put her on the spot like this, but we hadn't discussed it on our own yet. And if we were going to be in this weird, three-way relationship, we needed to learn to communicate in front of one another without jealousy or nerves flying around unchecked every time we broached a difficult subject.

I sighed. "It's okay if you do. I honestly just want to know."

"I want to feel comfortable showing both of you my love, in whatever way feels natural in the moment. I don't want you to consider it cheating if"—Liv licked her lips—"if Brighton and I find ourselves alone sometimes."

"And I don't want to keep putting you in this situation of being stressed out about it, either. I don't know what to call what we have. But I guess if we're going to go all in and do this, we need to go all in and consider each other equal partners, even if Liv and I are married. I don't want you to always feel like a third wheel, Brighton. That's not fair to you."

"I don't either," Brighton said. "So, it's settled then?"

I nodded. "Just excuse me if I get a little jealous sometimes while I get used to everything. I've had Liv to myself for so long. I never imagined sharing her for the rest of my life with another man. Not to say it has to be forever, or anything. You know what I mean."

"What if I want it to be?" Brighton pressed.

My stomach dropped because I wasn't ready for where this was going. It was one thing to open my marriage bed to another man and consider ourselves on equal footing in this unusual three-way relationship. It was another thing altogether to say *forever*. But then again, it already kind of was, wasn't it? The life we'd created changed everything quickly, putting us on an accelerated path of unity.

"Do you?" I asked him. I had to know.

Olivia looked over at Brighton, her gaze soft. I could tell by the way they looked at each other and the lack of her surprise that they must've talked about this before. That only made my heart ache a little more. It felt like a betrayal that they'd openly spoken of marriage already behind my back. Olivia was *my wife*.

"I know I can't marry Olivia. She's your wife, Ryan. But I want to feel equal in this relationship, and I want to be fully committed to her—and to you by extension. Especially when the baby is born. If we're both 'Dad,' then I want that baby to know I did everything I could to be committed to his mother."

"Or hers," Olivia said playfully.

Brighton winked at her. "Or hers. The point is—you know I love Olivia. I'm trying to be as transparent as possible here. But I also respect you. As my friend, and as someone I love." He grew quiet. "And as Olivia's husband."

"So, what do you suggest?"

"I want to marry her in a small, private commitment ceremony. It wouldn't be binding by law since it's not legal. But it would mean everything to me to be wed to Olivia by heart. Especially with a baby on the way."

"Can't you have that without an actual commitment ceremony?" I wanted to vomit thinking of Olivia walking down an aisle to another man. It somehow made it all too real. It felt like losing her more than I already was.

"I suppose," Brighton said. "But come on. You know I've always wanted to get married. To have a family. I choose you guys. But that also means I lose that dream of ever being able to legally wed. That's a lot to give up."

"But isn't she worth it?" I bit back. "You said you'd take her however you could. That she was worth the risk."

Brighton sat up straighter, leaning forward as he leveled me with his gaze. "And she is. And I would. But didn't you also say you would do anything to make Olivia happy? It's no different. We both love her!"

"It is different!" I said, standing up. "She's *my* wife. I've loved her for almost nine years now. You can't love her the same way yet, Kerrington. Not enough to want to marry her."

"You don't get to tell me how I love Olivia," Kerrington ground out. "Besides, doesn't she also get a say in this?"

I looked at Olivia, noticing her eyes were shimmering with tears. I ran a hand over my face and sighed, sitting back down and trying to cool my temper. I put my head in my hands, afraid to look at her. "What *do* you want, Livy?"

It felt too soon to be having a conversation about Kerrington co-marrying her. I'd just gotten comfortable with the idea of the three of us openly being together. Hell, I'd just told the man he could sleep with my wife whenever he wanted without me even being there. Didn't I get some credit? Why did he have to push this *now*?

"I—I'm honestly not sure," she said, looking up at Brighton. They locked eyes, and a million unspoken feelings, words, touches, and stories passed between them. There was so much love it hurt to watch.

"He only mentioned the possibility of it on Friday, and we hadn't really had a moment to discuss it any further. Plus, I wanted to talk to you about it privately first. But we haven't had a chance yet with the trip and all."

"But do you want it?" I asked again, deliberately annunciating each word. "It seems pretty simple. I need to know the whole truth, Liv."

Her body trembled with the heavy breath she exhaled. The pause hung heavy in the air between us. Our eyes stayed locked, and our life flashed before my eyes. The first time I saw her walk into my classroom—that pale blond hair falling in big, soft curls down her back. The effortless smile and mesmerizing blue eyes. The chemistry. God, the chemistry. Then it moved to our first kiss—stolen in my office at the university. Hotter and more combustible than anything I'd ever felt. I knew then that I was going to marry her. That no logic of being her professor could stop me from loving this woman or make me walk away from her. And that was less than a month after meeting her.

I remembered her on our wedding day, and the way she glowed from the inside out. We'd gotten married lakeside in the summertime. Her white, sheath-styled dress was made of lace and fit perfectly to the curves of her body. It was more casual than a traditional wedding dress, but that was Olivia. The wild to my holy. The dress had an open back, and I remember holding her in my arms for our first dance, my fingers trailing down her spine to finger the delicate buttons at the waist of her gown. The promise of our wedding night. The hope for everything to come.

How could I simply hand that gift over for someone else to take?

I glanced up, trying to fight back the warring feelings clawing at my heart and the control that was slipping through my fingers. The Olivia I remembered from the first day we met stared back at me. Then it dawned on me.

She was healing.

She was consistent in her therapy. She was openly sharing her feelings with me again. She'd apologized for the mistakes she'd made along the way. And now, here she was, bravely carrying our baby once again. Giving life to a future I'd begun to think wasn't in our cards. It had to kill her with fear. Instead, I saw hope on her face. And softness. And vulnerability.

All the things I'd been praying for the past year.

I held my breath, waiting for her answer.

...and I mean everything, becomes centered around that one simple word: No. Before that, our eight-year marriage was built on love, respect... the darkness loss after loss, the only thing that can set you free is the truth. It's as sacred as our wedding vows, and maybe even more so because it came after the loss... were one hundred percent honest with one another, that would be enough. That would be... —through another miscarriage. Until, finally, that fragile, false hope could shat... ...how honest, could bridge the hollow, gaping hole where my heart used to... ...to reach me. To save me. To restore me to the woman he'd fallen in love with. Even... ...ted. "And you fell in love with him?" Dr. Paul asked, his voice... ...through. Through the darkness that caused me to... ...I lifted my eyebrows and glared at... ...if I fell in love with a woman I... ...a nasty habit," I cried, wiping... ...respect. He wasn't back to work... ...Really, Eve...? ...you could n... ...did you say to... ...wasn't willing to... ...half into facts... ...and pray... ...in plenty... ...illuminate the... ...this was now... ...down. Here's what I st...

CHAPTER TWENTY-TWO

Brighton

I DIDN'T REALIZE I was holding my breath until Olivia answered.

"Yes."

One simple word and my life changed forever. She wanted to marry *me*.

The room stood quiet, holding all the weight of her response as we each absorbed it in different ways.

Ryan swallowed, as if coming to grips with what this meant. He shot me a glare from the corner of his eyes with a warning. "Then you better do it right, and you better not hurt her, Kerrington."

"I have your blessing?"

"I'm her husband, not her father," he snapped.

"Yeah, but you're the only other man who matters."

"I need time for all of this to sink in, okay? Can't you give me that?"

Olivia nodded, and I squeezed her shoulders with the arm I had around her.

"Look, I'm going to bed. We have to leave early in the morning so I can get home and grade papers. I'm not going to wait up."

Ryan kissed Olivia goodnight then took the stairs two at a time and disappeared to the second floor.

Olivia exhaled, slouching deeper into the couch as she leaned against me. I played with her hair, giving her space with the thoughts that must be running through her head. She was quiet for the longest time.

"Do you want to go to bed, too? Or talk about this some more?"

I thought maybe she'd fallen asleep, but she hadn't. She turned into me, holding onto my shirt with both hands. She put her forehead to my chest, and I could tell she was silently crying by the way her body shook. I scooped her into my lap and held her, rubbing circles on her back with my palm.

I never thought of the responsibility I was placing on her by wanting something like this. While I was elated that she said she wanted it, too, it must've been hard for her to say as much to her husband. Was I pushing for too much, too soon?

"Olivia," I murmured.

She rotated in my lap, so she was straddling me now. Her hands cupped my face, brushing against my three-day stubble. Her eyes were watery as they looked down into my mine, but they were full of love, too. It had been hard, but we were pushing through it to claim what had always been right here between us. In this space of what could never be. It felt forbidden, and in some ways wrong. But it also felt like the rightest answer in my life.

Olivia North Wells was going to be my wife.

She dropped her mouth to mine, softly at first. She just barely nipped at my lower lip, gently swiping her tongue across the skin. Then her tongue pressed forward, more assertive, sensual. Asking to tango. I had one hand on her hip and the other snaked up her spine to cradle the back of her head and pull her lips closer to mine.

The heat exploded between us with the permission that was now unlocked. I pulled her body down harder into my lap as I pressed up against her core to show her just how much I wanted her. Her head fell back as she rocked her hips back and forth over my lap.

I cupped her breasts, kneading them as she ground her hips a few more times, until I could tell the friction was too much to bear. I held onto her back and stood. Olivia's legs wrapped around my waist and she never stopped kissing me. I walked us to the stairs. I needed to get her into a bed. But we never made it. It was as if every feeling we'd ever had for one another came pouring out, unrestrained. With this new permission came freedom without guilt. I pressed her back against the wall at the bottom of the stairs and kissed her hard, slipping my hand inside her sweatpants and making her come. The first time we made love was hot, dirty, and sensual as fuck. I kept her pinned against the wall as we took greedily from one another. She'd have scratches on her back tomorrow from the brick, but she told me not to stop as I drove deep inside her, possessing every inch she surrendered to me.

We finally snuck upstairs well after three in the morning. Olivia's legs were shaking so badly I had to carry her. When we got to the room, Ryan wasn't there. It changed the mood instantly.

"I'll go check on him," I said, letting Olivia get ready for bed.

I walked down the hall and saw the door to the guest room ajar. Ryan was standing at the window, wide awake, his back to me. He'd never gone to bed. His hands were in his pockets as he stared out the window at the snow-blanketed woods beyond.

I started to step back when he called out to me.

"If you hurt her, I will kill you."

"I'd expect nothing less," I said. "But I'll never hurt her, Ryan. And I want to stop hurting you, too."

"It's harder than I thought it would be."

"I can only imagine."

"Get some sleep," he said.

"Aren't you coming to bed?" It didn't feel right without him.

"I need some time and space to process everything."

I nodded, shutting the door on my way out.

By the time I got back to our room, Olivia was sound asleep. I could see the shadows and light play across her face from the moonlight coming in through the big, open windows. How could it hurt so much and yet feel so right to love a single woman?

I'd give Ryan the space he needed tonight, but tomorrow I would talk to him one on one. I wanted to marry Olivia more than anything in the world, but I wouldn't if it alienated Ryan. This wasn't just about me and Olivia. It was about the three of us, and we weren't complete without him.

I wasn't complete without him.

CHAPTER TWENTY-THREE

Olivia

RYAN WAS SURPRISINGLY cheerful the next morning, considering the weighty conversation we'd had the night before. He greeted me with an arm around the waist and a loud smooch to the cheek while making omelets. Brighton wasn't downstairs, so it was just the two of us.

He set the table for three, pouring orange juice and setting out cutlery while I got a small mug of decaf dandelion tea.

"Where's Brighton this morning?"

"Went for a jog."

"In this weather?" I asked, looking outside dubiously. More snow had fallen overnight, and I couldn't see the floor of the porch anymore.

"Yeah. He was up bright and early. Think he just needed to get some energy out. You know how much he loves to run."

"Why didn't you join him?" I asked.

"Just wanted to get us fed before we hop on the road. Besides, I'm not thirty anymore, Liv. It's damn cold outside. I'm not trying to have a heart attack or anything. I'll leave that foolishness to Kerrington and run on the treadmill when we get home."

"Fair enough," I said, stirring some honey powder into my tea. We sat in companionable silence for a few moments. But some things still weighed heavy on my heart, and I wanted to clear the air. "Ryan, I'm sorry if I hurt your feelings last night."

He looked surprised when he turned to me. "I'm a big boy, Liv. I can handle it. I never thought this would be easy when we picked up where we left off with Brighton."

"Yeah, but it's moving faster now that a baby is on the way. As much as I'm excited about the baby and taking this next step with Brighton and the three of us, I don't want it to change *us*."

Ryan's half-smile was full of bittersweet truth. "It already has, baby."

I swallowed. I didn't want him to be right. I was so scared of losing my tether. Brighton was my wild to my wild. Ryan was my steady rock. He always had been.

"Things may change around us, Ryan. And we may grow with our love in this new—situation, I'll say. But *we* are still Liv and Ry," I said, not sure who I was trying to convince more.

"Yeah," he said softly.

I went over and wrapped my arms around his waist. "I will never love anyone more than I love you," I whispered.

He turned in my arms and dropped his mouth to mine, taking back what was his. I stood on my tiptoes, Ryan's hands holding me firm and steady in his grasp as I reassured him that I was, am, and always would be his first and foremost.

He placed his forehead to mine. "I needed to hear that, Liv. God, did I need to hear that."

I pulled back and looked up at him, my arms still wrapped around his waist. "I need us to be okay through all of this. If we're not okay, I'm not okay."

Ryan's eyes swept over my face. "We'll always be okay. Even when we've not been as okay these last few years, I never doubted *us*. You don't need to either. Now, let's eat so we can get on the road before this weather gets any worse."

When Brighton came in five minutes later, he shook off the snow from his coat and hung it on the hook so he could join us for breakfast. Things felt almost normal, with the three of us eating breakfast together and chatting about how our days looked once we got home.

The return trip was more subdued than car rides we'd shared in the past. Brighton made some work calls and texts that were pressing. And after a late night of making love to him that left me breathless and shaky, my body gratefully took the opportunity to fall asleep for the entire car ride home.

That night, Brighton stayed at his place to give Ryan and me some alone time. He understood that we'd thrown a lot at him over the weekend, and that Ryan probably needed a minute to take everything in. Even though I reassured him it wasn't necessary, he insisted on giving Ryan some breathing room and promised he'd see me the next day.

That night, Ryan and I lay in our bed, just the two of us, and talked quietly like we used to. We shared our hopes and fears for the new life growing inside of me. We made slow, delicious love to one another like only a husband and wife who've known each other's bodies for years could do. And we made promises to one another about our future once the baby came.

I felt more connected to Ryan and loved than I had in years. It's funny how much life can change so quickly. Yet some things withstand the test of time, no matter what's being thrown our way.

By the time I drifted off to sleep, I was confident that our marriage could survive any vows I made with Brighton.

CHAPTER TWENTY-FOUR

Brighton

NOVEMBER FLEW BY fast with December bearing down on us with more snowstorms than usual. The baby was right on target, and Olivia was finally showing. Somehow, she was even more beautiful with her blossoming belly and swelling breasts. She was friskier than ever, too. We often joked that it was a good thing that Ryan was okay with us both loving on Olivia, otherwise the poor man would never get any work done.

We were all looking forward to the time off around Christmas. The school closed for three weeks, and Olivia planned out her jobs to break between clients over the holidays. She was exhilarated with the work she was doing, and it showed. Even though we were keeping her up most nights and she was busy, gone were the bags under her eyes and the exhaustion. She was well into her second trimester and enjoying the energy that had returned.

Paige was happy that the house had sold, as were my cousins, who were splitting the proceeds three ways. I'd more than amply covered fair market value and then some. I insisted on paying Paige her normal fee, even though she returned the check at first. The sale of Uncle Isaiah's house brought her a big paycheck, and I didn't want to take that from the boys just because we were family. She helped me sell my house in Watertown, too. It was a starter home I hadn't gotten around to upgrading because I was too busy making everyone else's domicile dreams come true. It was easy to part with and made starting over next door to Ryan and Olivia that much easier. At the new house, Olivia helped me decide which staging pieces to keep and which furniture of mine to move down. Obviously, I kept the furniture I'd handmade that inspired the Northern Wells Bedroom Trio I sold this year to Erickson's, the upscale furniture store. Olivia and I giggled the day we moved it in, jumping onto the bed and making it even more special.

Things were growing even deeper with Ryan, too. I couldn't put my finger on it, but he relaxed even more into himself under the blanket of our three-way love affair. There was a wisdom, contentment, and joy that seemed more solid than it was when I'd first met them. And while he and I continued to express our deep feelings for one another through our occasional kisses, there was an unspoken understanding that it would likely never go any farther.

But every time we were all together, the three of us sank deeper into love and intimacy, and I'd never felt happier in my life. Olivia had an OB/GYN appointment the week before Christmas, and we decided to find out what the baby's gender was, as well as get the baby's DNA tested. We still didn't want to know the outcome, so we asked Dr. Chavez to keep it a secret. But we all agreed it would be better safe than sorry in case there were any emergencies with the baby's delivery. Between both of our experiences, we wanted to be as prepared as possible to bring our child into the world safely. Since my sister passed away from cancer at a young age, we also decided to store the cord blood to make sure he had the best fighting chance his whole life.

I was still convinced it was a boy, and Olivia was still convinced it was a girl. Dr. Chavez was used to our little arrangement by now, and we steadfastly agreed that at the end of the day, we cared less about what other people thought than we did about our own happiness and wanting to experience every milestone with Olivia.

"Are you nervous?" I asked Ryan as we waited for Dr. Chavez to come into the room.

"Nah. Are you?"

"Cool as a cucumber," I fibbed. The truth was all I wanted was Olivia's safety. Sam dying had been the single worst thing to ever happen to me. But losing Olivia . . . I couldn't even go there in my thoughts. Sam proved how much can go wrong during childbirth. As long as the baby was healthy, and Olivia was too, I didn't care what we named it. We could name it Cucumber for all I cared.

The door opened and Dr. Chavez came in, beaming. "All righty, kiddos. You ready to find out your baby's gender today?"

She scanned through our chart, then set it on the table. Olivia glanced up at Ryan and me, then nodded. We each held one of her hands and waited as the black-and-white screen came to life.

"The baby's being a little stubborn today," Dr. Chavez said, lightly pressing on the side of Olivia's tummy with the transducer to get the baby moving.

We all held our breath as we waited to see the baby move, and hopefully open its legs so we could find out the gender. It felt as if all the air had been sucked out of the room as we watched. And waited. Olivia squeezed my hand, and I squeezed hers back as if to say, "It'll be all right."

"Come on, Baby T," Ryan whispered. We called our baby that since it was created by our little "trio" and we hadn't settled on names yet.

After a few intense moments, Baby T finally started squirming. He probably didn't like being poked by the doctor's instrument. A little fist shot in the air, and Dr. Chavez clicked to save that picture as we all laughed. As the baby began to move more, the doctor was able to zoom in and take a look. To me, it all looked gray and fuzzy, and I couldn't see a thing. Olivia gasped, letting us know she could feel the first flutters as the baby moved inside her.

"Are you sure you want to know?" Dr. Chavez asked one last time. We all looked at each other, our excitement hardly contained.

"Yes!" we all answered at the same time.

"Congratulations, then! You three are having a . . . girl."

Olivia started crying, resting her head on Ryan's arm as the doctor took more pictures of the baby for us. "I told you so," she said, her laughter shaking through her tears as she joked with me.

I leaned over and kissed her fully on the mouth, drawing out the kiss. "We're having a baby girl, Liv," I said, rubbing my nose against hers. "I love you so much."

"I love you, too," she said.

Then it was Ryan's turn. He kissed her gently on her forehead. "Our rainbow baby."

"Our rainbow baby," she whispered back.

We were on cloud nine all the way home, Olivia talking animatedly about how she could finally buy clothes and think about the nursery. She made me promise to build the crib myself. I didn't tell her I already had the baby's bedroom set halfway complete. Erickson's jumped at the chance to acquire the pieces, so it paid for itself and then some.

I was handing more and more work over to my foreman, Rob, so I promoted him to general manager and instructed him to hire a new foreman for the time being. I wanted to put more focus on the furniture line and Olivia, because that kept me closer to home. After Ryan and I had beat the detached garage to pieces last summer during the reno, I'd restored it to a simple two-car garage but left most of it empty for the new owners to customize. I was glad I hadn't invested any more into it at the time, because now I was able to finally build my dream workshop, which doubled as my design studio.

Since Ryan was a natural with woodwork, I enlisted him to help with the crib when he could. That way, both of Baby T's daddies could claim having had a hand in building her nursery furniture. Things were falling into place, and only one thing would make that better. When we got home from the doctor's appointment, I made an excuse to run next door after our celebration dinner. Olivia said the baby wanted Juan and Don's again, so Mexican it was.

I hurried home like an eager schoolboy, setting the stage for my official proposal to Olivia. Ryan was in on it and would make up an excuse to send her over later. I lit dozens of candles in the entryway, leading up the stairs, and into the library. Every room held massive bouquets of the rich, purple tulips that were so special to us.

Because, tulips.

Olivia no longer bothered to knock when she came over, so I hung Christmas bells on the back of the knob to let me know when she arrived. I had our song playing softly on repeat in the background. The *Glee* cast sang gently about how the sun was coming in and everything would be all right. The first time we'd heard it together was during the summer when the three of us were just beginning. Olivia and I were wallpapering during the renovation, blasting music and dancing as we worked.

"Brighton?" I heard her call out from the foyer. "What is all this?"

I heard her taking the stairs. The third one from the top creaked, as all good staircases did in older homes. When she got to the second floor, I heard her sharp intake of breath. She must have gotten to my path of purple tulip petals. You would not believe how many tulips I needed to create that. But the look on Olivia's face when she opened the library door was worth it.

"Brighton," she sighed dreamily, looking around the library with wonder and awe. This was the first time she was seeing it decorated for Christmas. A twenty-foot Christmas tree commanded attention from the center of the library, covered in twinkling white lights and sentimental ornaments. Thick garlands of fresh fir spruced the fireplace mantle, woven beautifully around lanterns that housed softly flickering candles. Ryan had hand carved four stocking holders shaped like Christmas trees with a star on top for our new little family.

And my other sister, Becca, had knit matching stockings for each of us, including the baby.

Olivia squealed as her eyes landed on each detail. I still didn't think she really knew what was happening, but she was a mess from all the sentimental touches I'd added. "When have you had time to do this?"

I shrugged. "Here and there while you've been working."

"This is gorgeous!" she breathed out.

"Interior designer approved?" I asked hopefully.

"I think you could take my job!" she gushed. She ran her hands over the intricately carved stocking holders. "These are gorgeous!"

"Thanks. Ryan made those for us. We can keep them at your house next year once Baby T gets here."

"You mean *our* house, Brighton," she said, fisting my sweater with both hands and tugging me closer. "You are the sweetest. And here Ryan led me to believe you had some disaster happening over here with something I'd installed."

I shrugged sheepishly. "He was kinda in on it."

She stood on her tiptoes and brushed her soft lips over mine. That would never get old. I wrapped my arms around her waist and cupped her butt, lifting her into the kiss so I could take it deeper. A moan rumbled from one of us, but I pulled back. I needed to have my head on clear, and I was going all fuzzy-headed being kissed by her.

"This isn't everything," I said, taking her hand. I led her to the Christmas tree. "I want to show you some of the ornaments I added. I have a few special ones just for you."

"Oh, do you now?" She titled her head coquettishly and let me twirl her around. She threw her head back with glee, then gazed up at the tall tree. "This must have taken forever to decorate."

"I had some help. My sisters came down."

"Oh, boo. And I didn't get a chance to meet them properly?"

"We'll see them on Christmas Eve, remember? My whole family is coming down."

"I know! I can't wait," she gushed. "I hope they are able to get past the surface of things and really see how much we're in love. And why this works."

"My family is surprisingly understanding. I've already told them about the baby. They know this isn't negotiable. If they want me and the baby in their lives, they'll take the time to get to know you and Ryan."

An ornament caught Olivia's eyes as I was speaking, and she grinned. "Is that Stitch?"

"It is," I said, pointing to the ornament with the dog's face on one side and paw print on the back.

"That's why I saw white paint in his fur last week! I couldn't figure out what happened!"

"Guilty," I said. I also pointed out the one of Disney's Stitch, and one I had handmade from a seller on Etsy. I wrapped my arms around her and rested my chin on her shoulder as she gently lifted the ornament. "Ohana" was written in gold script across the front of a clear glass globe. A yellow-and-white Hawaiian flower filled the inside, and a delicate gold ribbon was tied in a small bow at the top. "You're the only family I'll ever need, Olivia."

She lifted her chin for a kiss, which I was happy to give her. But then I pointed out other ornaments like the ones I'd had made of our houses. They were miniature replicas of our actual homes hand painted on flat, wooden ornaments. She oohed and ahhed as she found each new decoration in the order I'd meant for her to. We'd almost gotten around the tree when she spotted two special ones. They were silver angel wings wrapped down so the bottoms touched and formed negative space between them where little charms hung.

"A piece of my heart is in heaven," she read, then choked back a sob when she flipped each charm over. One was inscribed with Laelynn and the other said Sam.

She turned into my embrace. "This is all too much. You shouldn't have. But I love everything!"

"I absolutely should have, Liv. This is our first Christmas together, with so many exciting changes on the way. But even as we move forward, we'll never leave them behind. They'll be Baby T's guardian angels, looking over their little sister from heaven."

Olivia bit back her tears. "Thank you. These mean the world to me."

"But wait. There's more!" I said in my best infomercial voice, making her laugh and lightening the mood. She gazed through several more ornaments and cooed over the one that said "baby on the way" with one of the ultrasound pictures nestled in its small frame. When we were just about done, I pointed out one last ornament, tucked away a little deeper than the rest.

"I think you missed one."

She leaned in, squinting to see what it was. It was a circular, mercury glass ornament that doubled as a trinket box with a small clasp. "Go ahead," I said, taking a large step back. "Take a peek inside."

Olivia opened the delicate ball hanging from the tree and gasped. I knew she'd seen the small wooden heart inside that I'd engraved with, "Olivia, will you marry me in heart?"

She spun around to find me down on one knee, holding out a white ring box. Nestled inside was the dark lilac diamond ring I'd gotten her. The band was white gold with tiny diamonds circling it. The same diamonds framed the square-cut diamond that I'd had cushion set. It was a stunning ring, but it wouldn't compete with Ryan's engagement ring or raise suspicion when she wore it on her other hand.

"Olivia North Wells, I have loved you since the day I met you—maybe even before then. When Sam died, I was scared I'd never find real happiness again. You were the most unexpected, beautiful surprise I never anticipated when I started the work on my uncle's house. I know this room holds bittersweet memories—but I don't regret anything. I wanted to make beautiful new memories in here. To remind us that nothing could've kept us apart.

"I want to thank you for fighting for me when you already had everything at your fingertips and could've lost everything. I'm not just here because of the baby, Olivia. I'm here because there's no other woman who could ever make me as happy as you do.

"I wish to god I could marry you on paper, with a proper minister in a church. This may not be that, but it holds the same weight to me, to my heart. When I say this, it's because I love every part of you. It's because I want to make vows with you before god, and my family, and Ryan. And Stitch," I added. Olivia's hands were now clasped in a prayer position by her mouth as she fought back tears.

"I want you for better or worse for the rest of our days. And I pray to god you'll have me, too. No matter what happens with the baby, or Ryan, or our jobs, or this house. I just want *you*. So . . ." I cleared my throat, getting choked up—so much so the box was beginning to shake in my outstretched hand.

I removed the ring and took Oliva's right hand. "Olivia North Wells, will you commit yourself to me before god and be a wife in all the ways that really matter? Will you marry me by heart and be mine forever?"

Her hand was trembling, her left hand covering her mouth in disbelief.

"Just so you know, I did get Ryan's blessing," I told her.

Olivia half-laughed and half-sobbed as she nodded her head. "Yes! Of course I will."

I slid the diamond ring onto her finger, and she gasped. It was a perfect fit, thanks to Ryan. "It's the color of our tulips," she noticed.

"Because, tulips," I said, pressing my forehead to hers. "I was so nervous, Olivia."

"Why? That was the most romantic thing I've ever heard."

"Did I do better than Ryan?" I teased.

She laughed. "Shut up and kiss me, Kerrington."

So, I did. Then I scooped her up and brought her to my bedroom and did all the things engaged couples do to celebrate. Morning would be soon enough to let her know the wedding was already planned for Christmas Eve.

d I mean everything, becomes centered around that

ne simple word: No. Before that, our eight-year marriage was built on one vspel

e darkness loss after loss, the only thing that can set you free is the truth. It's your

sacred as our wedding vows, and maybe even more so because it came after the loss

re one hundred percent honest with one another, that would be enough. That would

e—through another miscarriage. Until, finally, that bridge to balance and sha

ter how honest, could bridge the hollow, gaping hole where my heart used to be. The

pts to reach me. To save me. To restore me to the woman he'd fallen in love with. Even

ted. "And you fell in love with him?" Dr. Paul asks. I

rough. Through the darkness that caused me to lose

I called in sick and stayed at

if I fell in love with a woman I

a nasty habit I would regret

respect. Have at back in with

Really? Ov

you go say in the

it say'd with my to a

babi a h fact

and pray

ve place

estate. The

your. It's what I sa

CHAPTER TWENTY-FIVE

Olivia

I STRETCHED AWAKE, FINDING Brighton asleep beside me on his back, his arm thrown over his head. Even in slumber he was one of the most handsome men I'd ever met. Like a Roman god with his chiseled jaw and perfect nose. He had long, dark blond lashes that tickled when he gave me butterfly kisses. His lips were full, made for my kisses. I longed to reach out and run my hand along yesterday's stubble, but I didn't want to wake him. We'd been up late celebrating.

I stretched my right hand out and looked again at the lilac-colored diamond. It took my breath away.

"Did I do okay?" Brighton asked, his voice rough from just waking up.

I leaned over, laying on his bare chest as I looked up at him. "More than okay. Last night was so special. I can't imagine the planning that took."

"I had a lot of help."

"But it was *your* heart that created that moment to make it special for us. So, thank you." I reached up to kiss him. "Are you sure Ryan was really okay with all of this?"

"A thousand percent, Liv. Don't worry. Come on. He's making breakfast for us. Let's get dressed and go face the music."

I put on last night's clothes before we headed downstairs. We grabbed two mugs of coffee and made our way to the front door, stepping on a trail of beautiful rose petals along the way. I was laughing at something Brighton said when we heard someone on the sidewalk call out to us. I stopped dead in my tracks. I took a deep breath and turned, facing my husband's work colleague.

"Good morning, Kimber! What are you doing over this way so early?"

She was bundled up in a long wool coat sinched at the waist, a cowl scarf in the same hues of gray and soft pink wrapped around her neck. Her husband was beside her. He tipped his hat in our direction but said nothing.

"What are *you* doing out so early?" she asked, eyeing our coffees. We were clearly not dressed appropriately for being outside in the dead of winter. And I was sure I had sex written all over my hair, my skin, my face. I probably smelled like a brothel.

I swallowed, having no clue how to answer this woman.

Brighton held up his coffee mug. "She's just mooching off a generous neighbor to get her morning coffee fix. Their coffee pot is on the fritz. Thought maybe Ryan might like one, too, in exchange for some homemade pancakes. I don't get those too often anymore."

Kimber was not buying what Brighton was selling, but it was smoother than anything I could've come up with on so little sleep.

"How—cozy. And did I just hear you right? Did you say *neighbor*?" she asked slyly.

"You heard right," Brighton said cheerfully. "Look, I don't mean to be rude, but Ryan's coffee is getting cold, and I'm sure Olivia is freezing to death. It was good to bump into you again, Mrs. Shanahan. Mr. Shanahan." He nodded to her dour-looking husband.

I could tell Kimber was pissed that she didn't get the satisfaction she was looking for. And I still couldn't figure out what she was even doing in our neighborhood. But I didn't care. I just wanted to get away from her. As we made our way to the back door, Stitch barreled out to greet us. He jumped excitedly, as if he hadn't seen us in a week. Ryan stood there looking all handsome in his gray sweatpants and black Avengers T-shirt, holding the door open for us.

"Morning, babe," he said.

I raced up the steps and kissed him good morning. Brighton handed him his coffee, which brought a confused look to Ryan's face, his brows furrowing.

"Just go inside," I said.

When we got into the kitchen, I made my way to the sink. Sure enough, Kimber was still out there, staring at our house. She looked dead at me and a satisfied, knowing smile lifted the corner of her lips before she turned and walked with her husband in the opposite direction. *Shit.*

"What was that all about?" Ryan asked, handing Brighton his coffee back.

"Kimber," I ground out, slamming my mug onto the countertop. "God! That woman is such a troll."

Ryan looked amused. "You ran into Kimber? Outside? What in the world was she doing over here? I know for a fact that she lives near the university."

"I don't know, Ryan! But she saw Brighton and me sneaking back over here this morning. Thank god for his quick thinking. He told her our coffee maker was broken, and I was mooching coffee from him."

"Mooch anytime, gorgeous," Brighton said, taking a sip of his coffee.

I rolled my eyes in his direction. "Seriously, guys. This does not look good."

"What's she gonna do, Liv? It would be inappropriate of her to ask me anything point blank. And you gave her a plausible response. I'm sure it'll blow over and she'll forget all about it. If she doesn't, I'll have a word with her."

I chewed the corner of my mouth, still not happy that the situation was fully resolved. Kimber was nothing if not inappropriate, and I knew she wouldn't hesitate to find some sneaky way to bring it up to Ryan in the future.

"Why are we talking about Kimber anyway? Don't we have something to celebrate this morning?"

I looked into his eyes, meeting his gaze.

"Come here," he said, opening his arms. I fell into them, resting my head against his chest. He smelled like pine, and peppermint, and home. "I think this will be a good thing, for all of us."

He looked over my head at Brighton and nodded.

"Are you sure you're really okay with this?" I glanced up at my husband. His beard was neatly trimmed as it always was, but it was thicker in the winter, and I was here for it. His warm, whiskey eyes held nothing but love for me as he drank me in.

"Everything except missing you last night," he said, kissing my nose. "I don't like not sleeping with you. The house was lonely. I hope you don't mind, but I let Stitch sleep on your side of the bed."

I laughed, looking over at the spoiled dog. He was only a little more than six months old, but he'd already won over all our hearts. As if he knew we were talking about him he cocked his head, his brown curly ears lifting.

"Did Brighton tell you anything about last night?" I asked. "I'm not sure how much you want to know."

"Are you happy?"

"Yes," I whispered.

"Then that's all I need to know." He held out his arm for Brighton, who joined us. Ryan draped his arm over his shoulder and pulled him in for a half-hug since I was nestled against his chest in his other arm.

Brighton leaned forward and brushed his lips over Ryan's. It surprised me to see Ryan reach his hand up and bring Brighton's mouth closer for a deeper, more sensual kiss. But it still got me in the girl bits every time I saw them show their love for each other this way.

Brighton playfully bit Ryan's lower lip and slapped him on the ass before stepping back. "You're not getting your own ring, Wells."

"As if," Ryan chucked back at him. But the mood lifted, and Kimber was forgotten. We enjoyed blueberry pancakes and a fresh fruit bowl that Ryan prepared for us. I really, really didn't deserve the man.

"So, do you know what you're going to wear yet, or do we need to go shopping?"

"Huh?" I said eloquently, my mouth full of cantaloupe.

"You didn't tell her yet, did you?" Ryan asked, looking at Brighton.

Brighton made a cringey face, clearly busted with whatever he'd forgotten to tell me. "Since we don't have to wait on a marriage license, and it's going to be an informal ceremony just for our benefit, I thought we'd get married on Christmas Eve. My whole family will be coming down for Christmas and staying at my place. And I'd really like to get married before the baby comes, because I'm sure she's going to be a handful if she's anything like her mother—"

I lobbed a blueberry at Brighton, who was too late lifting his hands. The blueberry bounced off his solid chest.

"We're playing it like that are we?" he asked, a dangerous glint in his eyes.

I backed the chair up, ready to dash.

He grabbed my wrist before I could even clear the table and yanked me onto his lap. "You're being a very naughty girl. And here it is right before Christmas. What would Santa say?"

"I think he'd say I need to be punished by two very handsome elves."

"You mean two well-endowed, handsome elves?" Ryan quipped.

Brighton rubbed my bottom as I squirmed in his lap. "You're not getting punished until you tell me you'll marry me on Christmas Eve."

"This is the weirdest conversation," I said, looking back and forth between my fiancé and my husband. "But yes. We can have our ceremony on Christmas Eve. I assume we'll have it at your house?"

"Already have everything planned," he said, lifting his eyebrows salaciously. "Did I tell you Becca was an event planner?"

"Why, no, you didn't. Your sisters sure know how to save your butt."

"That's what sisters are for," he teased. Then he scooped me up in his arms like he would if he were carrying me over the threshold. My legs dangled over his arms as he carried me upstairs, Ryan close behind.

After our shower, the three of us tumbled into bed. We'd missed Ryan, and now that we were all back together, everything felt complete.

...nd I mean everything, becomes centered around that...

One simple word: No. Before that, our eight-year marriage was built on love...

the darkness loss after loss, the only thing that can get you...

as sacred as our wedding vows, and maybe even more so because... come after the...

were one hundred percent honest with one another, that would be enough. That would...

...—through another miscarriage. Until, finally, that tragic... even hope and she...

...how honest, could bridge the hollow, gaping hole where my heart used to...

...mpts to reach me. To save me. To restore me to the woman had fallen in love with...

..."And you fell in love with him?" Dr. Paul ask...

...ough. Through the darkness that someday to...

...I lifted an eyebrow and glanced at...

...if I fell in love with a woman...

CHAPTER TWENTY-SIX

Ryan

I'D PROBABLY NEVER do anything again for the rest of my life more awkward than meeting the family of the man who was about to "marry" my wife. But the Kerringtons were a boisterous, warm family, instantly putting us all at ease about the situation. Paige was the only one who was a little more reserved about the whole thing. But her husband, Vic, stayed by her side all night, keeping her away from Brighton as much as he could.

Liv and I didn't invite any family, since her parents died when she was a student of mine and my sister lived too far away. We both had plenty of friends from work and our college days, but we'd let those friendships lapse when we lost Laelynn. They wouldn't understand what we were about to do anyway, and we wanted to keep it intimate—surrounded only by the people we loved and trusted the most.

Brighton, Liv, and I decorated the downstairs of his house with a Christmas wedding in mind. The rooms were adorned with fresh, green garland, winterberry centerpieces, and floor lanterns of various heights filled with soft vanilla candles to warm the space. Brighton had recruited his mother's best friend to perform the "wedding" ceremony. She was a spiritual healer of deep faith and was accustomed to performing unconventional commitment ceremonies, as she did for years before same-sex marriages became legal in New York. She was happy to help Brighton and Olivia pledge their hearts before god and family.

I paced the kitchen, waiting for Olivia to come downstairs. I wasn't completely sure how to feel now that the day was here. Although it wasn't legally binding, it may as well have been for the deep commitment they were making. I knew I wasn't being replaced, but it left me feeling unsteady about our own vows now that she was exchanging them with Brighton.

As Olivia descended the back staircase, tears threatened to spill over. I suddenly had memories of her walking down the aisle to me at our wedding. She'd walked alone since her parents were no longer alive. She looked like a free-spirited goddess back then with her golden blond hair hanging long and straight, her skin sun-kissed and warm under the late day sun. She walked to me barefoot in the grass, carrying a romantic-looking bouquet of baby blue eucalyptus and white seafoam roses.

That was when she was mine, and mine alone.

I had no words for how beautiful she looked as she walked toward me in her wedding dress for Brighton. It was the palest of blush pinks with tiny, capped sleeves. Her décolletage was bare, leaving a long line of the soft, pale skin between her breasts exposed. While the top of the dress was lace and more form-fitting, the bottom tulle fell softly, expertly covering the bump that was getting harder to hide. She was barefoot again, which made me smile as she stepped into my arms.

"My god, Liv," I said, careful not to mess up her hair. She'd swept it back in some sort of sophisticated, loose bun with a singular braid framing her face like a crown. She had a small flower pinned into her hair and was wearing the diamond studs I'd bought her as a push present for Laelynn, before we knew of the awful fate that would change us forever. Tonight, they twinkled in the candlelight, as if Laelynn approved from above. "You never cease to take my breath away."

Olivia squeezed me hard before pulling back to meet my eyes. "I love you," she said. She was shaking, so I held her hand between my palms, gently calming her before we walked in to where everyone else stood in the front room.

"I love you, too, Liv. Till my dying breath," I reassured her, conveying everything I could in the look that passed between us. My heart hammered, but I had to be strong for Olivia. "Tonight is about your commitment to Brighton, though. And I promise you, I am okay with this. You have changed so much since he came into our lives. This feels right—to bring Brighton into the fold of our family. And I'm not marrying him. So, thanks for taking one for the team," I joked.

Olivia smiled then, bigger than she had since coming downstairs. I got it. She was worried about me. But there was a strange comfort knowing that between the two of us, Liv would never be alone. She deserved to be loved this much after all the loss she'd experienced in her life. And before Brighton, I was the only family she had.

"Ready to go get hitched? Again?"

"Ryan!" she said, laughing. She asked me to hand her the wedding bouquet she'd made herself. I walked to the box that was sitting on the kitchen island and lifted it out for her. She had a few sprigs of eucalyptus in her romantic bouquet of mixed wildflowers and evergreens. There were large, dusky pink roses, pale lilac flowers I didn't recognize, and purple tulips so dark they looked like the sangria we were having after the ceremony with our Christmas Eve dinner.

I noticed the bottom of the bouquet was wrapped with material, then covered with a thin layer of lace. "Your bouquet is beautiful, Liv. You did an amazing job."

"Thank you," she said. She angled the bottom of the stems my way. "I added a little piece of the kids and you to my bouquet."

"What is that?" I asked, looking closer.

"A small piece of one of Laelynn's blankets and one of Sam's is wrapped around the stems. The lace is from our wedding."

"You cut your wedding dress?" I asked, gaping at her.

"No! It was from my trousseau. But it reminds me of you."

"Good," I said, stealing a quick kiss.

She wiped the lipstick from my lips and adjusted my tie before we clasped hands and headed toward the curtains we'd hung to separate the back of the house from the front, so Liv could have her "moment."

I texted Brighton to let him know we were coming out. We heard the officiant say, "You may now rise."

Then I walked my wife down the aisle.

CHAPTER TWENTY-SEVEN

Brighton

SHE STOLE MY breath. Liv was everything I'd ever dreamed of, and she was walking toward *me*. To marry *me*. It didn't matter that we wouldn't have a piece of paper to legally claim our marriage. We were saying commitment vows under god, and before family. That was good enough. Ryan walked her down our small aisle lined with candles. Half my family stood on one side and the rest stood on the other half. I was so grateful that they'd all come and were willing to invite Liv and Ryan into our family as an extension of me.

I stood at the front of the room next to my mom's friend. I was grateful she could do this for us with such little notice and on Christmas Eve. Everything had fallen into place, and I wouldn't have wanted it to be any different, even if it were an option.

Ryan stopped in front of me, and he and Olivia had a silent exchange before he squeezed her hands, kissed her on the cheek, and then turned to me. He clasped my hand and went in for a half-hug. "Remember what I told you, Kerrington," he whispered.

"Never sleep with your wife?" I joked.

"Don't hurt her, or I'll kill you. I mean it," he said, then smiled broadly, his white teeth splitting his dark brown beard.

"You have my word."

Ryan sat with the rest of my family as the officiant began reciting the vows we'd written. We mingled promises from traditional vows with our own words, then sprinkled in some Celtic poetry to honor my family's heritage. We used "commitment" instead of "marriage," even though we all knew I was marrying Olivia with my entire heart and soul.

She placed a simple titanium wedding ring on my right ring finger, and I added a thin band in eighteen-karat white gold that matched her engagement ring from me.

When we were done, the officiant closed with, "By the powers vested in me as an ordained minister of the Universal Church of God, I now pronounce you formally committed and bound to one another under the laws of natural and heavenly love. You may now kiss your lifelong partner."

Everyone stood and cheered as I pulled Olivia close, wrapping an arm around her waist. She flushed prettily in front of our small audience before I leaned her back and kissed her like I meant it. Cheers erupted and my family surrounded us in a swarm of hugs.

It was the happiest day of my life.

We broke bread on the dining room table I'd built over the summer. It sat twelve and was more than enough room for the adults in our family. We sat the kids at the smaller table we brought in from the kitchen. Paige's older boys weren't amused at being placed at the kiddie table, but one stern look from Vic and they stopped protesting. Cheers erupted from Becca's younger kids, and we couldn't help but laugh. My mother and sisters made a lovely Christmas Eve dinner, and we stayed longer than we intended, enjoying ourselves as my family got to know Olivia and Ryan. There were a few small snafus as they tripped over how to refer to each of us in our unique relationship. We all laughed, knowing we'd have to get used to this, but I think we were all glad the kids were at a different table for that part of the conversation.

Sometime after midnight, we crossed the yard and headed home. I carried Olivia over the threshold of the backdoor where we once crossed hand in hand, the night we all first made love—not knowing what was in store for our future from that one small choice. For me, it was the best decision I'd ever made. I couldn't help but wonder if Ryan felt the same way.

Ryan chose to sleep downstairs with Stitch on our wedding night, since we couldn't have a modicum of privacy with family filling my house. I asked Ryan to stay with us—it only felt right. But he declined, insisting that a wedding night only came around once, and Liv and I needed this time together. It was easy to trust his wisdom, so I took advantage of the privacy and made love to my wife well into the morning. As long as I lived, I would never forget the way Liv's back felt under my hands as I unzipped her pale pink wedding dress and shrugged it from her body. She had gained weight with the baby and was filling out in all the right places.

I helped her take down her bun, laughing at the number of bobby pins it took to create such a loose, seemingly low-maintenance hairstyle. She stood before me, as naked and vulnerable as she'd ever been, trusting me to love her in all the ways I'd promised before god.

There are some things that are kept private between a man and his wife on their wedding night. It was a sacred evening that brought us closer than I ever could've imagined, so I knew I'd have to thank Ryan someday for his wisdom. As we lay in bed talking as the sun came up, I felt Olivia go completely still, then her hands went to her stomach. She sat straight up, and I immediately went into panic mode.

"Liv, what it is? What's wrong?"

"Nothing! I felt the baby kick, Brighton. Here, feel."

She placed my hand on her abdomen, on the left-hand side. I waited for what felt like forever, but to no avail. "What a little stinker!" she said, laughing. "It was such a solid kick."

"Did it hurt?" I asked. There'd been so much I didn't know about or think to ask with Caroline.

"No, I loved it," she admitted. "It's a sign of life. I'll never take one kick for granted." Olivia lay back down and rolled over, scooching her butt back so she was the little spoon to my big spoon. I wrapped my arms around her waist and snuggled against her back, burying my face in her hair. "You may want to watch how you're bouncing that curvy backside my way, Momma."

"Oh yeah? Or what?" she teased.

I never had time to answer, because right then the baby kicked again, and this time there was no mistaking it. "I felt that!"

Olivia placed her hand over mine and we lay there as the morning sun rose on Christmas Day, feeling our baby kick for the very first time.

"**RYAN! I HAVE** good news!" Olivia said, bounding down the stairs on Christmas morning. Well, technically, it was closer to Christmas afternoon, but I let it slide since they were still in that honeymoon phase.

"Merry Christmas, baby." I stretched my arms out for her, and Olivia sank into my embrace. I rested my chin against her head and inhaled deeply. Christmases would change forever once kids got here. I couldn't wait.

I'd dreamed of staying up late with Olivia after the kids went to bed, with music playing softly in the background. We'd be setting up god knows what—maybe a Barbie DreamHouse or a Matchbox racetrack. I couldn't help but think about how Laelynn would've been one this year. Probably walking and getting into everything under the tree. I never imagined anyone else being with us on Christmas

Eve as we prepared the magic, but maybe having two dads would be a bonus when we were in the toddler phase.

"Merry Christmas," she said back, grinning up at me. I lowered my head and kissed her good morning, just as Brighton walked into the room.

"Merry Christmas," he said groggily, scratching his head. "Any coffee yet?"

I slid his mug across the counter, made just the way he liked.

"Thanks, honey," he joked. He took an appreciative swallow. "Mmm. You're the best house husband a guy could ever hope for."

I snorted, keeping my arm draped around Olivia. "What are your plans today with your parents?"

"Well, they want to spend the day with me, obviously. It's been a while since I've been home—and forever since I've seen my nieces and nephews. I don't expect you guys to spend all day over there unless you want to. I thought maybe I could show my dad around the house and talk renos and such. The guys and Paige will want to watch football. And I'm sure I'll lose Kendra to the library."

"Yeah, sounds like fun, but we'll pass. We usually head to the cemetery on Christmas Eve or Christmas morning. We didn't yesterday because of the wedding. So maybe we can do that today, Liv?"

The color drained from her face, but a determined look flashed in her eyes and she nodded. The difference in how she responded today versus six months ago was evidence of her healing. I was so fucking proud of her for continuing to fight every day now, instead of retreating into herself.

She kissed my cheek again, then went to pour a small glass of the pomegranate juice she'd been craving lately. The doctor seemed to think it was a good thing, all these weird cravings she was having. She hadn't had as many with Laelynn.

"Can we meet you for dinner instead?" I asked. "What time did you say they were serving up?"

"I'll check when I get over there, but I think six maybe?"

"Sounds good. You hungry?"

"Famished," Brighton said, stretching his arms over his head in the air. He was padding around in an old pair of buffalo plaid pajama pants, with no shirt on. If I didn't love the guy so much—and feel so secure in Liv's love for me—I might've been a little jealous of the eight pack that defined his stomach, and the deep V that led to the drawstring of his pajama bottoms.

I watched as Liv's eyes traveled down Kerrington's torso and rolled my eyes. "I'd say to get a room, but I think you've had enough for one day."

Brighton grinned, wrapping his arms around Olivia from behind and kissing her neck. "Whatever do you mean?" he asked innocently. "And can you ever really have enough? It's Christmas morning, after all. Don't be a scrooge, Wells."

Olivia leaned back against his chest, unconsciously reaching back for him. I watched as Brighton ran a trail of kisses up her throat, while never breaking eye contact with me. He lifted his hands and cupped Olivia's breasts, pinching her nipples through the lacey pajama set she was wearing.

I groaned, setting down my coffee. "So, it's gonna be like that?"

Brighton winked at me as he slid his hands down Olivia's sides, finding the hem of her nightgown. I couldn't take it anymore.

I stalked over to where they stood, eager to have her back in my arms again. He'd had her all night. It was my turn, too.

Liv moaned my name, reaching out for me as Kerrington's fingers found their way home. And just like that, my Christmas morning got a whole lot better.

CHAPTER TWENTY-NINE

Brighton

WE LOST A good hour after our morning she-nanigans, but I was living the dream and having the best Christmas ever. Things got a little out of control in the shower when Ryan and I were kissing. It was the first time we allowed our hands to roam each other's bodies—we usually stuck solely to Liv. Even though it started innocently enough—I'd grabbed the soap, lathered up my own chest, and then used the rest to wash Ryan's tight abs—it shocked me how much I enjoyed feeling his skin beneath my fingertips. It didn't go any farther, but it opened a new level of trust and intimacy between us. We felt freer to embrace and explore during our kisses after that. I found kissing Ryan was much different than Olivia—Ryan having been my one and only experience ever kissing a dude.

I loved the way his beard felt rough against my face. It made me want to go harder on the kiss every time. His tongue was warm and sensual, but it was bigger, more demanding. Even when Liv was in control in the bedroom, she was softer. Ryan just took with confidence. The more we kissed, the more I was left with a wanting I didn't understand. He got a little handsy when I pressed deep inside Olivia. I didn't know what it meant, but the shower walls fogged up, and we all needed a shower after our shower.

After we dressed, I handed them each a small bag with their Christmas gifts. "Here, got you guys a little something for our first holiday together. I didn't know how big you went, so it's just this. I hope you like it."

"Thanks, man," Ryan said, unwrapping his first. I'd gotten them both brand-new Apple watches. After Olivia got hit by a car while running last summer, and us needing to get to the ER this autumn when she was admitted after her fainting spell, I just felt better knowing we'd all have access to call one another or 911 if we needed help.

I explained as much as I walked through the features with Ryan. "This thing tracks your sleep, monitors your heart health, reads like an ECG, makes phone calls, and streams music."

"This is awesome," he said. "I can't wait to set it all up."

"Yeah, we'll have to go for a run and try it out during the break."

Olivia opened hers while we looked on. Hers had a gold watch face and pink sand–colored band, while Ryan's was space gray and black. "It would've matched your wedding dress if I'd given it to you earlier," I teased.

"The perfect bridal accessory," she said, laughing. "Thank you."

"There's one more thing," I said, taking her hand and leading her from the room. "I have a wedding gift I meant to give you yesterday. It's downstairs."

"Brighton! This is too much."

It would never be enough where Olivia was concerned. I'd spend the rest of my life spoiling her rotten if she'd let me. When I'd purchased this surprise for Liv over the summer, I never could've dreamed it would one day be my wedding gift to her. Back then, it was a desperate attempt to show my love for her in the only way I might've been allowed.

When we got to the guest bedroom, I put my hand over Olivia's eyes. It brought back memories from the first day I'd met her, leading her into my uncle's library for the first time. I knew as an interior designer she would love that room as much as I did, and I wasn't wrong.

Ryan walked over to the windows and pulled the heavy curtains back, looping the tiebacks around them so they'd stay put. Stitch was running around our feet like a maniac, happy to have all three of us back downstairs. He did not like the baby gate at the bottom of the stairs, but we felt it was better to get him used to it now so that when the baby came, he wouldn't associate being kept downstairs when the baby slept as a negative thing or a punishment.

I removed my hand and leaned forward, whispering in Olivia's ear. "Open your eyes."

She was completely silent, and I worried maybe she hadn't loved the "king and queen" stained-glass windowpanes as much as she'd suggested at Babalu's when we were there last summer. Ryan and I decided to hang them in the window facing the side yard. It let in a lot of natural light and would brighten the muted blues, greens, and yellows of the faded glass. The center image on each held a torch with lilies winding up it, and Olivia had fallen in love with them instantly. The antique windowpanes were too exorbitant to use in a house I'd meant to flip, but I had Olivia in mind when I asked Louie Brightbeck, one of the owners, to secretly stash them in my trailer before we paid out and left.

Olivia spun around now and flung herself into my arms. "God, Brighton. I can't believe you remembered these. I love them."

I ran a hand over the back of her head as she burrowed into my sweater. Her body jerked a little, and that's when I realized she was crying. Ryan and I exchanged frowny faces, and I hugged her tighter. "Why are you crying? They were supposed to make you happy."

"They do!" she choked out. "I just—I *really* love them. I can't believe you got these. I think it's just my pregnancy hormones." She rubbed her face on the sleeve covering my bicep to wipe her tears away. "I need to run to the bathroom. This baby has no respect for my bladder."

"By all means."

Oliva stood on her tiptoes and kissed me. "You really get me," she said before dashing from the room to hit the upstairs bathroom.

"Good job, Kerrington. I think you've won the record for the number of times you can make Liv cry for sentimental reasons in one day."

I cracked my knuckles and raised my eyebrows. "Don't underestimate me. The day has just begun. Besides, I'm not the one taking her to a cemetery on Christmas Day, Romeo."

He grew serious, pursing his lips. "Today's going to gut Liv, so you need to be prepared. We haven't visited Laelynn's grave that often since the funeral. And her parents are buried there, too. But, yeah, once the baby comes, we're going to have to do this on a different day. I don't want Liv sad and depressed on Christmas every year around the kids."

"Kids?" Brighton asked. "You're already thinking of brothers and sisters for Baby T?"

Ryan ran his thumb over his bottom lip and nodded. "We always talked about having three kids. But with each loss, that seemed impossible. We talked about adoption or maybe using a surrogate. But after Laelynn, she shut down so hard. I knew it would be a long time before I could even broach the subject of having babies again."

"Guess god had other plans."

"Yeah, his intentions were good, but his timing sucked. I feel like someday our daughter's gonnna want to know which one of us is really her biological father. It's not an ideal situation, but I wouldn't change a thing."

"Me either. I haven't said it often enough, Ryan, but I really look up to you. You're the husband I hope I can be someday to Liv."

"Oh, so you think if you can't hit *her* today with more sentimental tears, you're gonna pull me down instead?" he joked.

"I mean it. I've never known a stronger, more loving partner. The way you love her is inspiring—and brave."

"Look, our marriage wasn't perfect. You know that."

"Nothing is. I'm sure in ten years we'll all be grateful to have the extra house next door for when one of us needs a breather."

Ryan chuckled. "It *is* awfully convenient. Though I think we seriously need to rethink whether you keep it or live here. It seems crazy to maintain both houses when you're always over here anyway."

I considered what he was saying, and he had a point. It was something we'd need to think about long-term. "Where do you see us in ten years?"

Ryan leaned back against the dresser and crossed his legs at the ankles. "For starters, I hope by then we're all living together here, under one roof."

I nodded. It would create gossip, but our family was priority number one.

Ryan ran his hand over his beard, contemplating our future. "I hope by then our daughter has two more siblings—if it's safe for Olivia. I'd really like us to consider planning the next two pregnancies, so we each have a chance to be a father."

"You've thought about that?" I honestly hadn't.

"All the time. I know we'll both love this baby no matter what, but I think we'll always wonder. And we both deserve the honor of biologically fathering a kid one day."

It made sense. "Think Liv will be up for two more?"

"Guess we'll find out."

I laughed. "You're an alright guy, Ryan."

"Just alright?"

I crossed the room, keeping my eyes trained on his intensely dark gaze. I was glad we weren't ever considering crossing the line and getting completely intimate with one another because I suspected with our matching testosterone and love for fucking, we would absolutely obliterate each other.

We stood toe-to-toe, our breath mingling in anticipation. I leaned forward, putting my hands on the dresser, and boxing him in. He flexed his chest and stood up straighter, his gaze dropping to my mouth.

I nipped at his bottom lip, drawing it in and sucking on it. Ryan groaned, which made me chuckle. He wrapped his arms around my waist and cupped my ass, pulling me hard against his body.

"Better than alright," I said, flicking my tongue out and tracing his lips. "My best friend. My dude soul mate."

He gaffed. "Dude soul mate? Is that really a thing?"

"I don't know. Just shut up and kiss me already," I dared him.

He tightened his grip on my ass and claimed my lips. His beard scratched my face as we widened our mouths for a deeper, more intimate kiss. It never stopped surprising me that Ryan could feel gentle too. While the kiss was intense, his tongue was soft and sensual, demanding, yet curious. It made me feel all kinds of things.

"Eh-hem," we heard from the doorway. I slowed the kiss but didn't end it right away. I was enjoying it too much. I'd had a lot of special alone time with Olivia lately, but not enough with the three of us. Things had gotten hectic after our weekend getaway, with Ryan grading finals, Olivia finishing a big She Shed renovation for a client, and me planning the engagement and wedding. I made a mental note to plan something special soon, so Ryan remembered how much he was needed in this trio and just how much I really did love *him*, too.

"So much for not being bisexual," Olivia teased. "He who doth protest too much."

Ryan cocked his head back, looking smugly over my shoulder at Liv. He winked, then shoved me off at the chest. "What can I say? I can see the appeal of Kerrington now."

I barked in laughter. "Only now? After all this time?"

"Boys," Olivia said, heading out of the room. "Brighton, it's two o'clock. Your parents aren't going to be happy with us if you don't head over soon."

I called Stitch to come with me. He'd be happier spending the day getting loved on by my family than being in his crate. At my house, we were welcomed into the fold, and things quickly fell into rhythm as Paige and Mom shooed everyone out of the kitchen to cook our Christmas dinner. Becca and Kendra were in the library reading. Stitch abandoned me to curl up on the floor at their feet, warming himself by the fire. Me, my dad, and my sisters' husbands grabbed beers and headed to my workshop. I was eager to show Dad what I'd built with my own two hands.

"Well done, Brighton," he said, looking around. He'd always been proud of me, but this meant a lot. "Looks like you're building yourself a nice little life here."

"I really am. I know it's unconventional, but it works for us." I took a pull from my beer. "I appreciate you and Mom being so open about everything."

"You didn't exactly give us a choice. Now did you, Son?" he chuckled. "Luckily, we care more about your happiness than what others think, and we would've been behind you anyway. But that told us how serious you were about Olivia. It's more confusing to us why Ryan would go along with all this than anything else. But he's a nice guy and seems like a good friend."

"Yeah, sorry. But there is no way in hell I'd share Paige with anyone," Vic added.

I didn't expect them to fully understand. Unless you were one of us, and felt the palpable love between us, I could see how it might be confusing. Hell, if truth be told, I knew if the situation was reversed, I wouldn't be able to share Olivia with anyone else. That was the hardest part for me to reconcile with. I didn't know if that meant Ryan loved Liv more than I did—since he would literally do anything to see her happy. Or if I loved her more. Because I'd rather die than risk losing her.

"What's it really like?" Becca's husband asked. "I mean, with the three of you. Do you take turns spending time with her? Or do you just like, *share* her?"

I know Joey didn't mean anything by it. He was simply curious. But if it were anyone other than my sister's husband, I mighta decked him for asking. Which meant I needed to formulate a simple comeback that shut this shit down quick, because I was sure we'd need to do a lot more of this in the future if we started living openly.

"For starters, I don't ask you and Becca about your love life, right? And that's my wife. I know you didn't mean anything by it, but don't disrespect her like that by asking such crude questions."

He held up his hands and laughed nervously while my dad said in a low warning, "Brighton."

"Sorry, man," said Joey. "I just—can't wrap my head around how this even works. Aren't you worried how your daughter will answer these questions some day? About why she has two daddies and one mommy?"

I did. I worried about it nearly every day. But I'd figured out that there was only one honest answer, so that's what I told Joey.

"She'll tell them it's because she's lucky."

...and I mean everything, becomes centered around...

...one simple word: No. Before that, our eight-year marriage was built on our respect...

...the darkness loss after loss, the only thing that can set you free is the truth. It's your...

...as sacred as our wedding vows, and maybe even more so because it came after the loss...

...we one hundred percent honest with one another, that would be enough. That would...

...—through another miscarriage. Until finally, that fragile, false hope and shame...

...ter how honest, could bridge the hollow, gaping hole where my heart used to be. Th...

...pts to reach me. To save me. To restore me to the woman he'd fallen in love with. Even...

..."And you fell in love with him? Dr. Pai ask...

...through. Through the darkness that caused...

...I called an egg... and granted...

...I fell in love with woman...

...a nasty twist. It...

...How did...

...you...

...you...

...my...

...and pray...

...pray...

...Here's what I...

CHAPTER THIRTY

Olivia

FTER BRIGHTON WENT next door, I grabbed a box of tissues and shoved it in my boho purse. I had a feeling I'd need a lot of them today. I filled two water bottles for me and Ryan and met him by the garage. Usually, he would have the car started and the seats warmed by now.

"Everything okay? Did we forget something?"

"No, I just wanted to give you my Christmas present when it was just the two of us. We won't have many more milestones to hit when it's just Liv and Ry," he said sadly.

"We can always have alone time, Ryan."

"You know what I mean," he said, tugging at my hand.

"Where are we going?"

"Through here."

He opened the garage door, and I gasped. Inside was a brand-new Honda Odyssey Elite in Obsidian Blue Pearl. The biggest red bow I'd ever seen was on the hood of the minivan.

I was speechless. We talked about getting a minivan when we were pregnant with Laelynn because it was far safer than my open-roofed Wrangler. But I'd been afraid to buy one before the baby was born—just in case. Turned out it had been okay to wait. Now? The timing was everything.

"I can't believe you did this!" I said, grinning from ear to ear.

"You're not upset with me? I was a little hesitant to make such a big purchase without discussing it first, but your safety comes first."

"How could I ever be upset over something as sweet as that? I'm just blown away. Ryan . . . this is too much."

He handed me the keys. "It's exactly what my girls deserve. Merry Christmas, Liv."

I flung myself in his arms and pressed my lips to his. He lifted me up, and I wrapped my legs around his waist. Then he turned me around and pressed my back up against my new car and kissed me until I was dizzy and breathless.

"We're so going to have to break this in before the baby comes," I said.

"I like the way you think. Promise me something?"

"Hmm?" I asked dreamily as I slid down his body to stand.

"I want to be the first to break it in with you. One last Liv and Ry hurrah."

"One might even say, one for the road?"

Ryan rolled his eyes. "I thought I was going to be bad with the dad jokes."

"You're going to be the best father, Ryan. I'm more sure of that now than ever."

"What do you mean?" he asked as we slid into the minivan and onto the smoothest leather seats my bottom ever graced.

I turned the car on, then looked at Ryan. "This past year, you have fought tooth and nail for me. When I was drowning, you wouldn't let me sink. Even though I kept shutting you out, you never gave up on me. That's what family means. Never leaving someone behind, right?"

"Never."

"I owe you my life, Ryan. I feel like I'm happy again for the first time since before we started trying to get pregnant. That doesn't mean that I don't think of our babies every single day. Or that something isn't going to trigger me tomorrow." I searched the knobs, turning on the seat warmers. "But before, I couldn't say I was happy. I felt broken. Like—all the way beyond repair broken."

"I always knew you'd survive, Liv. You're a fighter. I was just worried *we* wouldn't. And that scared me more than anything else in the world."

"I know," I whispered. "I get that now that I'm out of that really dark place."

"Do you think Dr. Paul is helping? So that if we experience loss again, you won't go back there?"

"I can't say it wouldn't set me back. But I'm not the same person that I was a year ago. I honestly believe I have the support I need and can trust that I'd survive whatever life throws our way."

Ryan knocked on the dashboard three times. It was a superstition of his. "Let's hope life is done throwing us curveballs. I think we've had enough."

"Amen to that," I said, feeling a little guilty for only getting Ryan a new juicer for Christmas. "I'm gonna get used to this backup camera really fast."

Ryan laughed. "Wait till you see everything else she does."

We chatted about Ryan's work on our way to the cemetery, to keep my mind off what we were about to go do. It was the absolute last thing I wanted to face on Christmas Day, when everything was going so well. But we visited my parents every year at this time. I just never imagined we'd be visiting our child there someday, too. A parent isn't supposed to outlive their kids. And Laelynn never even got a fair chance. We pulled into a front-row parking space. There was no one else around, which didn't surprise me.

I closed my eyes and took a deep breath. Ryan reached over and held my hand but didn't say anything. I knew we'd need to visit my parents first, because every time I saw Laelynn's grave, I was a waste afterward. I put my other hand over my belly and did some deep breathing exercises Dr. Paul recommended for when I felt stressed or sad. I tapped my thumb to each of the four fingers on that hand, slowly, one at a time. *Healed. Healthy. Happiness. Harmony.* I don't know how long we sat there while I collected myself, but Ryan never pushed me or told me to hurry up.

We got out and walked to my parents' graves. I closed my eyes and said a small prayer while Ryan rubbed my lower back. Then I talked to them in my head and told them all our good news, and how I was finally looking forward to something. As I was getting ready to leave, a red bird flew down, landing on the headstone. It cocked its head to the side and looked at me before flying away.

Laelynn's plot was in a different section of the cemetery, an older one where Ryan's family has been buried for centuries. They'd purchased extra land so only their family could be buried there. It was like a smaller cemetery within the bigger one. A fence lined with rose bushes circled the large perimeter as far as the eyes could see. It was in the oldest section, so a family of large oaks stood sentient over the Wells family, which I found oddly comforting.

Laelynn's headstone was placed in the part reserved for Ryan's branch of the family tree. A headstone already stood erected for Ryan's parents, who had died before I met him. We paid our respects before moving to Laelynn's small headstone. There was a gap between his parents' plot and Laelynn's— ones that were already paid for, for Ryan and me someday. Even though it was just earth beneath my feet, a shiver ran up my spine as my boots crunched through the frozen snow. It wasn't something I ever wanted to think about.

Ryan and I crouched down on our toes so we could get closer to Laelynn's miniature heart-shaped marker. I ran my fingers over the engraved stone where her name was etched like some kind of bizarre mistake.

Laelynn Gia Wells
Beloved daughter of Ryan and Olivia
Wrapped in our love. Sleep, little one. Sleep.

"Hey, baby girl," I whispered. Ryan placed his hand on my lower back as I talked to our daughter quietly. "You're going to be a big sister soon. But don't worry. This baby can never take your place. Only you could be our little wildflower."

A solitary tear slid down my cheek.

"It's Christmas today." I felt like someone was stabbing me in the heart it hurt so badly. "You should've been at home with us today. You would've been one."

My words died, caught in a strangled sob. I fell to my knees, no longer able to balance myself on the balls of my feet. The snow quickly worked its way through my jeans, but I barely noticed. I put my face in my hands and started crying. Ryan kneeled next to me, wrapping me in his arms and letting me break.

We sat there until the lower half of my legs felt like they'd gone numb from the snow and I began to worry about frostbite. Ryan lifted me as he stood, keeping his arm around my shoulders.

"I love you," I said shakily to Laelynn one last time.

Ryan did what he always did before leaving. He kissed the first two fingers of his right hand and placed them on top of the heart-shaped headstone.

We linked hands and headed to the car. When we got there, I handed Ryan the keys and didn't even need to ask. We drove home in silence with nothing more in the background than the soft whoosh of a powerful new heating system and the soft echo of my tears.

CHAPTER THIRTY-ONE

Ryan

WHEN WE RETURNED home, Olivia headed upstairs. It was an improvement over six months ago when she would've headed to the guest bedroom and locked herself in there alone. I was grateful Kerrington had Stitch, so we didn't have to deal with his excitable love right now. I texted Brighton to let him know we may not make it over for Christmas dinner, but that I would try hard to get us there.

I led Olivia to the shower because I knew from experience that she was suffering mild symptoms of shock. Between that, the cold snow, and her grief, she would need to warm up fast so she could get present in her body. Water was the best way to do that.

I held her in my arms and let the hot water warm us as it washed over our bodies. She was conditioning her hair when she began sobbing again, collapsing against my chest as she heaved. I rinsed her hair for her and got us out of the water and into bed, where I could hold her under the weight of our comforter to help her stay warm and feel safe.

"I'm trying, Ryan. I am. So damn hard. Every day. Then something like this happens. Is this what's going to happen every time I think of her? Every time I want to visit her?"

I ran my hand over her hair and kissed her forehead. "Shh, Livy. It's only been a year."

"I know. It just hurts so bad. It's still so raw. There are days when I feel so full and happy. We have things to look forward to again. A future. And I want so desperately to keep my body safe for this new baby to grow. I'm scared, Ryan. Really scared."

I tipped her chin, raising her face so our eyes met. I wanted to take it all from her. I would if I could. I would bear the entire weight of her misery for the both of us if god would hand it over to me.

"I want to promise you that it'll all be okay, that nothing will go wrong. But I can't. We know it can because we've had the worst happen to us. But we also survived it. I know you can't see it—you can only feel what's going on inside that incredibly large heart of yours. But you're night and day stronger than you were before. We can face this—and whatever life throws our way—together."

She bit her lip, fighting back more tears. I could see the tremble in her chin. "I'm just so exhausted, Ryan. I'm so damn tired of having to be strong."

"I know."

There wasn't much I could say. She had the right to feel emotionally exhausted. She was right to feel scared. I was just frustrated because I didn't know how to make things better.

"What do you need right now? Do you want me to let you sleep? We can skip this dinner tonight. I already texted Brighton and told him we may not be up for it."

She swallowed, taking a deep breath against my chest.

"What do you see, Ryan?"

"I see the most beautiful woman I've ever known lying in my arms."

"What do you smell?"

"Warm, vanilla undertones."

"What can you feel?"

"The softest skin under my fingertips."

"What do you hear?"

"The way the pillow crinkles when we shift."

"And what do you taste?" she asked, pulling herself up on her arm to look down at me.

Her blond hair hung in wet ropes over her shoulder. Her breasts were slightly fuller, and her neckline was smooth and fair. I reached my hand up, running it along her collarbone to her throat. She closed her eyes, and her breathing hitched.

"Forever," I said, pulling her down so I could kiss her. Her mouth was soft, compliant. Her lips parted easily and let me in. My tongue pressed forward, seeking hers. It was gentle, languid—like wake rolling across the surface of a lake.

We may not get everything right in our relationship—but where we were now felt better than it ever had. We *were* stronger together. I was confident there was nothing we couldn't face together—and now, we had Brighton, too. His family might not understand our love, but when the three of us were together, it was all encompassing.

When all of this began last summer, I teased Olivia, crediting her healing to the Brighton Effect. It felt like everything he touched turned better, warmer somehow. Like pavement under the heat of summer. As I made slow, gentle love to her, I realized it was so much more than that.

He was the spark that had ignited healing for our family. But instead of burning us alive like I'd feared would happen, it ended up transforming all of us into the sun itself. The truth was, I don't think we'd have gotten to this point without Brighton. But now that we had, I knew I never wanted a day without sunlight again.

"GO ON, HONEY," Mom said, kissing me on the cheek. "Olivia needs you."

Guilt stabbed at my heart. It was Christmas, and my family had come to town for me. No, I thought. They'd come to town for *us*. For our wedding. They'd embraced Ryan and Olivia and our unusual relationship, showing us more grace and dignity than I ever imagined possible in such a short amount of time. Paige must've had something to do with smoothing things over ahead of time because she'd known about us the longest and had busted my chops the most when I first told her. Since then, she'd come around. She even befriended Olivia. The two were scheming ways they might be able to work together in the future. And by scheming, I mean Paige had all kinds of creative ideas swirling around in her mind and was not so subtly hinting at how amazing a collaboration could be.

"Are you sure? I feel terrible. And Ryan's with her, so she's not really alone," I said, my heart torn as I thought of Olivia struggling and me not being there for her. How could I sit around the Christmas table and make small talk while Olivia was mourning the loss of Laelynn?

My mother put her hand on my shoulder and smiled sympathetically. "But *you're* not there. And if anything is clear to me after these last few days, it's that you belong with her. She's hurting right now, but you not being there with her is causing you to hurt too. I can see it in your eyes, sweetie."

"I love her, Mom. More than I've ever loved a woman."

"I know," she said, squeezing my shoulder. "Now, don't worry about us. We have a full table, lots of good food, and an amazing library to keep us busy. Now that you're married, you're going to learn fast that Olivia and Ryan are now *your* family. It doesn't mean that we aren't, or that we won't be here for you. But they're your people. And when your baby is born, it's just going to become more so. Nothing should be more important than *your* family now. Not even us. It's a rite of passage, Brighton. And I couldn't think of a better Christmas gift than to know how much love you have surrounding you. Don't ever let it go."

I was too choked up to speak, so I pulled my mom in with one arm and hugged her close. "Thanks, Mom. Tell everyone I'm sorry."

"There's nothing to be sorry for. Now go."

WE SPENT OUR first Christmas together talking long into the night about our lost babies. We imagined what they would be like if they were still with us. Sam would be well into elementary school by now. I wondered if he would like engineering and building like me. Would he have my dirty blond hair, or his mother's raven locks? I had an image in my mind of what Sam would look like, since I got to hold him after Caroline.

For as long I lived, I would never be able to erase the memory of feeling helpless as I glanced down at my newborn son, knowing I couldn't save him. Parents are supposed to protect their children. Yet there he was, small and perfect in my arms—only he wasn't wiggling or crying like he should have been. Or looking up at me with the blue eyes most babies are born with.

He wasn't there with me at all. I was left holding what could have been, a blanket full of broken dreams and love that I had no idea how to piece back together.

I tried to be there for Caroline afterward, but it soon became clear that we'd only stayed together for Sam. Instead of someone to lean on, I was left driftless in my grief. My sister Becca was the one who talked me into counseling, and it was what saved my life. I'd had the dark days Olivia was experiencing before I met her. I knew a little of what it was like to mourn what would never be. But I hadn't carried Sam in my body. My body wasn't responsible for giving him life. And I'd never know the miracles of pregnancy that only a mother can feel while growing a miniature human in her body.

So, I listened while Olivia shared her grief. I held her in my arms when she told me about visiting Laelynn's graveside.

And I cried with them both when they talked about her funeral and how hard it was to walk away when it was over, knowing their baby was laying there alone, beneath the freshly turned earth.

Nothing can prepare a heart for that kind of grief.

Even though I'd gone through something similar, hearing their story gave me more perspective around their individual grief. You never value life more fully than you do when you realize how suddenly it can be snatched away.

We made a pact that night, the three of us. That no matter what happened—with our baby, or in our lives—we would be there for one another. To hold each other up if we broke, to love one another back from the brink. It wasn't something any of us wanted to think about, but it was our reality, based on shared experiences.

When we were all talked out, and no tears were left to cry, we climbed the stairs to go to bed. Then we did what came naturally to us—we leaned on each other. We made love well into the early morning hours, making promises and commitments with our bodies.

If Christmas Eve was mine and Olivia's wedding night, this had been mine and Ryan's. Finally, the three of us felt truly united in matrimony, tethered by our hearts, and rooted in a love so strong I knew nothing could ever shake it.

"**Y**OU BOUGHT HER a freaking minivan for Christmas?" Brighton sputtered to Ryan as we stepped into the frigid morning air.

"Oh, did I forget to mention it?" I teased, blowing him a kiss. I was letting Brighton drive today because he had a surprise for us. We had less than a week left till Ryan's classes resumed, and Brighton wanted to take us on what he called a "babymoon"—which he explained was like a mini-honeymoon and a last romantic trip rolled into one before the baby came.

Even though we still had lots left to do to prepare for Baby T's arrival, it was better than sitting around at home. I'd had more than my fair share of that over the last six months. It felt nice to get away and take road trips again. It was something Ryan and I used to love doing together. Though, our road trips with Brighton were exponentially more interesting, with him having come from a large family and knowing from experience how to keep long trips fun.

Brighton's youngest sister, Kendra, agreed to stay at his house for a few more days while we took our trip, which meant Stitch had a closer, more familiar place to stay than Regina's farm. Neither Ryan nor I had a clue where we were going, but that was half the fun.

"What's one of the best dates you've ever been on, or taken someone on?" Brighton asked as we drove. We often played games like "what if" or twenty questions. It passed the time and helped us get to know each other even better. "If yours is with each other, you have to name separate ones if your first pick is already taken."

"Hmm," said Ryan, considering. I was in the front with Brighton, and Ryan was in the second row behind me. I pulled down my visor so I could see him in the little mirror. It wasn't quite as easy to twist anymore now that I was nearing the end of my second trimester.

"For me, I'd have to say it was the time I rented out a movie theater for a private prescreening of *The Hunger Games*. We had the whole theater to ourselves. They even let us go behind the counter and taught us how to use the popcorn machine. We made a huge tub of popcorn, got to pick out some candy, and watched the movie before anyone else. It was pretty cool. When we were done, we went and had dinner in the lobby. I had them set up a romantic table for two, complete with candles and Liv's favorite flowers."

I swallowed, and Brighton squeezed my hand. Peonies had been my favorite flowers for years. It was mostly because Ryan always gave them to me, and they came with a lot of love. One day, when Brighton and I were struggling with our growing feelings for one another at the beginning of all this, he admitted he loved me. It was a day that was both my wreckage and my salvation, because I loved him, too. But I would never betray my marriage to Ryan or risk breaking Brighton's heart any worse by admitting my feelings or making promises I couldn't keep. My heart had ached to say the words back, but I simply couldn't. So, I did the next best thing. I told Brighton how I loved tulips more than anything else, even though I also loved peonies. And it killed me that I couldn't have them planted all around me so I could enjoy them every single day. He understood exactly what my heart was saying, even though I didn't dare come right out and say it.

The next week, he planted hundreds and hundreds of plum-colored tulips all around the inside border of our fence. It was a visual explosion of his love for me, and something I would never forget. Now, when I thought of my favorite flower, it was always the tulips of my heart.

Brighton was laughing at some part of Ryan's recount of our date, pulling me from my memories. "You're up next," he said.

"Well . . . it *was* kinda hard to top that date, for sure."

"I didn't realize you liked movies like *The Hunger Games*," Brighton said. "We need to talk movies next."

"Are you kidding me?" Ryan piped in from the back seat. "Olivia's never met a young adult post-apocalyptic or dystopian movie she didn't like. Isn't that right, Livy?"

I laughed. "He has a point."

"Interesting," Brighton said. "And here I thought I *really* knew you."

I smacked his arm playfully. "Moving on to *my* best date. I guess Ryan setting up a threesome doesn't count?"

The guys burst out laughing.

"I mean . . ." I scrolled through all the best, most romantic memories I had with Ryan over the years. There had been so many it was hard to choose. "Okay. I've got one. When Ryan and I first started living together, he made me get up early one morning—like at the butt crack of dawn. I'm not a morning person, but he promised it would be worth it. He ended up driving me to this nearly empty pasture in the middle of nowhere. The sun was coming up, and we saw the most breathtaking sunrise. All these brilliant pinks and purples and dusky blues. Then we went around the back of this barn. I had no clue where we were going. That's when I saw this giant hot air balloon lying on its side in the grass. We got to help hold it while this guy and his crew lit the fire and righted the balloon—which is a lot more work than you'd think. I'd never flown in a hot air balloon before, so I was a little intimidated with how small the basket was. But it was breathtaking once we got in the air," I said dreamily, transported back to that morning.

"Have you ever been in a hot air balloon?" I asked Brighton.

"Can't say I have. Though it's a bucket-list item."

"I hate that term," said Ryan, laughing.

"How come?" Brighton asked.

"You're making a list of things to do before you die. I mean—how morbid is that? I'd rather make a carpe diem list or something."

"It's pretty much the same thing, isn't it?" I asked.

He leaned forward between our seats. "Not at all. One's focusing on the fear of dying, making you feel like you're running out of time. So, the items become things you *think* you should do, if you had no time left, rather than the things you *want* to do, knowing you have this huge, glorious, open life ahead of you. It's about possibilities, instead of fear."

"Hmm. A carpe diem list. I like that. We need to make one then," Brighton said. "One for just the three of us, and one for our family once the baby comes. Let's carpe the fucking diem out of this beautiful life we've been given!"

The rest of the drive flew by with both meaningful conversations, and silly ones. We spent more time than I cared to admit discussing the pros and cons of whether we'd rather walk around for the rest of our lives with two noses or live with no ears. I chose two noses.

I found out that Ryan's favorite flower was a hydrangea because his grandmother grew them in her yard when he was growing up. And Brighton's were sunflowers because they never failed to make him happy. Now I understood why he'd bought them for me the first time the three of us were intimate together. We laughed as Brighton recounted his story of standing in the grocery store, stumped over what flowers were best to bring for a threesome. He went with what made him happy.

We were so engrossed in the fun we were having we didn't notice when Brighton pulled into the main entrance at the Watkins Glen International racetrack. Ryan and I had only been one other time, though admittedly, it was for a beer festival. We camped with a few friends along the boot side of the track and, overall, the weekend was hazy.

"What in the world are we doing here?" Ryan asked. "There aren't any races going on right now, I don't think."

"Nope. You're right about that," Brighton said mysteriously. "Come on, let's go!"

He was jumping around like a kid, and the enthusiasm was contagious. When we approached the main entrance, a nicely dressed older woman greeted us with a golf cart. We all hopped on, even though we had no idea where we were going. She gave us a tour of the track and all the facilities— which were plentiful. According to her, it was voted the best racetrack in North America, and it was one of the original three circuits to host Formula 1 Grand Prix racing.

We still had no clue *why* we were there, but it was fun getting a private behind-the-scenes look at the track. We took the tunnel through to the infield and made our way to the Tower Suites, where a reserved parking spot was waiting for us. The private facility was the opposite of any experience we'd had at the track before. During race season, corporations rented it out so they could schmooze their clients and watch the races from the luxury of their own suite.

"Yo, Skippy!" Brighton hollered as we neared the two men waiting for us outside the building. There was obviously a friendship there as Skippy grabbed Brighton's hand and shook it, slapping him on the back in a half-hug greeting. He was tall, wide, and boisterous. "These are my friends, Ryan and Olivia."

We shook his hand and Brighton continued with the introductions. "Skip here is Becca's old high-school sweetheart," he explained. "He manages a bunch of shit at the track."

He pointed to another man. "And this guy right here is why we're here today. I want to introduce you to Russell Tierney, the head of the Upstate New York BMW High Performance Driving Academy. He's going to teach Ryan how to safely drive an M2 around this track."

"Are you shitting me right now?" Ryan asked.

"Nope," said Brighton, a contagious grin taking over his face.

"You can just call me Russ," the man said, shaking Ryan's hand.

"Holy crap." Ryan looked back and forth between me and Brighton. "Did you know about this, Liv?"

I shook my head. "Not a clue. You sure this is safe?" I asked Russ.

"I've been teaching people to drive racetracks all around the country for the last twenty-five years. Used to race myself a little back in the day. Now I focus on the upstate area exclusively, and Watkins Glen is one of our main tracks. I've trained hundreds of people in high-performance driving. He's in safe hands. I won't just throw him on the track and say good luck."

"What *do* you do?" I pressed.

"I'm taking Ryan over to another building, where I'll teach him everything he needs to know about high-performance racing, and things he specifically needs to know about driving the M2 on *this* course. A helmet's required, and I have one for him, so no worries there." Russ turned to face Ryan. "The best way to learn after that is by experience. I'll be driving in front of you in a lead car so you know what turns are coming up and can pace easier. After you're comfortable driving the course, we'll pick up some speed until you're ready to let 'er loose on the back straight."

"Sounds amazing. Aren't you driving too?" Ryan asked Brighton. "I'm guessing Livy shouldn't."

"Nah. I've driven with Russ more times than I can count," Brighton explained. "While you're in driving school, Liv and I will grab a bite to eat in the Tower Suites. You guys will meet us back here for your lunch before you start driving. We'll watch you from up here. If it gets warmer later, we can even head to the rooftop so we can catch you on the back straight, too. That's the fun part."

"I can't believe you did this for me," Ryan said. I could tell he wanted to say more, but he held back in front of our company.

"Carpe diem, right?"

Ryan grinned. "Hell yeah. All right, Russ. Let's get started." He leaned over and gave me a quick kiss before heading off with the driving expert.

Meanwhile, Skip opened the door to the Tower Suites, and we followed him to the viewing room Brighton reserved just for us.

"How far along are you, darling?" Skip asked.

I nearly stumbled. It was the first time anyone outside of our little enclave noticed I was pregnant. I'd done a good job hiding it from my clients so far, and I wasn't on social media much anymore. I had no one else to tell.

"Just about six months," I said, rounding up.

"Well, congratulations. Got four myself. All under eight. Wife started popping 'em out right after college. They're fun. Just expensive as fuck. Noisy, too. People don't believe me when I tell them I come to work to get a little peace and quiet."

I laughed. It was hard not to relax around Skip.

"So, you know Becca? How's she doing these days, Brighton? She still with that douche bag?"

"You mean her husband?"

"Yeah, that's the one."

"Happier than ever. Sorry."

"No harm, no foul. I screwed up." Skip turned to me. "Don't ever let the right one get away. That was my lesson in life."

"I'm sure your wife made up for it," I said gently.

"She's a right pain in my ass, but I do love her."

I laughed, but the sound died on my lips when Skip opened the door to the private suite. It was bigger than I expected, and a huge window afforded us an amazing view of the racetrack. Several tables were already set up and covered with a lavish Italian spread typical of upstate New York. There was also a huge tin bucket filled with ice and a vast array of cold drinks and freshly chopped fruit in small plastic cups. My favorite part, though, was the separate table full of more sweets than I could count, including my not-so-secret weakness—Half Moon Cookies.

"Wow," I said eloquently, not sure where to start. "This is amazing!"

"Well, take all the time you need and enjoy your lunch. Ryan's going to be a while. You have the place to yourself, but we're just a phone call away if you need anything at all."

"Thanks, man. I really appreciate everything," Brighton said, shaking Skip's hand as they said their goodbyes.

When the door finally closed, I turned to Brighton. A big grin spread across my face as I looked up into his beautiful green eyes. "What in the world has come over you with all this?"

A dangerous glimmer filled his gaze as he stared back at me, hungry for something other than lunch. My breath hitched and I knew what was coming before he cupped my face and kissed me, walking me back to the closest wall. I'd wanted to feel his mouth on mine all morning, so I took greedily. It wasn't long before our kisses became deeper and more urgent. His hair was soft under my fingertips, and my breathing hitched when his mouth moved to my neck, then to the open skin just above the swell of my breasts.

"Making up for lost time," he growled as his hands cupped my now-generous breasts. "This is what I'd do if I were wooing you guys. We kind of skipped over that part. Now, get your clothes off, hot momma."

"What? You expect me to get naked here?" I asked, looking toward the extremely large viewing window.

"We have time, Liv. No one's coming in until we're ready. And no one can see up here into the suite. Trust me."

He locked the door to prove it, then stalked back over to me and began removing layers of my clothes one at a time, kissing every inch of my body in the process. By the end of the day, I wasn't sure who had the better driving experience—me or Ryan.

CHAPTER THIRTY-FOUR

Ryan

"**H**OLY SHIT THAT was amazing!" I said for about the hundredth time since we'd left Watkins Glen. I still couldn't believe Brighton set up such a thoughtful and extravagant experience for me. Olivia seemed more relaxed, too. It was nice to see her at ease for the first time since visiting Laelynn's grave on Christmas Day. The excitement of the afternoon caught up with her though, and the moment her head hit the pillow on our over-sized bed at the Hilton Garden Inn, she fell fast asleep. The look the receptionist gave us when we asked for their king-bed suite was priceless.

Brighton and I ordered appetizers and beer from room service because our quick dinner of subs on the way to the hotel wasn't cutting it. Plus, beer. We closed the door to the bedroom and sat in the suite's living room to eat and chat about the day, careful to keep our voices low so we didn't wake Olivia.

"I really appreciate what you did for me today."

"It was nothing. I know people, so I was able to pull a few strings."

"That's not what I meant."

"I know. I just didn't want to embarrass you by letting on that you were getting all mushy and shit."

I took a long pull of my beer and really looked at Kerrington. He was so different than the man I met that first day at his uncle's house. Or maybe I'd just finally gotten to know the real him. The one Olivia saw all along. The one she was able to fall in love with, even though she had me. We were different, I got that. We each gave her something special in our relationships with her. I knew she never intended to fall in love with the man. But after spending the last six months with him, I was starting to see how it could happen. I may not have fallen in love with him the way she had, but I loved him, nonetheless. I couldn't remember the last time I told a guy friend I loved them. Had I ever?

But I was lying to myself. Kerrington was more than just a friend now. That was the part that confused me the most. Luckily, no one was asking me to figure it out—including him.

"So, what do we have planned for tomorrow?"

"It's another surprise."

"You're just full of 'em."

Brighton snorted.

"Seriously though. What is all of this?"

"You really don't get it, do you?" he asked, leaning forward to place his elbows on his knees.

"Guess I'm slow."

Brighton stood and slowly walked over to me. He ran a hand through my hair, then down the side of my face. He traced my beard with his thumb till it found my mouth, swiping over my lower lip. I stood, putting us toe-to-toe, facing one another. The air in the room felt heavy—like it does just before a storm drops.

"Let me catch you up to speed."

I swallowed, unable to stop my eyes from falling to Brighton's mouth. I'd gotten familiar with it lately. I knew he could be rough, biting and taking, just as easily as he could be soothing, as if each languid kiss would make me forget that it was with a man. It confused me because I wasn't attracted to men.

But I was attracted to *him*.

"What the hell is it about you that makes you so fucking irresistible?"

"You think I'm irresistible?" he postured.

"I'm standing here, aren't I?"

"I did all this because I love you, okay? When I say I love you, it's not because I also happen to love Olivia. It's because I love *you*—Ryan Marshall Wells. I don't want this to just be about Olivia and me, or you and Olivia. I want our life to be about *all* of us. When I say I want both of you, it's because you fucking matter to me."

His mouth was so close I could smell the stout on his breath.

"So, you're wooing me, then?" I joked, the corner of my mouth rising just a smidge.

"I guess I am."

"I hope you don't expect me to put out after our first date."

"I'm able to wait," he said.

Fuck.

I swallowed. This was unchartered territory. Something we agreed would never happen.

But how do you love at arm's length? I couldn't help where my heart was leading me anymore than I could control my breathing. It somehow veered me onto a path I never expected, never wanted for myself. It had always been about Olivia. I didn't know what to do now if it wasn't.

The truth about love is—you don't choose it. It chooses you.

Who knows? Maybe I really had fallen in love with Brighton just as hard as Olivia had. There was only one way to find out. I leaned in, our faces touching with the tenderest ache of what stood between us.

His hand lashed out, gripping the back of my head. I could feel his chest rising and falling against mine, his warm breath on my lips.

In that moment, I made a choice.

I surrendered to whatever this thing was that was pulsing between us. I *needed* more.

I *needed* Brighton.

"I'm not," I said.

His mouth crashed down on mine, fierce and unrestrained with the permission I'd just given. He pushed his hands into my hair, yanking my head back as he pressed his tongue in deeper, making me open for him as he explored the terrain of my mouth. I dropped my empty beer bottle to the floor and reached for his hips, tugging him closer.

We had moments during our shared time with Olivia when we'd let our hands explore each other's bodies—but it was always a safe caress here or there. A firm hand gripping an ass as we kissed. A slow exploration of each other's chests during a shower. But then, inevitably, we'd redirect the surging arousal I knew we both felt back onto Olivia.

It was safer there.

Tonight, there was no Olivia. She was sleeping soundly in the other room. And now, our touches became a little bolder. Brighton walked me backward until my shoulders met the hotel room door with a soft thud. He pulled back and our eyes met in the heated tension that hung thick between us—the air clouded with feelings we'd been fighting for too long because we simply didn't understand them before now.

Now, I understood exactly what this was. It was love. And for the first time, I stopped questioning and surrendered. Brighton wanted to woo me? Game on.

I grabbed the back of my T-shirt and yanked it over my head, tossing it to the floor when I was done. Brighton's eyes dragged over my chest, which had a light covering of dark hair leading in a thin line down my flat stomach to the V below. He thumbed his lip as his eyes slowly dragged their way back up to mine. He leaned in again, slower this time. A promise crackled in the air around us. When I leaned my head forward and sucked his lower lip in between my teeth, he hissed, pressing his hips forward and grinding them against me on instinct. A spear of lust unlike anything I'd ever experienced shot through my body, making my dick ache. This was new terrain, and I had no idea how to explore it. But I let my hands slide over Brighton's ass, finding the back hem of his jeans. I slipped my palms inside, cupping his bare skin as he pressed his body even closer to mine.

"Fuck," he growled, his fingers gripping my beard just as tightly as my hands gripped his backside. Our chests heaved between us as we tried to catch our breath. "We really doing this, Wells?"

I pulled him even closer so our hips were pressed together, leaving no doubt where this was headed and how turned on I was. He chuckled, dropping his mouth and tracing his tongue along my lower lip slowly, sensually.

When his palm slid down the front of my stomach, my abs tightened under his touch. I closed my eyes when it passed under the top of my jeans, his rough grip meeting the smooth skin of my shaft. There was no going back, and I knew I never wanted us to.

That night, our relationship changed, melting even deeper into a range of feelings that defied everything we thought we knew about our capacity to love one another. There were no barriers left between us anymore—and we knew it would deepen not only our connection, but our relationship with Liv.

To say this trip changed our lives was an understatement.

That night, Brighton made me realize this "thing" between all of us was truly a forever thing. A commitment not just between Olivia and Brighton, or me and Olivia, but *all* of us. He took his time with me, to make sure I knew that. That I *felt* that. That I felt loved.

That's what this trip was all about.

And it worked.

That night, I fell even deeper in love with Brighton Kerrington.

CHAPTER THIRTY-FIVE

Ryan

WE SPENT THE next three days in New York City—including New Year's Eve. Brighton surprised us with a cooking lesson with a renowned chef who taught us how to make organic baby food from scratch. She also taught Brighton and me recipes for a few go-to meals we could easily make after the baby was born so it didn't all fall on Olivia's shoulders. Since we didn't know many people in the city, and it was like a separate world unto itself, it was easier to be openly ourselves there. That felt unusually freeing and brought out the playful side in all of us as we explored how our relationship could work—both in and out of the bedroom.

We did all the things tourists in love do together and Liv somehow managed to sweet talk some last-minute tickets from a scalper to see *Hamilton*. The cherry on the cake was when we went to the infamous Studio 54 for a New Year's

Eve concert with Michael Bublé. It was technically owned by the Roundabout Theatre Company now, but it was still cool knowing we were gracing the same space as so many legendary artists, actors, singers, and models who partied hard there in the seventies.

Brighton and I were already tipsy from our dinner at Feinstein's/54 Below, and high on hearing Bublé sing in person, when we stumbled from the club, laughing. We were eager to get back to the hotel and away from Times Square. We had no interest in watching the ball drop with a million of our closest friends.

Olivia was holding onto Brighton's hand while I tried to hail a taxi. When it sped by me, he doubled over laughing, draping his arm loosely over my shoulder and pulling me in for a kiss. He dropped his mouth down on mine and claimed it. It was over before it started, but my lips burned for more.

"You think it's so easy, you do it," I said, laughing.

That's when I thought I heard someone call my name. There was still a crowd outside the theater, but as I glanced around, I didn't see a single familiar face. Maybe I'd had too much to drink.

But no, a hand reached out and tapped my upper arm. I turned to shrug it off when my eyes landed on the cold, calculating stare of Kimber Shanahan. Her husband was nowhere to be seen, but an older woman stood next to her.

"Kimber! What in the world are you doing here?" I spun back to get Brighton and Olivia's attention before it was too late. It was too late. Brighton was enthusiastically kissing Olivia's neck, and she was swatting at him, telling him to hail a cab already.

Fuck.

"Guys, look who I just ran into," I said louder, tugging the back of Brighton's tuxedo jacket. They parted, confused. That's when Olivia saw Kimber, the blood draining from her face.

Kimber looked confused as she gazed between me and Brighton, then Brighton and Olivia. Then her eyes dropped to Olivia's stomach, which protruded under the gold-and-teal swingy cocktail dress she was wearing. Kimber already knew we were pregnant from our run-in after the ultrasound. But it was poor timing to be reminded of the fact after she'd just seen an obviously sensual kiss between my wife and my best friend.

"Kimber!" she said, trying to recover. She unconsciously wiped at her bottom lip, which only made it worse. "Happy New Year!"

"Uh, yes. Happy New Year to you three, as well."

"Thanks, Mrs. S!" Brighton said, trying to lighten the mood. "And who's this pretty little lady with you tonight?"

Kimber waved to the woman behind her. "This is my sister, Maxine. She lives here, and I thought I would visit for New Year's Eve. We just don't have anywhere nearly as fun to celebrate back home. Maxine, this is Ryan Wells, my colleague, and his *wife*, Olivia."

Her sister didn't seem as interested as Kimber did.

"And this is my best friend, Brighton. He's a little drunk," I whispered loudly. "Don't mind him. He gets a little touchy when he's had too much to drink."

"I'm right here you know," he said, laughing too loud and playing it up. "I was just trying to show Ryan here how to hail a taxi in the city. You can tell he's not from around here."

"Yes, I saw. You have an . . . interesting technique."

"Why thank you," he said and bowed a little at the waist. "Now, if you'll excuse us, Olivia's a little tired and we're a little drunk. It was good to see you as always. Maxine, nice to meet you."

"Yes, well . . ." Kimber glanced back at Olivia's stomach, then acted surprised. "Olivia! I'd almost forgotten you were pregnant. I didn't realize you were so far along. No wonder you look so tired. You must be ready to pop! When are you due?"

I could tell Olivia was about to pop something all right. I wrapped my arm around her, drawing her closer to me and farther from Brighton as subtly as I could. Poor Maxine looked uncomfortable and bored at the same time.

"Early April," I answered for Olivia since she was quietly seething next to me.

I heard Brighton whistle from behind us, then call out my name. "Let's go, Wells."

"Sorry to be rude and leave so fast, but it looks like we got lucky."

"Indeed," Kimber said, raising a brow. "Have a good evening, Ryan. I can't wait to catch up back home."

I'm sure she couldn't.

The cab ride back to the hotel was quiet, though Olivia held my hand tightly. It wasn't until we closed the door of our hotel that she finally brought up what happened.

"How bad was it?" Olivia asked. She kicked off her heels and moaned, rubbing her aching soles before changing into her pajamas. Brighton jumped onto the bed, still in his tuxedo, and leaned against the headboard. He patted the bed for Olivia to join him and grabbed her feet, putting them onto his lap when she did. She lay stretched out across the bed with an arm flung over her eyes.

I shrugged off my dress shoes and lay down next to her, turning on my side so I could face her. I ran my fingers down the front of Olivia's body from her chest to her stomach, where I slid my hand beneath her soft cotton T-shirt to rub her rounded stomach. It was so damn cute.

I ran my hand gently back and forth, unable to get enough knowing our baby girl was in there. "It wasn't our finest moment," I answered truthfully.

She moved her arm just a tad to peek out of the corner of her eye at me. "Did she see Brighton kiss me?"

"Uh, yeah. Everyone at the theater saw that kiss. It was kinda hard not to notice."

Olivia groaned.

"Hon?"

"Yeah?"

"She saw Brighton and me kiss, too. I just thought you should know."

She sat up on her elbows and looked at me. "What in the hell are we going to do, Ryan? This seriously isn't good."

She plopped back down onto the bed. "Why? Of all places in all the world, how did we end up in the same city, and the same place, at the same time as that woman? For god's sake! There are like eight million people in New York City!"

"A lot of people come here for New Year's, Livy. It's just shitty coincidence that we both did this year. Don't worry about it, though. There's nothing we can do about it now. We'll worry about it another day."

Right then, I felt a little thump under the palm of my hand. Olivia's eyes lit up as she looked at me. "Did you feel that?"

I nodded, grinning from ear to ear.

"I forgot to tell you at Christmastime! We got sidetracked like we always do," she said, rolling her eyes. It was true. The three of us got distracted by each other in the best way possible quite a bit.

I put my ear to her belly and started singing Michael Bublé's cover of the song we'd heard him play in person earlier. "Birds flying high, you know how I feel . . ."

Brighton swung around, resting his head on the side of Olivia's stomach. "It's a new dawn, it's a new day, it's a new life . . ."

Olivia shimmied between us. "Mmm, and I feel so good," she finished sweetly.

I got up, turned on my Bublé playlist from my phone, and turned off the lights in our hotel room. Then I joined Brighton and Liv in bed and helped them both know just how little I cared about the Kimber situation, and just how good my new little family really made me feel.

CHAPTER THIRTY-SIX

Olivia

THE NEXT TWO months flew by fast. I was enjoying getting back into the swing of things with my work, and Live Well Interiors was doing better than ever. Ryan had studiously avoided Kimber since returning home. Not without her trying, though. Ryan said he didn't care if anyone found out, but I had my reservations. It's one thing if it was just us to consider. But it was a small town, and I was already protective of Baby T.

One weekend, about five weeks before our expected due date, Brighton and Ryan decided it was finally time to decorate the nursery. Fear had held me back from decorating it sooner. Even though I knew it would make things easier if it was done before the baby's arrival, it became all too real when we moved out the few items we'd stored in the near-empty room. All the loss I'd experienced with Laelynn rushed back. I thought it would paralyze me, but I felt oddly at peace. Maybe because I was no longer so empty inside. I'd made room for love this past year, even after unspeakable grief. It was time to make room for our new daughter, too. She deserved that.

Dr. Chavez moved me to every-two-weeks visits a month ago and every appointment was a blessing because it made me feel that much more confident in her safe arrival. I was finally letting myself feel *hope*. And Brighton was living with us all the time now. He and Ryan were getting even closer, and the two often teamed up to make sure I wasn't overdoing things.

So, I let them install the tall, cottage-inspired chair rail I'd dreamed of using in a nursery someday. They painted it white, and I paired it with the fairest of blush pinks for the walls above. A pale cream rug covered most of the hardwoods, and Ryan already hung the wispy ivory curtains I ordered. Everything I chose was in soft shades of peaceful neutrals, including the club chair that doubled as a gliding rocker and the modern, faux-leather ottoman I found. The pallet made me feel calm and happy when I finally saw how it all came together.

But the pièce de résistance was the modern white crib Brighton handmade for Baby T. I walked over, running my hand over the smooth side rail, my heart heavy with gratitude for this gift of love from father to daughter. *Fathers*. Ryan had a hand in it, too, creating the custom rails and legs for Brighton's design. It all worked in perfect harmony.

I turned, overwhelmed with the emotions flooding over me. "You guys . . . this is beyond anything I dreamed of."

"She deserves it," Brighton said, looking relieved. "I also made the dresser, the small bookcase, the changing table, and the toy chest. I thought it might be nice to add one to a collection that has happier connotations."

A tiny woodland bunny in soft beige, blush pink, and cream was hand painted on the toy chest above the opening clasp. I ran my hand over the top of it.

"The inside hinges self-close slowly, so you won't have to worry about it slamming down on top of her. And Ryan helped with all the detail work. Couldn't have done it in time without him," Brighton said, cramming his hands into the pockets of his jeans.

"Is it everything you wanted?" Ryan asked.

"More," I breathed out, inspecting all the items I'd ordered but hadn't seen in person until today. The table next to the rocker was a wooden tree trunk, the bark completely removed and the pale, cream-colored wood inside sanded and soft. A lamp shaped like a bronze rabbit with its tall ears poking through the top of the shade added whimsy without losing design aesthetic.

There was a set of six pictures framed in white that hung rows of three above the changing table. Each frame held a painting of a woodland animal's face, as if popping up from the bottom of the frame to say hello. They were painted in watercolors and matched the neutrals in the room. "Where did you get these?" I asked. I hadn't picked them out, but they went perfectly with the nursery.

"Becca painted them as a baby gift. She's very artistic and wanted to do something special for her new niece."

Niece. It suddenly dawned on me that because of Brighton, our baby was inheriting a small brood of cousins. She would grow up with even more love surrounding her than I ever thought possible. The idea warmed me. She'd have cousins to play with and spend Christmas with. Goose bumps ran over my arms in a good way.

The last thing my eyes landed on was another print, this one standing on top of the bookcase and resting against the wall. The bookcase already had a few books on its shelves, as well as some baskets for toy storage. Whitewashed bookends spelled out the word LOVE, with LO on one side and the VE on the other. I couldn't help but smile.

But the print was what drew me closer. It was framed in a soft, natural wood, much like the end table, but a few shades richer. The print had geometric gold lines surrounding a special quote I'd always loved, with delicately painted flowers of all shades, like the ones I'd carried at both weddings. *God is within her. She will not fall. Psalm 46:5.*

It had been years since I'd been to church, but that didn't mean that god wasn't with me every day. I knew that. I also knew I wouldn't have survived the last few years without that knowledge. Even on my darkest days, when I was fatigued from crying and broken with pain, that tiny seed of buried truth was what held me from splintering completely apart.

"This is beautiful," I whispered, running my hand over the frame. "Whose idea was this?"

"That was all Ryan. Well, Ryan and Becca. But his doing."

Ryan crossed the room and folded me into his arms. "This has been a long time coming, Liv. I never wanted you to forget that this baby girl is going to be so loved and so strong. She already is. She'll be okay. She *will not* fall. We won't let her. She has a whole family to catch her.

"Here, I got you this, too. I know you've always loved that quote, and I want you to remember that no matter where you are or what you're going through, it applies to you, too. My girls will be protected, no matter what. This past year has proven that," Ryan said, holding out a small gold cuff bracelet. The same psalm was engraved on it, bringing tears to my eyes. I put it on my wrist before throwing my arms around Ryan. After the longest, tenderest embrace, I opened one side of our hug and waved for Brighton to join us.

"I was so scared to walk in here," I admitted. "Afraid it would remind me of everything we lost with Laelynn. It does make me think of her, but it makes me happy, too. And relieved knowing that when we bring our daughter home, she'll have her own beautiful room waiting for her already."

"We have one more fun surprise," Brighton said, heading to the closet. He opened the door with great flourish. Even though it was an old house, the closet was deep and square. It used to be a boring brown wood—one of the few spaces we hadn't worried about updating until we converted the room to a nursery.

Floating white shelves now lined the three closet walls making a U-shaped bookcase for more toy storage. Behind those, the walls were painted a rich shade of dusty rose, brightening it up. A fluffy, soft-white carpet now covered the closet floor, creating a mini reading nook or special place to hang out. Two rods were installed higher, making room for the baby's new clothes.

"You can rearrange anything you want. And we can return any of the clothes if you don't like them. I asked Paige for help. And Ryan and I picked out some together online from stores we don't have here."

I fingered through the soft material, and my heart hitched for the first time. I had to bite back the melancholy that fought for real estate, focusing instead on how lucky I was to have two men who loved our baby this much already. But the tender ache that pinched my heart was there, under all the joy. I knew it always would be. I would never not think of Laelynn. I flipped through the clothes just to see what they'd picked and burst out laughing. At the end was a white onesie that had a tiny blue tutu sewn around the waist that said "Duke" in cursive across the chest. Next to it was a matching one with "Syracuse" and the tutu was a warm tangerine.

"You guys get serious points for this," I said, turning to face them. "These are great."

"She can wear the Duke one home from the hospital," Brighton said.

"And by Duke, he means SU," Ryan said.

"Or maybe the other cute outfit you have in here, with the tiny sage flowers on it."

Brighton rolled his eyes and smacked Ryan's arm. "Of course she'd pick one of Becca's."

I lifted my hands in the air as if surrendering. "Switzerland," I joked. It was best to remain a neutral territory when you had two confident husbands who loved making you happy and outdoing one another.

"I know you wanted to have the baby's name spelled out over the crib, but since we haven't agreed on one yet, we'll let you figure that out after we bring her home."

"It's hard with three different opinions," I joked.

When we were in the city for New Year's, Ryan, Brighton, and I popped into a local bookstore (because, books). Ryan found two first-edition childrens' books he wanted to buy for the baby. We also picked up a baby name book, a sleep solution guide, and *What to Expect the First Year*. On the ride home, we had a heated, good-natured debate over possible names. It helped keep my mind off the whole Kimber situation and passed the long car ride home.

She was always in the back of my mind, though, and I couldn't help but wonder when she was going to use this to her advantage. I placed my hands over my much larger bump and rubbed. I would do anything to protect this little girl. As days passed, and we got closer to her due date, I became increasingly more aware of our unusual situation and how difficult it was going to be every step of the way as the baby grew older.

More than that, it was unfair—once again—to Brighton. To the outside world, everyone would naturally assume she was Ryan's daughter. We still didn't know how to have conversations with her in a couple years when she became confused over who to call Dada, or to explain why she called them both that.

Then there was a more pressing matter. One we continued to disagree on about how to best handle: Who's name would we list as the father on her birth certificate?

...nd I mean everything, becomes centered around...

One simple word: No. Before that, our eight-year marriage was built on love, respect...

the darkness, loss after loss. The only thing that can set you free is the truth. It's g...

as sacred as our wedding vows, and maybe even more so because the...

were one hundred percent honest with one another, that would be enough. That would...

...le—through another miscarriage... Until, finally, that tragic, false hope would sha...

...tter how honest, could bridge the hollow, gaping hole where my heart used to b...

...mpts to reach me. To save me. To restore me to the woman he'd fallen in love with. Eve...

..."And you fell in love with both?" Dr. Paul ask...

...rough. Through the darkness that caused us to...

...I felt an eyebrow and glanced ...

...fallen in love with a woman...

...I found mys...

...pect. He...

...Riley...

...going...

...you give...

...wanted...

...in fact...

...mate...

CHAPTER THIRTY-SEVEN

Ryan

I T WAS A beautiful Sunday afternoon, the kind that felt almost holy. I woke up to the most beautiful sunrise, and the weather was expected to hit almost fifty degrees—a veritable heatwave for upstate at the beginning of March. I'd been a little fatigued the past two weeks, but I chalked it up to sympathy exhaustion and everything I had on my plate at work. I was taking at least two weeks off when the baby was born, so I was busy getting everything ready for the sub—who was luckily a retired professor I knew who would be able to slip right in and cover for me without a hiccup.

On top of that, Brighton and I decided to babyproof both houses before the baby came, just in case. We might've gone a little overboard, as Olivia pointed out that the baby wouldn't be able to do anything for the first few months—especially not Houdini her way into our toilets. Still . . . better safe than sorry.

But today I felt great. We did what we did most Sunday mornings: brewed coffee, made a big breakfast, and curled up together in the sunroom to read for a bit—Olivia had a new rom-com paperback from one of her favorite indie authors; Brighton liked to read news on his CNN app; and I still enjoyed looking through an actual newspaper, even though I got grief for it.

"What's on your plate today?" I asked Olivia.

Brighton was taking a shower and getting dressed so he could meet his sister, Becca, at a couple properties she and Joey were considering buying. Since she owned her own event planning company and Joey managed the business side of it, they could work from anywhere. Many of her clients were from all over upstate, and she had connections with just about everyone. We often joked that she and Paige were the Kevin Bacons of our area because everyone we knew could easily be mapped back to one of them in fewer than six degrees.

Now that Brighton was staying, for good, she was also thinking of moving her family here, so our kids could grow up closer to each other. The conversation choked up Liv and me, since Baby T's only cousins were coming from his side of the family.

We still hadn't chosen a first name for our little one, but I had an idea I wanted to run by Olivia this morning after Brighton left. Stitch's ears perked up and he cocked his head, but he stayed by her side. Lately he was glued to her, and we all noticed the change. I hoped he would adjust once the baby came.

Stitch started wagging his tail, and I turned to see Brighton standing in the doorframe, his muscular arms stretched out like a T. My eyes trailed over his biceps to his chest, which strained against his shirt. At least he was wearing one today. I'd never met anyone who liked to go shirtless so much.

"You heading out?" I asked.

"Yeah, but we had a change of plans. I was supposed to meet Becca and Joey at the first property, but he's staying home with the kids since one of 'em has a low-grade fever. It'll be easier to drive together now. We might stop somewhere and grab lunch afterward, so don't wait for me to run."

"Sorry to hear that. Hope the kids feel better."

"Thanks. It'll give Becca and me some quality time, anyway. I rarely see her without Joey or the kids glued to her side."

Brighton crossed the room and leaned against the arm of my chair. He ran his palm over my upper back, rubbing it as he glanced over at Olivia. "Becca wants to throw you a baby shower, but I told her I didn't know how you'd feel about that. You don't have to answer now. Just think about it, okay?"

Olivia visibly paled. She hesitated, but finally said, "That was nice of her. Tell her I'll think about it. And give her our best. Hey, does she want to join us for dinner? I was thinking of making Ryan's favorite lasagna."

"As long as you don't try to sneak spinach in there again like last time," I joked. "Lasagna's no place for greens."

Brighton chuckled, squeezing my shoulder before he stood up to leave. He leaned down and planted one firmly on my lips first.

"What was that for?"

"Just miss you," he said.

He'd worked late every night this week on an issue at the new residential community his company, Brighton Design and Build, was constructing in town. It was like his gated community in Watertown with exclusive lakeside access. But a few problems were piling up. He came home exhausted, sometimes crashing in the guestroom so he wouldn't wake Livy.

Sunday afternoons were normally reserved for hours of lazy lovemaking and a chance for all three of us to connect. We knew once the baby came, it would be harder to have afternoons like this. So, we were bummed when we found out he needed to meet his sister so early. Otherwise, I would've dragged his ass upstairs and made love to him till we were all sweaty and breathless. My love for Brighton, separate of Olivia, had only grown deeper since our babymoon. I still couldn't believe the turnabout since that first day I'd met him—when I mistakenly thought he was a young punk—cocky and too handsome for his own good. Now I knew all the complexities and layers that made Brighton the anomaly that he was.

I stood and wove my hand in his hair, pulling him to me. We stopped just millimeters from one another's lips and stared into each other's eyes. We both loved the tension and the precipice right before we kissed—a sacred moment that feels a little taboo—then the freefall that comes from following your heart and giving into your desires, letting your warm lips meet.

With the late morning sun streaming in through the sunroom windows, Brighton's eyes were an even more beautiful and translucent green than normal. "Goddamn you make it hard to say goodbye."

"Then don't," I said simply.

I could feel his breath warm on my lips and couldn't wait any longer. I crashed my mouth to his, tightening my grip on his head. My heart rate accelerated, thumping wildly as I opened wider, taking, pulling all I could from this one kiss.

I wanted to be seared on his lips while he was with Becca, making it hard to think of anything but coming home to Liv and me. The truth was, I'd missed him this week, too.

Over dinner, I planned on asking him to sell his home and come live with us for good. Now that we knew for sure that Becca was serious about moving here, I wanted to ask him before he left. Maybe, if the properties didn't pan out, Becca could buy Brighton's place so they could keep it in the family. Nothing would make Liv happier.

Brighton cupped my ass and growled into my mouth, nipping at my lower lip. He ended the kiss, but we stayed forehead to forehead, our chests rising and falling with exertion and promise.

"Thanks a lot. My sister's here, and now I have a boner for days," he growled.

He adjusted his pants, and I couldn't help but laugh. "It's your own fault. You should've told her a later time."

"I'll make up for it when I get back," he promised, kissing my lips more gently this time. He held the side of my face. My beard was significantly shorter now because I was trying out a new look. His fingers scratched through the scruff and he groaned, adjusting his jeans again.

I laughed, swatting him on the ass as he made his way over to Olivia.

"Screw you, Wells. I'm glad my discomfort gets you off."

"That's not exactly what gets me off, Kerrington," I chaffed. "But I'll show you what does when you get back."

"Yeah, you will."

When he was done saying goodbye to Liv, he scratched Stitch's favorite spot behind his ear and was almost out the door when I remembered to mention the house.

"Hold up," I said, making my way over to him.

He was already three steps down when he turned. His hair was blonder in the sunlight, making him look even more like the Greek god we always teased him to be. I stood in the frame with the door ajar, my hand resting on the same glass pane I'd had to replace near the end of last summer when I let my jealousy over him get the best of me during a fight with Liv. I'd smacked my hand against the doorframe in frustration, hitting the small square windowpane instead and shattering it. It was the argument that sent Olivia running to Brighton for comfort, and ended with them sleeping together alone, without me.

At the time, it felt like my life was over.

It's funny how that single moment, a lie that had nearly shattered our marriage, ended up exposing the greatest truth of all—Brighton Kerrington was destined to be in our lives.

Which made it easy for me to ask him this. "We want you to live here with us. Permanently."

"Aren't I already? Or is my lease up?"

"You're funny, Kerrington." I took a step down. "But no more of this back-and-forth bullshit. We want you forever. No excuses. You belong *here*, with us."

"What are you saying?" he asked, running his tongue over his bottom lip, swollen and red from our kiss and the chafe of my beard.

"I'm saying I love the fuck out of you. Liv does, too. The baby's about to be here. Your family is *here* now—not over there. We want you to move home, to be with us," I said, my voice catching. "Sell your house. Maybe Becca could buy it—then we could have Baby T's cousins right next door. Either way, just move in with us already."

I held my breath. For some reason I was nervous he'd say no. That he wasn't ready. My biggest fear used to be losing Olivia. Now, it was losing her other husband from our lives. The man I now called mine, too.

He chuckled, taking a quick step back up to my level. "You had me at 'we want you forever.'"

"Smartass." It didn't stop me from claiming his mouth one last time. "So, is that a yes?"

"Yeah," he said, sounding relieved. "I was scared things would change once the baby came. That you'd change your mind and not want me in the picture anymore. It'd be so much easier for you and Liv if I weren't around to complicate things. It just got in my head, I guess. So, I wanted to wait until after the baby was born before even considering selling."

I fisted his shirt and pulled him back to my mouth, searing him, leaving him with no room to doubt. "When I said forever, I meant forever. Just like Olivia did when she said her vows on Christmas Eve. You're stuck with us, Kerrington," I said, swiping my tongue over his lip one last time.

"By the way, your sister's here."

Brighton laughed, then bound down the stairs to where Becca waited in the driveway. She waved, so I waved back. I had a fleeting image of him bounding down the steps of his uncle's house the first time we met. Remembered the way he waved to me before turning the corner in his pickup. Even then, I'd known Kerrington was going to be trouble.

"Did he say yes?" Liv called from her perch on the bench swing.

I nodded, wishing he wouldn't go. But I never took my eyes off his as he got in the car. The last image I had of him before turning back to Olivia was that brighter-than-life smile—the one that somehow changed us both.

It was seared into my brain, even as I took Livy's hand and led her upstairs to get back into bed.

CHAPTER THIRTY-EIGHT

Ryan

"**A**RE YOU SURE** you really want to go for that run?" Olivia teased, tempting me from bed. I'd already dressed and laced up my sneakers, double-checking my new watch to make sure the battery was charged. Olivia was kneeling on the bed in nothing more than my ratty old SU T-shirt. The collar was fraying with age, but it was her favorite of mine to steal. She claimed it was the softest one, but I also knew it was because I'd worn it the first time I told her I loved her.

I'd taken her to my favorite place—the Hole. When I was a kid, we spent our summers camping and hiking. Everyone in the area knew about the reservoir, and before long, me and my sister were flinging ourselves over the edge, too. It scared our poor parents half to death. When I got older, it became a favorite place to hang out and drink with friends on the weekends—which I no longer recommended and would ground Baby T for life if I ever caught her doing that!

By the time I met Liv, I'd been jumping off the cliff for over twenty years. I expected her to be scared like most women I'd brought there over the years.

Olivia and I were dating a few months before going, and I already knew I was in love. And not just in love. But *in love*.

"Do you remember the first time I brought you to the Hole?" I asked, feeling sentimental.

She grinned, tugging the shirt away from her body and showing it to me like, *duh*. "Of course, I do. It was the day you told me you loved me."

"It was the first day I *told* you, but not the first day I loved you. I'd already fallen head over heels by then. And then I go asking you to hurl yourself off the side of a cliff, to trust me just because I said it was safe."

She ran her hand along my bearded cheek, and I leaned in, closing my eyes. As long as I lived, I would never be able to get enough of my wife.

"I never once felt unsafe with you, Ryan. It's why I fell in love with you. My birth parents gave me up. Then my real parents died. Instead of seeing my damage and being afraid of it, you ran in, guns blazing, ready to fight my demons with me. You were always my hero in our story."

"Even now?"

"Especially now."

She leaned forward and peppered me with kisses. I inhaled her fresh citrus smell mixed with the afterglow of our love-making. It was a deadly combination and almost had me second-guessing my run.

"We had some good times, didn't we, Liv?"

"We did. And we'll have so many more. I can't wait till

Baby T is old enough to go to the Hole. I can't wait to teach her how to fly."

"You'll be the best teacher, Liv. And the best mom. You've always been my safe place to land. I know you will be for our kids, too."

"Have I been, though? Because this past year doesn't feel like it. Without even meaning to, I left you to hang out to dry on your own after Laelynn died. I realize now how self-centered I was not to notice how much you were hurting, too. I wasn't your safe place, Ryan. Because I couldn't even hold myself afloat. I regret that every day."

"I understood, Olivia. I never held it against you. My god, I just wanted to help make all your pain go away so you could be happy again. Not for my sake, but for yours. The world needs Olivia North Wells healthy so she can show up and be a safe place for others to land. And you have me and Brighton in case the burden ever gets too much to carry on your own again. That's one of the benefits of this whole thing that brings me peace at night."

"Which part?"

"Just knowing that no matter what, you will always have someone to love you. You won't ever have to feel alone again like you did when your parents died. You will be surrounded by love every single day. When one of us is flailing, we each have more support to buoy us back up."

"I still don't know how I got so lucky," she sighed.

"I think we all did."

She leaned in for a kiss again, making me triple-guess my need for exercise. "Hey, before I go, I want to run something by you."

"Shoot away," she said.

"I know we haven't decided on the baby's first name yet, but I was thinking . . . what if we gave her the middle name Samantha, in memory of Sam? Do you think Brighton would like that, or would it make him too sad?"

A sentimental half-smile curved Olivia's lips up as she looked at me with those damn blue eyes of hers. "I love it. I think he will, too. Don't you?"

I nodded. Baby T would have our last name, that much was already decided. It just made sense with Olivia's last name being Wells, too—besides other obvious reasons. We hadn't worked everything else out just yet, but we had our whole lives to do that. We'd cross each bridge and hard decision as it came. Together. All three of us.

"You're an amazing man, Ryan Wells. Do you have any idea how much I love you?"

"I could use a refresher later," I teased.

"I'll be waiting."

I kissed her one last time on the nose and brushed her hair from her eyes. We were forehead to forehead, and a wave of nausea and melancholy washed over me. I didn't want to leave her.

"Go!" she insisted. "I promise I'm not going anywhere. You'll be back before you know it. Besides, I may need a nap while you're gone. You know how to tire a girl out in bed, Mr. Wells."

"Fine! I *do* need the miles. Get some rest. You're gonna need it for later. Brighton's not working tonight, and I'm already ready for round two. Or was it three today? Four?"

She laughed, sitting back on the bed. "Go! You're incorrigible."

"But you love it," I said, backing out of the room. "You love every little thing about me."

"More than you know," she said, blowing me a kiss. "But don't let it go to your head!" she hollered after me as I made my way down the stairs.

It was much warmer now that the sun had time to warm the day. I checked my watch. It said 52 degrees. I wouldn't need a hat today. I jogged a mile to get out of our neighborhood and warm up, then stopped in a grocery store parking lot to stretch like I always did. It was going to be a long run. After stretching, I headed out, making my way along side streets to avoid traffic. I glanced down to check my stats and to set my watch to log the run. Lately, my heart rate had been a little on the higher side, so it was important to know what I was starting with before I increased my exertion. Looking down while I was running made me a little dizzy and I didn't want to eat asphalt today, so I made a mental note and got back in the zone. Stiffness gave way as the miles wore on, and I focused on my breathing so I wouldn't blow myself out. It was all about pacing so you had the endurance to finish, even if it meant slowing things down periodically. If I pushed my exertion too hard, I'd get winded and end up having to walk home, and I didn't want to do that. I was maintaining a consistent ten-minute pace, which was slower than normal, but that didn't surprise me either because of how tired I was lately. I'd made an appointment with my primary care physician for next week just to make sure it wasn't something I should worry about. The last thing I wanted was to cause Liv any stress these last few weeks of her pregnancy.

Fuck! I stumbled, having to bend over and take a series of deep breaths. A pain shot through my chest like a knife, causing my heart rate to accelerate. My new watched beeped, and I looked down at the notification that popped up. It warned me that my heart rate was too high. No shit, Sherlock. I'd pushed it too hard.

I did a few rounds of deep breathing, even though the crushing weight wouldn't go away. It was like heartburn but a million times worse. I was almost done with my run anyway and was only a few miles from home, so I slowed to a walking pace and headed in that direction.

When another pain tore through me, I started to worry. I made my way into a convenience store to grab a bottle of water and get something salty to eat just in case. I'd had things happen like this to me in the past on long runs.

As I was walking from the drink cooler to the front of the store, my heart did this weird fluttering thing that made me feel it all the way up in my neck. *Whoa.* I was debating whether to call Olivia for a ride home when, of all people, I spotted Kimber rounding the corner. There was no place to hide in this small store.

"Ryan! It's been forever. I've been trying to get a hold of you. Have you been avoiding my calls for some reason?"

I didn't have the time or patience for this. My watch beeped and I glanced down. It was alerting me of my changing heart rate again. Only this time, it was probably my company causing it. "Just staying busy. The baby's due next month, so we have our hands full getting ready for it."

"Oh, I bet you do!" she said, a little too gleefully. "Look, I know it's none of my business, but it's pretty clear what's going on over there on your street. I just want to warn you to be careful. You know how the school is. A scandal is the last thing they need right now."

"And how exactly is my marriage a scandal to anyone, Kimber? What happens privately in my home is my business, just as what happens in your home is your business. Though, from everything I've heard, the things happening with Mr. Shanahan seem to be *outside* your home, and they aren't so private, are they?"

Her face flushed, and she grew uncharacteristically quiet before she lashed out at me. "This has nothing to do with *my* husband, Ryan. He's a good man, and we have nothing to hide. Unlike you." She dropped her voice an octave. "I *saw* that man kiss you, Ryan. And I also saw him kiss Olivia, too. And they were sneaking out of his house early one morning with yesterday's wrinkled clothes on and bed head, no less. I don't know what in the world is going on over there, but it does have me thinking. I mean, I'm *worried* about you."

I was so angry I could scream. She cared about no one other than herself. She wasn't fooling anyone. And I didn't have time for this. I started to brush by her, no longer caring about social etiquette, when she asked, "Are you even sure you're the father of Olivia's baby, Ryan? You should know I'm only asking as a concerned friend."

I felt another flutter. Then a deep ache filled my chest, like someone punched me from the inside. *Fuck.* It was so strong I almost doubled over. I needed to pay for my shit and get to the parking lot so I could call Olivia. I'd have her pick me up so I could go home and nap. Maybe I was more dehydrated than I thought, and my electrolytes were way off. Better safe than sorry.

I knew I needed to get out of dodge, but first, I was ending this charade of civility with my coworker once and for all. "You have nothing to worry about, Kimber. We're all just friends. New York was harmless fun, so drop it. My personal business is exactly that. Personal." My arms had been tingly from coming in out of the cold into the overly warm store, but now I was starting to worry that wasn't the only reason why. And it hadn't been *that* cold to begin with. My heart rate increased as my concern rose.

I leveled Kimber with my gaze. "This is the last time I will ever say this to you, Kimber. It's unbecoming and unprofessional for you to have such a profound interest in my love life. It's completely inappropriate to be constantly harassing me in and out of work about my sex life and my marriage. Don't make me file a formal complaint with the university because I will. That's my next step if you don't drop this. Are we clear?"

She squared her shoulders, and I watched as her jaw set hard, her nostrils flaring as she tried to swallow her anger. Yeah, she didn't like to be called out on her shit. Too bad.

"Crystal clear. However, it would be a shame if the school received an anonymous tip on their hotline about one of the *darlings* on their faculty." She ditched any preamble and went straight for the jugular. "You and your kind *sicken* me, Ryan."

I almost laughed. If she was more worried about my kiss with Brighton or my kink for being in an open marriage than she was about losing her career, she deserved everything that was coming to her.

"Bring it, Kimber," I said leaning in closer to her. The sudden movement made me sway. "You come after me and my family, making these nasty threats, I won't hesitate to take you down. No one and nothing comes between me and the people I love."

I turned to walk away, dropping the items I had in my hand on a nearby shelf. My arm felt like it was going from tingly to outright numb, and my neck and shoulders ached now, too. What in the world? My watch beeped again.

I knew I needed to call Liv, but now I was starting to wonder if I needed to call an ambulance as well. I glanced down to see how high my heart rate was, and I felt like I was going to throw up. The dizziness got worse, and I could only vaguely process the new alert. It was too long to read but the first part sounded bad: *Your heart rate has shown signs of an irregular rhythm, suggestive of atrial fibrillation. If you have not been diagnosed with AFib by a physician*—

Kimber's shrill voice faded into the background. The aisle started to blur as black seeped into my peripheral vision. Before I could understand what was happening, my body gave out on me, collapsing. I reached for the shelf in front of me and couldn't quite catch myself. Instead, I heard cans tumbling off the shelf and rolling away on the slick linoleum floor as I started to fall. Everything felt as if it was happening in slow motion.

Then, what felt like a lightning bolt shot through my chest, and an iron grip closed around my heart. The last thing I thought of was—

nd I mean everything, becomes centered around...

One simple word: No. Before that, our eight-year marriage was built on love, respect

the darkness loss after loss, the only thing that can set you free is the truth. It's ge

as sacred as our wedding vows, and maybe even more so because it was after the los

were one hundred percent honest with one another, that would be enough. That would

ile—through another miscarriage. Until, finally, that fragile, loose hope and sha

tter how honest, could bridge the hollow, gaping hole over my betrayed the b

mpts to reach me. To save me. To restore me to the woman he'd fallen in love with. Eve

help cotinue sted. And you fell in love with him? Dr. Paul ask d

through. Through the darkness that caused me to

I lifted an eyebrow and glanced a

the I felt more until woman

easy hole I found my

expect. He would bett to

ger. Kratey D

and you tru th

d you get caught th

anted with my th

takes, he said

and pro

in pla

lonate. Th

was ne

re. Here's what

CHAPTER THIRTY-NINE
Olivia

MY BOOK NO longer held my interest because I'd been lying around in bed too long and my back was starting to hurt. I showered and was about to get dressed before deciding I needed a small project to keep my hands and mind busy over these last few weeks. I looked in my closet to pick out something to wear when I realized how cluttered it was. Ryan and Brighton would kill me if I did anything too strenuous. But I could certainly sort through my wardrobe and donate a few pieces I no longer wore.

I put on music and started going through my clothes, tossing the ones I no longer wanted into a pile on the bed. I was having so much fun I didn't even realize more than an hour had flown by. I stretched my arms above my head, my shirt riding up over my round belly. Just for fun I'd put on an old T-shirt that was a gag gift from a sorority sister. It was a still picture from the Twilight movie of Bella riding on Edward's back through the woods. I looked in the mirror and giggled. The shirt was too small now, and it said: "This is my ride or die . . . and he sparkles!"

I ran my hand over my protruding baby bump, reminding me that I wanted to get pregnancy pictures at a park or by the lake before the baby came. It would be a nice way to freeze this special period in time when it was still just the three of us—and we didn't have much time left.

"We're almost there, Baby T. I just need you to hang on at least two more weeks, okay? But I'd prefer four. Then we'll finally get to meet!"

It was as if the baby heard me and answered with a swift kick from within. Laughter bubbled over. I could see my belly move now every time she moved. That was something that never got old. *Movement*. This baby was active, and that brought relief to my worried heart—even if the little booger did keep me up at night.

I looked at the bed covered in clothes. *Crap*. I wouldn't be able to move everything off until Ryan or Brighton got home. I checked my watch. Ryan was doing a ten-mile run, so I wasn't expecting him home for at least another thirty minutes or so. Especially since he liked to stop and do warm-up and cool-down stretches. He was always better at that than I was.

I padded downstairs, knowing I needed to eat again. Hours had passed since breakfast, and I'd burned plenty of calories with Ryan. Our early afternoon hadn't been as lazy as it normally was. I giggled again.

As I made lunch, I couldn't help but notice how quiet and lonely the house felt without the guys home. It's funny how not that long ago, all I wanted was to stay inside by myself. I never liked the quiet though. When it was too still, I had time to sink down long, dark rabbit holes of despair.

Then one little thing would trigger me, setting off a chain reaction that was hard to recover from. I never even signed back up for the baby newsletters I'd subscribed to the first time around, even though the information would probably be helpful. After seeing *And Baby Makes Three: A Newsletter for First-Time Parents* in my inbox when I returned home from the hospital with no baby, well, that had sent me right over the edge.

As I was adding diced celery to my tuna salad, my phone rang. I glanced down, hoping it was Brighton. I frowned. Why on earth would Kimber Shanahan be calling?

I declined the incoming call, sending it straight to voice mail. Stitch was following me around the kitchen on my heels, so I put him in his crate. I didn't need to be tripping over him and falling on my ass. I could hear my phone ring again while I was in the other room, but I had to go to the bathroom for the fiftieth time that day and nature wouldn't wait. I padded to the guest bathroom and went, straightening the items on the countertop before heading back to the kitchen for my sandwich. I'd been craving tuna on pumpernickel lately. It had to have a slice of baby swiss and some romaine lettuce to be good though. Sometimes, I even added a squirt of spicy mustard on top.

Before I made it to the kitchen table with my lunch, my phone rang again. I looked down. Kimber had called twelve times in the time it took me to put Stitch away and go to the bathroom. I rolled my eyes. Maybe it was time for a restraining order.

I started to text Brighton about what was going on when the phone rang *again*. This time, I picked up, ready to give Kimber a piece of my mind.

"This better be important," I said. "And Ryan's not here, FYI, in case you're looking for him."

There was so much noise in the background I could hardly hear Kimber's normally loud and obnoxious voice. "Olivia! Where are you? Are you sitting down? There's been an emergency. The ambulance just left for the hospital. We were talking and—"

"Whoa, whoa, whoa," I said, stopping her. "Slow down. I can hardly hear a word you said. Where are *you*?"

"I'm at the Byrne Dairy. I was stopping in for some—oh, Jesus. Never mind. I ran into Ryan while I was here. We were having a delightful conversation when he suddenly looked peaked. I asked him if he was okay, or if he needed to sit down, but he shook his head no. I couldn't tell if he was sweaty from his run or if something was wrong. The next thing I know, he was clutching his chest, stumbling. I think he had a heart attack, Olivia. He fell to the floor, and I screamed for help. A nice lady ran over and said she was a nurse. Someone else called 911. But the lady couldn't get Ryan to respond, and he looked too pale, Olivia. One minute we were talking, and the next minute he's on the floor getting chest compressions. It was awful—"

The blood drained from my face as Kimber droned on, and my lunch fell from my hands. Ceramic splintered as the plate hit the floor. Stitch barked from the other room. I started to hyperventilate.

"Where did they take him?"

"To the hospital, Olivia. That's what I just said. Aren't you listening!?"

I hung up, even as she continued to talk. Then I slowly slid down the kitchen island and sat on the floor, trying to get my breathing under control. She had to be wrong. I would know if something happened to Ryan. He was my ride or die, for god's sake. I would *know*. I called his phone and heard it ring from the sunroom. *Shit!* He didn't take it since he had his new watch. I immediately called Brighton.

He picked up on the first ring. "Hey, beautiful. What a nice surprise. Guess what? Becca—"

"Brighton! Stop. Listen to me. I think Ryan had a heart attack while he was running. I need to get to the hospital, but I don't know if I can drive myself right now. Where are you?"

"Wait. Olivia. This doesn't make sense. Why would he have a heart attack? He's fitter than—"

"I don't know!!" I yelled. With great effort, I hefted myself up from the floor, trying to think of what I needed in case I was at the hospital for a long time with Ryan tonight. I threw a phone charger and a granola bar in my boho bag. I already had tissues inside. I looked for my phone, remembering I was on it.

"Never mind. I'll drive myself. I've got to get there now. If anything happened to him, I don't want him to be alone. I need to be there for him."

"Liv, I'm less than fifteen minutes away. Stay put and wait for me."

"I can't," I whispered. "I have to go. Just meet me there. God, I hope Kimber was lying."

I hung up, grabbed my keys, and ran outdoors as fast as I could. My hands were shaking, and I had a hard time getting the keys in the ignition. I looked down, realizing I was trying to shove Ryan's Jeep key in the wrong car. Every minute wasted was a minute he was there without me. If he really had a heart attack, would he be coherent? Could I go in to see him? I just needed to know he was okay, and I didn't trust anything that came out of Kimber's mouth.

I reversed too fast, using the camera to guide me. I rolled onto the grass and clipped the curb at the bottom of the driveway, making the minivan lurch when I came down off it and peeled out of the neighborhood. My phone rang again. It was Kimber calling back. I ignored it until the ringing stopped. Not even a minute later, Brighton called back.

I'm sorry, I thought, ignoring the incoming call. I couldn't answer while driving anyway, and I didn't trust myself to get it on speaker phone. Not when I could hardly read the street signs through my tears. A car slammed on its brakes next to me and honked its horn, alerting me that I just blew through the stop sign on the way out of our neighborhood. My hands trembled so badly I didn't know how I was even holding onto the steering wheel.

Please, god, if you never do anything else for me ever again, please just let this all be a mistake. Let Ryan be okay. I promise I will never treat him badly again or go back to the place I was last year. I will never wallow another day about what I don't have. I just need him to be okay. Please, god. Please, please, please.

Tears slid down my cheeks, but I had no napkins to wipe them with, and my tissues were in my purse. I looked at the empty seat next to me and realized I never actually grabbed my purse once I put the charger in it.

As soon as I got to the hospital, I jumped out of the car and ran into the ER. I was huffing and puffing from the exertion and naturally put one hand on my lower back to support it, while the other cradled my baby bump. A nurse frantically rushed over with a wheelchair.

"Here, sit. Are you in labor?" She looked me over from head to toe. A strangled noise laced with hysteria gurgled over when I realized I was still in my Team Edward T-shirt. In public. And I still didn't know where Ryan was or if he was okay.

"Where are your shoes?" she asked.

I looked down at my dirty bare feet, confused. There were still patches of snow outside, even though the sidewalks and parking lot at the hospital had been shoveled and sanded. I'd traipsed through it all, none the wiser.

"I—my husband. It's not me," I explained. "It's my husband, Ryan Wells. I think he came by ambulance. Has it gotten here yet? I need to see him or talk to somebody who knows what's going on. Someone called me and said he had a heart attack, and—"

The doors whooshed open, letting in a cool burst of air, and making me nauseous as it mixed with the warm air in the triage area. I felt faint.

Arms caught me, helping me to a chair. They were familiar. I could smell Irish Spring and sandalwood. I turned in my seat, looking up. Brighton was there with his sister, looking as wrecked as I felt. Becca was on the phone with Joey, telling him she wouldn't be home tonight. Why was she here again?

"Liv—look at me."

There was too much going on. A mother dragged three whining kids through the lobby in front of us—a dirty baby was on her hip, a sullen-looking girl trailed behind her on a Nintendo Switch Lite, and the poor woman was literally dragging a little boy across the floor by his hand. He refused to stand up and help her by walking. Then he cried when she snatched the candy bar from his hand that he just picked up off the floor. The doors whooshed open again, sending another cool gust of air our way. An ambulance screamed in the background. Was Ryan in there?

"I can't get an answer, she won't tell me what's going on!" I wailed. The nurse was gone, and I started to panic. "Where did she go?"

I stood, spinning around to search for her. I felt woozy. I immediately fell onto my ass on the hard chair with the thin plastic cushion. How difficult was it to make better chairs for people who were feeling so bad they had to come to an emergency room?

"The nurse went to find a doctor and track down what room Ryan's in. She said the ambulance that picked him up was in the bay empty, so he's here somewhere."

"I can't believe this is happening," I moaned, dropping my head to my hands. "He's so healthy. How could he have a heart attack? He couldn't, right? Wouldn't we have *known* something was wrong?"

"I don't know," Brighton said, cradling me the best he could with one arm while sitting in a different chair. "We'll find out together."

Becca hung up the phone. "I know a few people at the hospital. Let me go see if I can hunt anyone down and find out what the hell is going on. This place is crazy right now."

A nurse came by at one point to give me some disposable surgical booties for my bare feet and confirm what we mostly already knew. He was admitted by ambulance due to cardiac arrest and was rushed into the emergency room. I needed to fill out paperwork for him while we waited. And, of course, she had no update on his condition. Brighton went with me to the admissions desk, where a woman took our information and was understanding when I told her I forgot to grab my purse on my way out of the house. She looked up our insurance information from my most recent visit, so we were set. When she noticed my condition, she handed Brighton an apple juice box and some peanut butter crackers in case I was feeling lightheaded. Then she led us to a separate waiting room that was a little quieter than the triage area. Brighton texted Becca and told her where we were and asked her to meet us there. Minutes ticked by, and I couldn't stop my legs from bouncing. Brighton sat with me, draping his arm around the back of my chair. I dropped my head to his shoulder and started crying again. I couldn't lose Ryan. I couldn't.

After what felt like a long while later, that's how the doctor found us. I didn't even realize Becca had rejoined us until she stood up next to Brighton.

I was afraid to greet the doctor walking toward us or look him in the eye because I was too scared that I wouldn't like what I saw there. Too much time had passed since Ryan was admitted.

"Are you Olivia Wells?" he asked. I finally looked up, meeting the darkest brown eyes I had ever seen. They were impossible to read.

I blinked. "Yes."

He reached out his hand, and I stared at it. Was he really trying to shake my hand right now? I didn't care about anything other than Ryan.

"Where's my husband? Can I go see him?"

"I'm Dr. Patel," he started.

When I just stared at him, Brighton reached over and shook the doctor's hand. "I'm Brighton Kerrington, a family member of Olivia's and a friend of Ryan's. How is he doing?"

"Why don't you both come with me," he said briskly as he scanned the room. Several other families had come and gone, and there was no privacy in the waiting room. Becca said something to Brighton and sat, but I couldn't focus on anything other than where the doctor's white coat hit the back of his calves and how one of the heels of his black shoes was scuffed.

I'd been hopeful he was taking us to Ryan's recovery room, but instead, he turned into a small conference room. The doctor held the door open for us to enter first. He flicked the lights on, and they shimmered for a moment before settling into a dull off-yellow hue.

It was uncomfortably silent as the door clicked into place and I waited for him to say something—anything. I suddenly felt claustrophobic. Dr. Patel sat across the table from Brighton and me and clasped his hands together in front of him. They were strong hands, with graying hair on the backs of his knuckles. Had he been with Ryan? Were those the hands that saved his life after his heart attack?

Dr. Patel cleared his throat, wasting no time. "I'm sorry to tell you both that Ryan died at 4:46 p.m."

I froze, my leg no longer bouncing.

I couldn't have heard him right. Brighton clasped my hand under the table. I couldn't breathe. It was impossible.

"I'm sorry. What?"

"Mrs. Wells, I know this may come as a shock because of Ryan's age and overall physical condition. Have either of you noticed any unusual behavior lately? Fatigue, dizziness, nausea? Did he have any heart arrhythmias that you are aware of? Any complaints of being out of breath or winded with minimal physical exertion?"

Dead.

This stranger just said my husband was dead. He couldn't be.

At 4:46 p.m. What was I doing then? What time was it now?

I heard Brighton answering the doctor the best he could, but I couldn't speak. I felt like I was going to throw up. I clutched my stomach. No! *No, no, no, no, no!*

The doctor and Brighton were looking at me, and that's when I realized I'd just screamed that out loud. I shook my head. He couldn't be dead.

"He was perfectly healthy," I answered. I didn't even know if we were still on that question.

"Though, he has been tired a lot lately, but he has an aggressive, demanding schedule and they were preparing for the baby's arrival," Brighton said. "I've been staying with them to help, so I know he's been burning the wick at both ends. But nothing more than usual."

The doctor nodded, adjusting his black, wire-framed glasses. He lifted them onto his head where they stood out against all the grays. He rubbed the bridge of his nose.

"I'm deeply sorry, Mr. Kerrington, Mrs. Wells. We did everything we possibly could. Cases like these with someone so young are rare, but not unheard of. Especially if he's had a previous unchecked heart attack or blood clotting that you didn't know about. We think he may have had hypertrophic cardiomyopathy. Based on what you've told me, if he did, it was undiagnosed—which isn't uncommon for someone who is otherwise healthy and hasn't required MRIs or anything of that nature."

That's when I started shaking, my entire body going cold. My hands felt as if they were turning blue, and I couldn't formulate a response. How had I missed this? Had I been that self-absorbed?

The doctor texted something on his phone, and a few moments later, a nurse entered with a bottle of water and a warm blanket.

Brighton wrapped it around me and opened the bottle for me. I didn't even know tears were streaming down my face until Brighton handed me some tissues. I looked at his outstretched hand. "Is he really dead?" I rasped. "I was just with him earlier today. We made love twice, for god's sake. Then he went on his ten-mile run. He couldn't do that if he were sick, right? He wasn't sick!" I insisted loudly, slamming my hand on the table and causing some of the water to sloosh over the top of the bottle.

"I understand that this comes as a complete shock. I wish I had better news for you. We did everything we could, Mrs. Wells."

"What now?" I asked hysterically. "That's it? You're just going to walk out of this room and go eat dinner? What do we do? I can't just leave him here. We're having a baby in less than a month. I *need* my husband."

"I understand your concerns," the doctor said quietly.

"Can we see him?" Brighton asked.

I gaped openly. Would they let us? "Yes! I need to see him. Please."

"You may. You can wait in here while I make sure his body is ready. I'll send a hospital coordinator in while you wait to discuss any logistical questions you might have about what steps come next."

"Of course I have questions! My husband left our house today in a perfectly good mood. He never once said anything about not feeling well. Now all of a sudden you expect me to believe he's dead? We just buried our baby the November before last. Now I'm supposed to bury her father too?"

I turned to Brighton, my eyes searching for any truth. He wrapped me in his arms and covered the back of my head with the strong palm of his hand. "I can't do this again, Brighton. I can't."

Dr. Patel stood, offering Brighton his hand once again. "I'm sorry about your unexpected loss, Mrs. Wells. Mr. Kerrington."

It was too cold. So final and matter of fact.

Why couldn't he reassure me that Ryan would be okay?

"It isn't fair. It isn't fair," I repeated, rocking back and forth against Brighton's chest as he cradled me in his arms. "Nooooooo!" The blood-curdling wail ripped through me, nearly tearing me in half.

...d I mean everything, becomes centered around that...

One simple word: No. Before that, our eight-year marriage was built on one...

the darkness loss after loss, the only thing that can't you live is the truth. It's...

's sacred as our wedding vows, and maybe even more so because it came after the loss...

ere one hundred percent honest with one another, that would be enough. That would...

le—through another miscarriage. Until, finally, that fragile, false hope would sha...

tter how honest, could bridge the hollow, gaping hole above my heart aged to g...

mpts to reach me. To save me. To restore me to the woman he'd fallen in love with. Even...

...ed. "And you fell in love with him?" Dr. Paul ask d...

...rough. Through the dark ess that carged me to...

...I felt invisible and starved a...

...if I fell in love... th a woman...

...a nasty habit. I found myself...

...ect. He sat back I wonder...

...you mo th...

...you giv ng to...

...l smiled noth ng to...

...ball. In fact...

...and pray...

...implo...

...intimate. Tog...

CHAPTER FORTY

Brighton

THE THING ABOUT losing a loved one is that life doesn't stop just because you do. Even as your entire world crashes down around you, death and its ugly soldiers march onward, demanding even more than they already stole from you. The days immediately following Ryan's unexpected death were the worst of my life. I thought I was prepared for anything after losing Sam. Surely, if you can survive the death of a child, you can get through anything.

I was wrong.

Every movement became a chore, every decision a crippling roadblock. Olivia was catatonically quiet, and I wasn't sure what was worse—that, or the way she'd screamed and raged as soon as we returned from the hospital. The kitchen was her victim as we staggered in from the mudroom that night. I poured us each a glass of water because I had no idea what to do with myself and I was in shock, too. Olivia accepted the glass with trembling fingers, clutching the kitchen island with her other hand. Her fingers were turning red, and I was about to suggest going upstairs when she threw the glass across the room. It shattered and splinters of glass flew everywhere.

Stitch was barking from the other room, slamming against the crate to get out.

"Olivia—"

"Don't." Her chest heaved as she looked down at the countertop.

"Did you know that I hate these countertops?" she whispered.

"No."

"When we moved here, the previous owners had perfectly good granite ones. But they didn't go with my 'perfect' little design vision. So, I special ordered new ones, even though they cost us an arm and a leg, and we couldn't afford them at the time.

"They were delivered the weekend I was away on a girls' trip. Back when I still had friends," she said remorsefully. "Ryan only had a vague idea of what they looked like based on a picture I'd shown him before I ordered them."

She swallowed, her head hanging between her arms as they supported her against the island. "When I got home, and saw that they'd installed the wrong ones, I went ballistic."

She laughed, and I was starting to worry about her.

"Over fucking countertops."

She looked up at me, tears streaking her face. She was wearing some bizarre T-shirt I hadn't even realized until now, and her hair was a wreck, despite being pulled back in a low ponytail. "I lashed out at Ryan, as if the entire thing were his fault just because he was the one who was there when they were installed. He should've *known* they were the wrong ones. Right?" she asked hysterically.

I didn't think she really wanted an answer.

"The ones I wanted had a delicate gold veining in them, and these—these were so . . . *plain*," she said, as if it were a dirty word. "Ryan sat there and took it, offering to replace them even though they were well over seven thousand dollars. He would do fucking anything to make me happy," she half-moaned, half-sobbed.

"Turned out the mistake was my fault all along. Somehow, I'd given the dealer the wrong order number—and that one difference cost me the countertops of my dreams. Instead, I got these. There's barely any marbling. And you know the shit of it all? These look way better. It was a happy fucking accident. I never told Ryan that. Or that I was sorry for flying off the handle and blaming him when it was in no way his fault."

She hiccupped as she inhaled too quickly. "And now, I can never tell him that."

She went to the nearest cupboard and swiped everything off the shelves, throwing it to the floor with a satisfying shatter. "Aaaaaaah!" she screamed, picking up a large oval serving platter. She threw it flat down in front of her.

"Liv—"

"I said don't, Brighton! You don't know how I feel right now, okay?" *Smash.*

"He gave me everything I ever wanted." *Smash.*

"He wanted to live in the country, but I was the one who had my heart set on the city. I grew up longing for an older, historic home, even though they're expensive and drafty, no matter how much money you pour into them. They squeak and creak and come with all kinds of problems. But I love every single thing about them. So, he got it for me.

"And I couldn't even give him one freaking child before he died!" She wiped the back of her mouth with her hand, looking around for more ammunition. "What the fuck is wrong with the universe?" she yelled, looking up at the ceiling. "Whyyyyyyyyyyy?"

"Liv, stop!" I ordered. "You have to calm down for the baby. The last thing we need is for you to go into labor early."

She paused cold in her tracks. Her chest heaved as she took a deep breath and inventoried the kitchen. She lifted her head and met my eyes. "He's never even going to meet his daughter, Brighton. After all this time waiting and giving so much to everyone else." Her chin trembled, and I knew she was trying hard not to start crying again.

"He was wrong," she said, ripping the bracelet he gave her from her wrist. "There is no god if he could take Ryan from me, too. And if there is, I've certainly failed them both."

She turned to head upstairs, and I didn't stop her. I needed to clean the kitchen so Stitch didn't get hurt on a stray piece of glass. I heard the water through the creaky pipes above and was glad Olivia was getting in the shower. It would help calm her. It always did.

I cleaned the mess, then let Stitch out to go to the bathroom. I spent a few minutes soothing him and hated to put him back in the crate when I knew he was worried about Olivia. But I needed to go check on her. I dragged my heavy legs up Ryan's stairs. When I got to the landing, I stopped and leaned against the wall. I closed my eyes and pictured his face, thinking of how he smiled up at me this morning in the sunroom. *Fuck!* I ran my hand over my face. Had it really been this morning?

Pain knifed at my heart, and I finally cracked.

My body heaved silently as I stifled my tears. I slammed my fist back against the wall.

I understood how Olivia felt—about being robbed. We'd finally worked through all the knots in our messy, tangled relationship. And I loved Ryan more than ever. I loved him with a fierceness that scared me. I couldn't imagine a life without him in it. And if I felt this way after knowing him for such a short amount of time, I couldn't begin to pretend to understand how Olivia was feeling. I didn't know how I would get us through this unspeakable pain. But I would try. I had to. We had a baby on the way.

Time doesn't slow and life doesn't stop just because death marches in.

ad I mean everything, becomes centered around that...

One simple word: No. Before that, our eight-year marriage was built on love, respect...

the darkness loss after loss. The only thing that can set you free is the truth. It's as...

as sacred as our wedding vows, and maybe even more so because it came after the loss...

were one hundred percent honest with one another, that would be enough. That would...

le—through another miscarriage. Until, finally, that fragile false hope would sha...

matter how honest, could bridge the hollow, gaping hole where my heart used to b...

empts to reach me. To save me. To restore me to the woman he'd fallen in love with. Com...

...ted. "And you fell in love with him?" Dr. Paul asked, ...

...rough. Through the darkness that caused me to be...

...I lifted an eyebrow and glared at...

...if I fell in love all over again I...

...nasty habit I found myself...

...respect. How it used to...

..." Rather th...

...you...

...gave my to th...

...wanted nothing...

...babies. In fact...

...and once...

...ultimate. Tog...

...was now...

...It is what I s...

CHAPTER FORTY-ONE

Brighton

UNSPEAKABLE DECISIONS WERE made, and I was the one to make them. Olivia couldn't face everything just yet, and I wanted to do right by Ryan. Before we left the hospital the night of Ryan's death, we signed paperwork to authorize an autopsy and release his body to the coroner. I asked Liv for the passcode on Ryan's phone so I could call his sister and do what I could to get his affairs in order. The university knew what happened, thanks to Kimber, but they sent their condolences and offered to help in any way they could.

We decided to hold off on a funeral or memorial service until later in the spring. The ground was still too hard to dig from the winter, so bodies were stored until the ground could thaw, which usually ended up being in late April or early May, depending on the year.

The baby would hardly be a month old when it was time to bury her father. The weeks ahead scared me. Every day brought a new challenge—something we didn't want to face, or something that would trigger us and make us miss him all over again so much it hurt. Some days, we spent the entire day in bed crying together. On other days, Olivia frantically cleaned the house to prepare for the baby's arrival.

What surprised me was Olivia continued to see Dr. Paul after Ryan's death. That brought me more hope than anything else. I'd been terrified she was going to tell me she changed her mind and that she no longer wanted to be with me now that Ryan was gone. Had we *only* worked because it was the three of us? I couldn't help but wonder if we would survive this and come out on the other side together.

I'd helped "save" Olivia once. What if I couldn't do it again?

I called all of Olivia's clients to let them know what happened and to make sure nothing was slipping through the cracks. I knew other interior designers and passed along names for those who couldn't wait. Olivia was the executor of Ryan's will, but she gave me power of attorney so I could handle everything.

I signed the paperwork and sold my house to Becca and Joey. Paige graciously handled every detail, so it was one less thing I needed to worry about. Thanks to my sisters, our refrigerator was constantly stocked, even though Olivia couldn't keep anything down. I forced her to drink protein shakes because those were at least tolerable, and she needed to take care of herself and the baby.

And our nights . . . they were interesting. Instead of turning away from me like I thought she might, she became the aggressor and was infinitely insatiable. I knew it was a distraction, a way to feel *something*. I didn't take it personally because I knew it was helping her stay tethered—just enough to prevent the spins from starting again. But I couldn't help but wonder who she saw while she was fucking me.

One afternoon, about two weeks before the baby was due, we sat in the sunroom together, trying unsuccessfully to read. Stitch was curled up on the bench swing next to Olivia. When my phone rang, I picked it up immediately. We were expecting an update on Ryan's autopsy results.

I mouthed to Olivia who was on the phone and asked if she wanted me to put the call on speakerphone. She nodded, though she immediately bit her lower lip.

"We're both here," I told the coroner.

"Mrs. Wells, I'm terribly sorry about your husband. We have the preliminary findings but won't have a full written report for several more weeks. When we do, Mr. Kerrington can come pick it up from our office."

"What did you find out?" Olivia asked.

Over the last few days, she'd frantically searched through Ryan's things to find anything we might have missed. We knew Ryan wouldn't intentionally hide anything, but we also knew he wouldn't want to upset Olivia if any abnormalities started popping up here or there.

I ended up finding a health app on his phone that tracked his heart rate since Christmas, and a clearer picture began to emerge. I'd spotted a troubling trend of arrhythmias and an accelerated heart rate. Cross-referencing the dates on his calendar, they didn't always align to high-exertion activities or events. That was the concerning part. What we didn't know was how *aware* Ryan was of all this, or if he had reason to believe it was serious.

He'd been concerned enough to make an appointment with his primary care physician. They called when he didn't show, and Olivia spoke with the doctor, since she was listed on his HIPAA forms. The doctor let Liv know what the receptionist had noted on his chart when she made the appointment. *Worried about heart rate. PVCs? General fatigue.*

That was all. Not enough for the doctor to bring him in early or recommend a trip to the ER. There was no way to know what was lurking inside that huge heart of his.

"We confirmed the hospital's assessment of hypertrophic cardiomyopathy, and cardiac arrest is listed as his cause of death. HCM is a rare condition that causes the heart muscles to become hypertrophied—which means they're abnormally thick, making it harder to pump blood. It can also cause stiffness, which prevents the heart from pumping enough blood to meet the body's needs. Most of the time, it goes undiagnosed because the person never experiences any of the common symptoms, or they chalk them up to anomalies rather than a pattern. There's no cure for what Ryan had, but people with this condition *can* live a normal life-span."

"So, what happened to Ryan then?" I asked.

"Well, for a small subset of people with HCM, it can cause shortness of breath, chest pains, or a problem with the heart's electrical system. In Ryan's case, the septum between his bottom two chambers was enlarged, causing obstructive hypertrophic cardiomyopathy, which is exactly what it sounds like. It was obstructing—or blocking—blood flow out of the heart. He also had myofiber disarray, which is what caused his arrhythmias."

"Why Ryan? If others can live their whole lives without complications, what made it worse for him?" Liv asked.

"I can only answer that from a medical perspective, Mrs. Wells. Ryan was one of the few affected by the chest pain, shortness of breath, and arrhythmias that can come with HCM. He probably started noticing a few of these symptoms in the months leading up to his death, even if it wasn't enough to say anything. Unfortunately, biology doesn't discriminate, and HCM *can* cause sudden death in seemingly fit, young people—sometimes even in those younger than Ryan."

"So—he died right away?" Olivia asked. "He didn't really stand a chance, did he?"

"They tried to revive him and did everything they could. It was just too late, Mrs. Wells."

"You said it can happen in people younger than Ryan," I said, a troubling thought occurring to me. "Was Ryan's condition genetic?"

"Yes, it is usually inherited," the coroner confirmed.

Olivia gasped, covering her mouth.

"If a parent has HCM, their children have about a fifty percent chance of inheriting the genetic mutation that causes the disease," he explained. "Do you and Ryan have any children, Mrs. Wells?"

"We—I . . . I'm pregnant now. Our daughter's due in a couple of weeks."

"Try not to worry. Just be aware that doctors recommend that if a child has a first-degree relative with HCM, they get genetic testing to be screened for this condition. In some cases, testing doesn't detect the mutation. So, if your little one ends up being an athlete, you'll want to screen her once a year for the mutation. If not, adults should get screened every five years."

"His sister," Olivia mouthed over the phone at me.

I nodded, thinking the same thing. "Thank you for letting us know," I told the coroner.

"Certainly. As I said, my office will contact you if anything else comes up, but it was a pretty straightforward case."

A case. Ryan had lived a whole, vibrant life. He had a wife, and a child on the way. He had *me.* And in one, cruel moment, he became a fucking case.

"I can't imagine how hard this is for you, Mrs. Wells. But try not to worry about this part of it yet. You have enough to deal with, and it's not even a given that your daughter will be affected by this. Most likely, she has a perfectly healthy life ahead of her. Ryan's case was a tragic exception."

Those words would echo in my heart for years to come.

CHAPTER FORTY-TWO

Olivia

"**P**USH!" THE DOCTOR said for the tenth time. I sincerely wanted to punch her in the face right now. I knew from experience that childbirth wasn't a walk in the park, but I'd forgotten it could hurt *this* much. Brighton was standing next to me, holding my hand.

A strangled, primitive sound emerged from somewhere deep inside my throat as I clenched my eyes and pressed down again. It felt like trying to shit a basketball from my vagina. Sweat covered my brow, and I was exhausted after hours of labor. Somehow, I'd gotten it in my head that this might be my last pregnancy, and if it were, I wanted to have a natural childbirth to have the complete experience.

Here's what I say: SCREW THAT SHIT.

It's completely overrated. I would give my left tit to go back and change that decision.

"That's it," Dr. Chavez said. I wasn't sure what her job was at this point, other than to be a cheerleader between my splayed legs. It was a vastly different experience than the last time I was in this position.

Then it felt like something was tearing my body in half. A burning sensation ripped through me before there was a gushing feeling, and our daughter slid from my body. It felt like I just peed everywhere, but I didn't have time to care. My vagina stung like it had just been attacked by a thousand bees, and it was all I could feel until I finally heard my baby's healthy, loud wail for the first time.

Relief escaped my lips in the form of laughter, and Brighton leaned down to kiss my forehead. We were beyond caring at this point. "You did it, baby. I'm so proud of you."

I started crying. Every time I heard a new howl from our tiny, mighty baby, my heart slowly rearranged, falling back into place. My person was right over there, and I couldn't wait to hold her. This was a long, agonizing time coming.

The nurse brought our daughter over to me, and my heart softened as I held her against my chest for the first time. I laugh-cried as I looked down at her chubby, beautiful face. I barely registered when I heard the nurse tell Brighton she was eight pounds, two ounces and twenty-one inches long. Her head circumference was thirteen-point-something inches, and I wanted to scream, "Yes, I know! See? Basket. Ball."

Brighton was running his fingers through my hair, his eyes soft and teary as he looked down at his girls. Even if we hadn't finally decided to ask Dr. Chavez to confirm the DNA results, there was no mistaking that this was Ryan's daughter. She had thick, dark hair with the same small cowlick Ryan had. She was the spitting image of her father, and it only made me love her that much more.

"She's perfect," Brighton said, running his hand gently along the side of her face. "Just like her mother."

"Do you want to hold her?" I asked, leaning into Brighton's arm, and kissing it.

He looked nervous, and I realized he may not have held many babies in his life after Sam. That would soon change, and like everything Brighton did, I knew he would become a pro. Even though my life was in shambles, completely flipped upside down from how it used to be, I was starting to love some of the messy pieces as I navigated our new surroundings.

Not a day went by that I didn't think of Ryan or yearn for him in a way that would stay with me for the rest of my life. I'd taken so much for granted with him, and as much as it hurt that I couldn't make it up to him, I vowed not to do the same with Brighton and our daughter.

Because even if she were Ryan's biological daughter, Brighton would be the only father she grew up with. We would make sure she knew and loved Ryan, but if anyone understood the real, permanent bond that comes with adoptive parents, it was me. She would love Brighton just as fiercely and wholly as I'd loved my daddy.

When Brighton held her for the first time, my heart bent a little more, twisting into a brand-new shape. I once thought that my heart was irreparably broken—and I'd told Ryan as much. He taught me, by loving me completely and unconditionally through the good times and the worst days of my life, that it wasn't really broken.

Love heals even the worse scars.

If Ryan could redefine his definition of love so drastically, I knew there was nothing that love couldn't overcome. Brighton and I had a lot more healing to do, especially after Ryan's sudden and unexpected death. But as I watched him coo over the baby, kissing her forehead just like he always did mine, I knew we would somehow be okay.

I didn't spin out like I did after Laelynn's death. I worked with Dr. Paul on healthier ways to work through my new grief so I could still be present for Brighton and our daughter. It wouldn't always be easy—I wasn't so naïve to think it would be. But Ryan had left his legacy behind, showing Brighton what being an amazing husband looked like. And I had no doubt he'd live up to Ryan's memory and fill those big shoes before long. He was well on his way, which was the only reason I was able to get through the last four weeks.

"I love you so much," he whispered to our daughter. "Baby, what if we name her Ryan?"

Everything shifted into place. *Ryan*. It was perfect. My heart felt almost "right" for the first time since my husband's death. I smiled, remembering his dark, rugged looks. His thick, brown hair with the cowlick over his forehead. The dimples, and bearded jaw. His strong yet tender hands, the ones that felt as if they were made specifically to hold me. They'd reached back to save my ass more times than I could count. And his eyes. The same ones I hoped our daughter would have one day—kind, wise, fiery, and passionate. But most of all, confident and brave.

If Ryan had been the holy to my wild, what would our daughter be?

"Do you have a name in mind?" the nurse asked, as she took care of all the post-birth tasks that were necessary, if not fun.

Brighton handed Ryan back to me, and I snuggled her tightly to my chest, wondering how it was possible for my heart to expand this fast, even in the middle of grief.

She'd been born from the overwhelming love of three people stumbling their way through a storm of pain, until they finally emerged on the other side, better versions of themselves. If the past few years had taught me anything, it was that love really *was* worth the risk. Our daughter was proof of that.

"Her name is Ryan Samantha Kerrington Wells."

...nd I mean everything, becomes centered around that...

One simple word: No. Before that, our eight-year marriage was built on love so pu...

the darkness, loss after loss, the only thing that can set you free is the truth. If y...

as sacred as our wedding vows. And maybe even more so because I came after the los...

...re one hundred percent honest with one another, that would be enough. That woul...

...le—through another miscarriage. Until, finally, that tragic false hope and sha...

...tter how honest, could bridge the hollow, gaping hole where my heart used to b...

...mpts to reach me. To save me. To restore me to the woman he'd fallen in love with. Eve...

..."And you fell in love with him?" Dr. Paul ask...

...through. Through the darkness that carried me to the...

...I lifted my eyes and stared a...

...I fell in love with a woman I...

...vestige left? I found myse...

...expect. His first look in m...

..."Katy. D...

...d you m...

...d on your way to th...

...d wanted a thing t...

...but in fact...

...and pra...

...in plan...

...intricate...

...it was nec...

...How's what I se...

CHAPTER FORTY-THREE
Brighton

THE FIRST MONTHS of Ryan's life were a bittersweet blur. We were exhausted from our new sleep schedule and having such a steep learning curve. Luckily, Becca and her family had already moved in next door, becoming not only a good friend to Olivia, but a godsend to our entire family. When we didn't have the answers, she did.

Olivia and I were getting the hang of things, slowly but surely. I hesitated to say that though, because it seemed like every time I did, Ryan's sleep schedule changed, and we were having to adjust all over again. We were happy that Stitch was doing so well with the big changes in our house. He seemed to miss Ryan a lot, and we often found him curled up on the sofa of his home office. We knew by the way he already seemed protective over the baby that they would become fast friends one day.

Ryan's memorial service was the hardest day of all since the baby was born. We kept the ceremony small and intimate, as Ryan would've wanted. And he was buried in his family's plot alongside Laelynn.

I worked from home as much as possible to help care for Ryan and focus on the design side of my business. I officially turned all day-to-day operations over to Rob, who seemed to be running things like a champ. It's not that I wouldn't ever go back, but I had everything I needed in this house. At first, I was afraid it would be too hard on Olivia—being surrounded by all the memories of their marriage and what she'd lost. But she said it was comforting to know that their baby was not only conceived here, but that she would be raised here. Memories of Ryan still hurt, but they also healed.

We decided to renovate the room that was once the guestroom where Olivia used to escape on some of her darkest days. We turned it into a playroom since it was adjacent to the kitchen and sunroom where we spent so much time. Olivia let me handle the bulk of that but had a few design ideas of her own to contribute, of course. When I was clearing out the room, I asked Olivia what she wanted to do with the memory box I made for her. We moved it upstairs, deciding to store it in her closet. It held so many important memories, but we were also ready to start taking baby steps to move forward.

Before she put the box in her closet, she ran her hand over the surface one last time. I loved the way she smiled at the flowers I painted on the lid. Purple tulips. Our flower.

She was ready to add Ryan's things to the box, as well. The death certificate and his autopsy report. The watch he was wearing at the hospital and his wedding band. One day, we would share everything with our Ryan. But today, we needed this closure.

Olivia paused when she lifted the box's lid, staring into it as if she'd seen a ghost.

"What's wrong?" I asked as I folded and put away my socks.

"There's something in here, with Ryan's handwriting on it."

I joined her by the bed and looked down. Sam's items had joined Laelynn's, though they each had their own special boxes to keep everything separate. They rested on top of two blankets, one that had belonged to each of our lost babies. But on top of those little boxes lay three legal-sized envelopes, each bearing Ryan's small, neat print on the top.

"What do you think these are?" I asked, lifting them. There was one addressed to each of us, including the baby.

Olivia's hand shook as she closed the lid and sat on the bed. "I don't know. I'm afraid to find out."

I set the envelopes on the bed and moved to stand between her legs. She wrapped her arms around my waist, and I held her against my stomach. "We've already lived through the worst."

She took a deep breath, and I saw her tapping her fingers in the silent relaxation mantra she used when she was stressed or anxious. Then she looked up at me, her eyes trusting, curious, and full of so much love. "What should we do with Ryan's? Should we open it?"

"No. Whatever it is, let's save it for her. We can give it to her when she graduates. She'll be old enough by then to handle whatever's inside."

So that's what we agreed on, setting our daughter's envelope back inside the box.

"Would you do me a favor?" Olivia asked quietly before we opened ours.

"Anything."

"Would you mind painting a hydrangea on the memory chest one of these days?" she asked. "For Ryan."

"I'll paint it tomorrow," I promised.

I leaned forward and kissed her forehead. I knew whatever was in these envelopes, it would be bittersweet. I didn't know if I was ever going to be ready for something like this. I just prayed it gave us both some closure. Therapy only goes so far. It was the rebuilding of our life day by day that was helping the most. Staying open with each other. Learning to communicate. And me taking diaper duty. That helped a lot, too.

"Do you have any idea how much I love you?" I asked Olivia, nipping gently at her lower lip. It was too soon to make love again, but we were counting down the days.

"I might have a pretty good idea," she said.

And that was all I ever wanted. To be able to love Olivia.

The funny thing about love is we think it's something we can control. That we can choose who gets our heart. But love is elusive, effusive, and permanent all rolled into one. Our ideas about what we all wanted from one another had changed over time. I went from trying to wrestle my feelings for Olivia to the ground to stealing whatever feelings I could get when I was around her, as if that would ever be enough. As if I could live with anything less than Olivia's entire heart.

But it was Ryan's love that surprised me and changed me most of all, questioning everything I thought I knew about love—friendship, romantic love, sexual love, soul mates . . . they were such mucky waters to wade in. How do you compartmentalize love?

You can't.

When I stopped trying to control my feelings and how I thought I was supposed to define love, an entire new world opened for me. I know it did for Ryan and Olivia, too. We all benefited from this new definition of love in the end. Because the truth is—the more you love, the more you love.

Look, I never claimed to be Shakespeare. That was Ryan's forte. All I know now is—Ryan left us with the greatest gift of all. His daughter. And every day we were redefining what love meant and trying to love a little harder than the day before.

I wrapped my arm around my wife's shoulder—only now, Olivia was my wife in every sense of the word. Some thought it was too soon, but we knew it was what Ryan would want for us, and for his daughter. The second time we said our vows was in a ceremony even more simple. It was in the county clerk's office with just the two of us, plus Becca and Joey to act as our witnesses and hold the baby. We already exchanged rings the first time, but I wanted to give her something special for our wedding. It was a bittersweet day for Olivia, and I wanted to remind her that just because we were making it official, it would never erase the importance of their marriage. It didn't mean Ryan was any less a part of our lives.

Every day since then, Olivia wore the locket I gave her. An engraved tulip and hydrangea pom were entwined on the front of the necklace. It opened like a clover to reveal miniature pictures of our entire family: Ryan, Olivia, me, and our daughter.

I gently squeezed her shoulder before picking up my envelope from the bed. "Are you ready to do this?" I asked, nudging her.

"As ready as I'll ever be."

So, we sat there in silence and read the letters we found in our envelopes, one at a time. They were full of all the love Ryan had for us. I knew it would be something we would cherish forever and return to repeatedly throughout the years. Because in the end, in typical Ryan fashion, he held none of his love back.

And if Ryan's life had revolved around anything, it was his heart.

Dear Brighton,

If you're reading this, it probably means I kicked the can. Which means you're probably celebrating because now you finally have Olivia all to yourself. (Calm down, it's a joke.)

After Laelynn died, I knew life could change in the blink of an eye. Nothing we think is ours is permanent. Which is why I spent so much time doing everything I could to make Liv happy, no matter how that looked to anyone else. Because if I only get this one precious life with her, why would I waste it doing anything but that? She was my everything, Kerrington. I know you know that. And I can see she is your everything, too. So, don't chum it up.

I have a confession to make. Ever since you got us those watches for Christmas, I was afraid to use mine. I did, but I avoided the app at all costs. The reason why is because I've noticed some changes in my health lately, and it scared the fuck out of me. Especially when I have more to lose now than ever before. It could be nothing, and that's what I'm hoping it is. But you know what I say—better safe than sorry. I have an appointment next week. Liv would be so proud that I finally made a doctor's appointment for myself without her having to ride my ass about it.

Which brings me to this letter.

It's silly, I know. After my appointment, when I know more, I'll figure out what to do with them. But it felt important to get these feelings down on paper just in case. If now's not my time to worry about this kind of stuff, I'll happily destroy them and spend the rest of my life

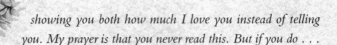

showing you both how much I love you instead of telling you. My prayer is that you never read this. But if you do . . .

I love you. And I don't just love you. I've come to love love you. I don't care what anyone else calls it. I know it for what it is. Perfection. You are the first time I ever loved without expectation, without limits, and without a promise of anything in return.

For as much as I busted your balls about Olivia, I finally understood why she was so drawn to you—you're like a force of nature neither of us could deny. And you know what? I'm so glad we didn't. I don't know what in the world possessed me to ask you what I did that day at the Crown and Feather. Maybe all along it wasn't just about Olivia. Maybe my soul recognized that we would both be safe with you. And maybe, even then, I craved you a little bit, too.

I was so angry then when you and Liv did what you did. (Don't even get me started on that from beyond the grave.) I needed you to know that it hurt me, deeply. But I'm not telling you this now to make you feel guilty over something we can't go back and change. I think everything happened for a reason. And I'm quickly realizing that it was more than just what happened, or the lie Liv told to cover it.

I was scared. Terrified, actually.

I was scared that you and Olivia would fall head over heels into a love so deep neither of you needed me. Not as a friend. Not as a husband. I know how stupid that sounds now, after all we've been through. But at the time, it was raw and brutal and terrifying all at once. I forgave you both a long time ago. And now? Like I said, I'm grateful.

You see, I've done a lot of thinking recently. I've come to realize that mine and Liv's truth pact was made from a place of fear. As a way for us to control our love when we were spinning out dangerously. Is honesty a critical part of every marriage? Yes. But if we'd really been honest, instead of making a truth pact, we would have talked more openly about our fears. Our wants. Our needs. We were too busy worrying about losing each other that we didn't realize the only way not to was to choose love. Every day. Day after day. No matter how hard it got.

That's what I want you to take away from this, Brighton. Because that's what you taught me. I hate that stupid quote about how if you love something, you're supposed to set it free. If it comes back to you, it was meant to be. But maybe there's some truth to it. What I think the author was saying is—when you stop trying to control your love for someone else, and simply love, that's when you know you've finally gotten it right. Things work out as they're meant to.

I let Olivia fly free, and she did come back. Only she came back even better, dragging your sorry ass along with her. By giving up my need for control, by really listening to her when she told me she wasn't ready to end things with you yet, that's when I finally got it right. By trusting that her love for me was bigger than anything I was trying to control. And what ended up happening was that we all loved more for it. Not less.

I never thought, in any version of this universe, that I would be able to love another man—never would've even entered my mind to consider it. Then you came into my life. (I blame your killer abs, disarming smile, and cocky swagger for not being able to resist.)

I don't know how to even label what we are to one another. Best friends? Lovers? Soul mates? Brother husbands? (Sorry, not sure what the dude version of sister wives is.) All I know is that—independent of Olivia—I love you, Brighton Kerrington. I loved you so much it hurt, because I was afraid of what my loving you would do to Olivia. But she saw it—she wasn't stupid. Do you know we had a conversation once, just her and me, about this very thing? It was before you and I were physically intimate.

She said, "Ryan, you look at Brighton the way you looked at me when we first met." Which made me snort laugh, because the first time Liv met you in person, that was exactly what ran through my head. I actually thought, Oh, crap. I'm fucked. Because some things are stronger than our control. Some things are fate.

Just as surely as Olivia was my destiny, so were you.

Now, before I lose my man card for admitting all this, let's talk practical things. Not like I'm trying to control anything from the grave. I would never do that. But . . .

Don't purposely hurt Olivia. I realize now it's impossible not to hurt each other in love. But there's a difference in intent. I know you and Liv never meant to hurt me. Don't purposely hurt her, or you can bet your sweet ass I'll be haunting you for the rest of your days.

Get your ass over to our house already. Don't be afraid to make it yours.

Love our daughter with everything you have, but don't try to control her. Let her learn how to fly. I hope she's every bit as wild and fierce and brave as Olivia. And as funny, kind, and generous as you. Oh, and study up on the dad jokes, okay? Olivia thinks she has the market on those, but we dads need to represent and stick together.

That's all I've got, Kerrington. I could tell you a million other little things to make life easier, but where's the fun in that? Some things you need to figure out on your own. Just you and Liv. Just promise me something? Immortalize me, okay? I wasn't kidding when I said I was terrified about not being a part of Liv's life, or your life. I want to be the butter between your bread for the rest of your days. Okay now, see? That is exactly why you need to practice your dad jokes before Baby T comes.

And Brighton? Everything's going to be okay if you just love one another.

I was worried for a good reason when I first met you. It's because I was worried you and Liv were meant to be together. And you know what? I wasn't wrong. I just never knew that we were, too.

Carpe diem, Kerrington.

Love, Ryan

Dear Olivia,

How do I even start a letter I think you might read one day when I'm not around? There was never any version of our future where we weren't together. Not even after everything went down. When we said our wedding vows, I meant them. And I feel good knowing I did everything I could to live them in practice.

But, Liv, it was wrong of us to make a truth pact. Not because honesty isn't important. But because there's inherently a lack of trust if we felt the need to make that kind of promise to begin with. Every time I asked you "truth?" it was because I was afraid—which meant I was untrusting and didn't have enough faith in us. And that wasn't fair to you. I thought it would bring us closer, but instead, it caused one of the biggest rifts of our marriage, because you were afraid, too. Which is why you lied to me. I understand everything so much better now.

I'll let Kerrington fill you in on the reason why I'm writing these letters right now. Like I told him, I pray you never see them.

Not just because you're having our baby, but because I want to spend the rest of my very long life with you—and Kerrington. You once thanked me for being brave enough to let you love two men. You know what? I could say the same. You were brave enough to let me explore my love for Brighton, even when neither of us knew what that meant. You didn't feel threatened by it. You trusted me. Just like I should've done with you all along.

Do I have regrets? Yes. I'm not going to waste my last words on them, though. Instead, I want you to know that you were the single best thing to ever happen to me. I was happy, Livy.

Even when I was acting like a rage ball because I'd stuffed all my feelings down like one of those clown cans with the crinkly snakes in it. Sooner or later, the pressure had to release. I hate that you saw that and pray you never remember me in that way.

Because when I think of my life, I think of you. I don't care that I had a wall full of diplomas or was a professor of anything. (Though, yeah, I did like teaching. Make sure my students know that, okay? Maybe glorify me with a scholarship or something? Yeah, I'd like that. Make Kerrington pay for it though. He's loaded.)

Seriously though. It was always you. Everything in my life started and ended with Olivia North Wells, and I wouldn't have it any other way. It was a life well lived.

Now, I know you're probably pissed at me for dying, and for leaving you when our baby was finally on the way. (Insert biggest regret here.) But like I said before, I am forever grateful that you won't be alone now. Kerrington will love you as deeply, fiercely, and protectively as I did. Do not be afraid to love him back just as hard. Don't ever let the memory of me hold you back from having the biggest, best love affair of your life.

You will go on, *Liv*. And I expect you to. God is within you. You will not fall. *And don't forget, you can always call on me like a force ghost.*

Please make sure Baby T knows me. Make sure she knows I wanted her. That if I'm gone, it wasn't by choice. Nothing could've dragged me from my life unless it was out of my control. Just like with love, I'm trying to surrender the outcome of my life. Whatever the doctor tells me next week, I'll deal with it. I hope I just have to eat more broccoli or something. And you know how much I hate that shit. But I would eat all the broccoli for you, Liv.

Well, I've got to get to the hardest letter of all next: our daughter's. I sure wish I knew what we were naming her. I guess fate will decide that, eh?

I'm not saying goodbye because I believe you are my person, Liv. I believe we will see each other again someday in another lifetime, another dimension, or in heaven itself. All I know is, my time with you isn't over. It never will be. (But don't let that stop you from having fun with Kerrington while I'm gone. A girl's gotta live a little.)

I love you, Livy. My wild, wild heart. Put your grieving behind. And enjoy all the beautiful, little moments of your life. Because we all know those are really the big things.

For now, I am going to lie down in the blanket of your love and sleep.

Until next time, all my love, Ryan

PS: Liv + Ry 4ever

EPILOGUE

Ryan

WAVES OF NAVY blue swarmed the sky, rising, rising, rising before being suspended in a moment of time against a backdrop of clouds, then plummeting back to earth unceremoniously. I would never be able to find my graduation cap. I scowled. I searched for the one with the hand-painted hydrangea on the top and the words: Carpe Diem! Which is exactly what I planned to do as soon as I found my stupid cap.

"Looking for this?"

I turned and grinned, flinging myself into my dad's arms. "Thank you!" I squealed. "I mean, I *had* to throw it. It's tradition. But . . . "

"I know, Ry," Dad joked. And he did. He knew me better than anyone. Even Mom. Maybe that's because my other dad, the one I was named after, was his best friend. He says I remind him a lot of my OG dad (my nickname for him since he was my "original" dad). I wish I'd had a chance to meet him, but then I remind myself if I'm *that* much like him, then I kinda already do know him pretty darn well. And that's kind of cool.

I ran my finger over my graduation cap, getting a little teary eyed. It felt like my senior year flew by way too fast. Before I knew it, I'd be off to Duke. I looked around, trying to spot Mom in the crowd. She was standing in the bleachers waving at me, her sleek, blond bob brushing against her shoulders as her face burst with excitement. I grinned and put my hands together and made a heart. She did the same. It was kind of our thing.

Munch was slouched next to her, his black hoodie drawn over his head as he texted furiously. He hated when I called him that, but it was my nickname for him since he was a baby. To me, he would never be Marshall. And despite his recent front that he didn't give a crap about much in life if it didn't have pepperoni, a game controller, or boobs—I knew the real Munch.

We may've had different OG dads, but we were as thick as thieves. He caught me looking at him and flipped me the bird, but I saw that cocky smile of his lift the corner of his lips.

"So, where are we going for lunch?" I asked, checking my watch. Dad insisted I wear one. Back in his day, it was called a "smart watch." These days, every watch has the same basic features, though hardly anyone I know wears one anymore. The only reason I did was because I was a cross country runner, and my parents were constantly worried about me. Since that's how my OG dad died, it's the one thing I don't push back on.

We made our way to the school parking lot, and I found Mom's blue minivan easily enough. It was the same one she's had my whole life. It's so embarrassing and *old*, but she says it's dependable and safe. And my dad always says it's better to be safe than sorry.

But not for me, and not today.

Before I left this small town, I had one last thing to do. And today was the day. I was afraid if I didn't get moving, I'd get cold feet. Mom and Dad have been giving me more freedom since I turned eighteen, and I tried not to take advantage of it. But tonight was different. I didn't want them to know about it, because I was afraid if they found out I lied, I might lose my graduation gift—which was a week at our beach house for me, my six closest friends, and their boyfriends. I'd be bringing my girlfriend, Hannah.

When we got to the car, Mom wrapped me in a hug and held on tight. Her hugs were the best. "How do you feel?" she asked.

"Relieved."

"I can imagine. You should be proud though. You busted your ass to be valedictorian." What she didn't say was inherently implied: *especially with dyslexia.*

It had been a challenge, and I had to work harder than my friends, but Dad told me all the ways it actually made my brain superior. I tried to remember that when I got discouraged and wanted to give up. Now that I'm older, I know it wasn't necessarily superior, it was just *different*. And if my parents taught me anything, it was that different is okay. In fact, it was superior.

"Can I go now?" Munch asked, pointing to a group of his friends. They were all holding skateboards and phones. Mom always says some things never change.

"Can I get a hug first?" I challenged him.

He rolled his eyes but wrapped an arm around me and squeezed my neck. He was already taller than me, and he knew it chapped my ass. "Congrats, Sis," he said before running off to join his friends. Munch was a man of many words.

"So, are we going to lunch or not?" Mom asked as we all piled into the minivan.

"I hate to ask, but would you be too mad if I took a raincheck instead?"

Mom swallowed, but then met my eyes in the review mirror. "Of course not, Ry."

I watched as Dad squeezed her hand over the center console. "Thanks, Mom. Hannah's meeting us at the house. Her graduation already ended."

The only reason we weren't at each other's graduation ceremonies was because we went to different high schools. I went to a small private one and Hannah went to the city school. She didn't hold it against me though. I only went because I got better differentiated learning services there than I would in public school. Guess Mom was right. Some things never change.

"Where are you girls headed, if you're bailing on lunch with us?"

"It's kind of a surprise. Can I tell you later?"

"Sure," she said. "It's not anything dangerous, is it?"

"Not from what I hear."

"All right then. I'm going to trust you, Ryan."

"I promise I'll be safe, Mom," I said, softening.

I knew no matter how much she and Dad tried to be the cool parents, they worried about us. It took Mom a long time to get pregnant with me. So, I understood. Life was precious to my parents. It's one of the things that made them so different from my friends' parents and was what I loved the most about them. They *truly* loved one another and never took each other for granted. They made it look easy, but Mom admitted it's not. She told me early on that love takes work, and it's always a choice, but it's worth it.

When we pulled up to the house, Hannah was waiting for me on our back porch. She was in a bathing suit already and sunning on a lounge chair. She popped up the minute she heard our old minivan pull in. Cars nowadays didn't sound like this. In fact, they were completely silent. Mom's dinosaur was a dying breed. Not many cars even ran on gasoline anymore.

I jumped out of the car and went over to my girlfriend. "Hey, Han."

"Hey, Ry." She looped her arm over my shoulder and gave me a big smooch on the cheek. It's not like we hadn't gone farther than that, but we usually kept things pretty PG in front of my parents.

"Nice bathing suit. Is it new?"

"Yep! Just for this special occasion."

"So, it involves water, then?" Mom teased. "Does that mean you accepted the invite to the pool party?"

"Mom!" I said, rolling my eyes. "Stop trying to play detective and *trust* me."

She laughed, holding up her hands. "Okay, okay. You haven't let us down yet. Do you need me to make sandwiches or anything before you leave?"

"I brought a picnic lunch for us, Mrs. Wells," Hannah said.

"Okay. Well, if you don't need us, we'll probably go take a nap. It's been a long day, and we didn't get much sleep last night."

It was true. I heard her and Dad come in later than they normally did. Their company was about to go public, which meant all eyes were on them. Mom and Dad linked hands and went through the back door. When we were alone, I turned back to Hannah. "So, you have everything?"

"Sure do!" she said, winking. Then she wove her hand through my long, brown hair and cupped the back of my head, pulling my mouth to her lips. Kissing Hannah would never get old.

"Let me go get my things and I'll be right back," I told her, squeezing her hand.

I went to my bedroom and grabbed my backpack. I didn't need much, just a blanket, some bug spray, a little music, a towel, some sweatpants and a hoodie in case it got cold overnight, a flashlight, some Swedish Fish, and of course—the letter.

I changed into my bathing suit and threw on a pair of jean shorts and my favorite retro T-shirt that I'd "borrowed" from Mom. It was a soft, worn-in one from my OG dad's alma mater, SU. It made Mom weepy in a happy way because it was the T-shirt he wore the first time he told her he loved her.

On my way out the door, I scratched Peeta's head, and he immediately dropped to the floor and rolled over onto his back for a tummy rub. "Who's a good boy?" I said, laughing.

I could hear Mom and Dad giggling from their master bedroom. When we were in middle school and no longer needed a playroom, they moved their bedroom from the second floor to the first. They blew out the back of the house and made a giant master suite, with a walk-in closet that was bigger than Hannah's entire apartment. And don't get me started on the bathroom! It would make any future loo of mine feel like a Porta Potty. I was happy for them, though. They deserved it. And lord knows I was happy when they no longer shared walls with me. There are just some things a daughter doesn't need to hear. And I wasn't stupid. I knew what "nap" was code for.

I got a little case of guilty conscience after hearing them and decided to leave a note, so they didn't worry. Better safe than sorry, I guess.

> *Mom & Dad,*
>
> *I didn't want to tell you because I was afraid you'd get mad at me, but Hannah and I are going to the Hole today instead of the pool party. We're camping out there overnight. I'll have my phone if you need me, and I have my watch on. I just didn't want you to worry. But I'll be okay. I'll be with Hannah. And before you ask, yes, I'm bringing the letter. Sorry to do it alone, on my terms. But you always told me to follow my heart. And this feels right, opening it there.*
>
> *I love you guys!*
> *—Ry*

Hannah and I enjoyed the drive up to the Hole. Mom says it takes less time to get there now because the road systems and transportation infrastructure were overhauled when Munch and I were younger. Hannah and I talked the whole way there and played a few rounds of Would You Rather? It was a game my parents played with us on car rides when we were kids. It was so nice not to have to actually *drive* Hannah's car. They were so self-sufficient now. I still thought it was funny that my mom *enjoyed* driving. I mean—what's to enjoy? It was only something to get you from point A to point B.

We programmed Hannah's car to park where my mom showed me once. I never had the nerve to jump into the quarry before, but today—I was taking the plunge! We hiked upward, the climb steep. Hannah had never been, so I couldn't wait to show her. When we made it to the top, I stopped, taking in a huge lungful of air out of habit. Mom and Dad always told to me to check my breathing after exercise to make sure I wasn't having any shortness of breath or chest pains. So far, all my genetic screening came back negative for the mutation. But still, they worried.

I felt amazing and couldn't wait to spend the afternoon with Hannah. We laid out our blankets, and she pulled out the picnic lunch she made for us. She also showed me the tattoo pen she'd borrowed from her brother. We were giving each other matching tattoos today, and it would be so cool because they'd be in each other's handwriting, which was rare to see these days.

When my OG dad and mom were married, they had this amazingly romantic love affair. They'd still be together if he hadn't died. "Liv and Ry forever" was their thing. They even wrote it all cute-like: *Liv + Ry 4ever*. So, Hannah and I decided to give each other matching tattoos that said: *Han + Ry 4ever*. We knew we were young, but if my parents taught me anything, it was that when you met your person, you knew. And Hannah was my person. We were going to the same university, and we planned to get married someday. Mom would *kill* me if I did it anytime soon. That's okay. We could wait. We had our whole lives ahead of us.

But I had two things to tackle first: the jump and the plunge. Jumping from the cliff would be far easier than the plunge I was about to take into my past. I'd waited my whole life for both, so it seemed only right that on the precipice of this important junction in my life, as I hung balanced between the last summer of my childhood and the rest of my life, I took a leap of faith and trusted that I would be okay after both.

"Let's do this," I said, standing. I pulled Hannah up with me, and we stripped down to our bathing suits.

"You sure you're ready?" she asked. I squeezed her hand.

Up here, in the mountains, time stood still. Not much had changed since my parents used to come. It was the same big clearing, the same big tree, and the same quarry. The only thing that changed over the years was the rope.

"It's now or never."

Hannah laughed when I still didn't move. "Would it be easier if I went first?"

And that was just one of the bajillion reasons why I loved her. I hadn't told her yet. I was saving it for today—just like my OG dad had done. "I feel like it's something I've got to do," I explained.

"Go get 'em, Ry," she said, pulling me in for a kiss. This time it was deeper and longer since my parents weren't around. The good kind of shivers raced over my skin, causing goose bumps to form even though it was warm outside. I knew it was time.

"Hannah, I need to tell you something first," I whispered when our kiss ended.

"It's okay if you're afraid to go. We can just chill instead. Do our tattoos. Wait—" she pulled back and looked at me. "You *do* still want to do them, don't you?"

I laughed. "Of course. In fact, that's sorta what I wanted to tell you."

"Okay."

"I'm all kinds of smooth, aren't I?" I joked. Maybe I *was* a little nervous. I'd grown up living with the best examples of love you could find. Our parents taught me and Munch early on to trust our instincts, put yourself out there, not to fear love, and when you found it—hold on with both hands.

"I love you," I said, letting it spill out before I lost my nerve. It was the first time I ever said it to anyone in *this* way.

Hannah grinned, pulling me in close to lay one on me again. She kissed me until I was breathless and dizzy and didn't know which end was up. "Girl, I love you too. I've been waiting for you to say that for*ever.*"

"You could've said it first, you know."

"Sometimes, a girl likes to be wooed," she joked.

"Uh, yeah, but I'm a girl too."

"Well, good thing we don't have to worry about it anymore."

Then she swatted my backside before giving me space. I took a deep breath. The rope was thicker than I expected and coarse. I prayed I could hold on long enough and drop at the right time. Mom told us when we were younger how long to count before letting go.

Images of my mom and dad played through my head like a movie as I psyched myself up to go. We'd heard all their stories while growing up. So much so it sometimes felt like I was there. I pulled the rope all the way back and closed my eyes, then thought of my OG dad. Even though I'd never met him in person, we had a special bond that transcended time. I couldn't explain it, but I felt like I really *knew* him. I couldn't wait to read his letter and get to know him even better.

Ryan Marshall Wells.

I opened my eyes and smiled at Hannah.

"This one's for you, Dad," I said. I ran as fast I could toward the edge of the cliff.

Then, I flew.

My Darling Daughter,

They say pain ebbs and flows over time, until one day, you find yourself accidentally living in joy again. Then each step from there is a little bit easier. The end goal? Being back to normal, I suppose. There's an old saying that goes—maybe you aren't really buried in a pile of manure; you're really just waiting to bloom.

Your mom and I had a few rough years before I died, ebbing and flowing through more pain than one couple deserves. This is the story about how your mom and I found ourselves living in joy again, despite all the manure life tried throwing our way.

Now, this isn't a typical love story. It ends with my death, after all. But here's the truth about love, kiddo: love never dies.

And you were our bloom.

So, sit back, get cozy, and keep an open mind.

It all started with what I like to call, the Brighton Effect . . .

The End

♡

If you loved *The Truth About Love* duet, you'll love my *Arden's Glen Romance* series, where small town meets big heat, leaving readers believing in love again. Start with Faith in Love today. Flip the page for a sneak peek at the first chapter.

And let's keep in touch! My Colleen's Angels VIP Readers' Circle on Facebook is full of amazing, kick-ass women like you. It's where I hang out the most to share inspiration, excerpts, sample chapters, cover reveals, giveaways, memes, and more! Mwah! Xoxo

FAITH IN *Love*

CHAPTER ONE

"FOR THE LOVE of God," Egan groaned, smashing his fist down onto the snooze button a little harder than necessary. He pulled a soft feather pillow over his head, wishing to delay the inevitable: the start of another boring day in Corporate America. He jumped when a small, feminine hand lifted the corner of the pillow, Macy peering in at him.

"Hey, sleepyhead. Thought you had a big meeting today? I hear there's this sexy PR babe who's meeting with your firm." Her blue eyes crinkled as her lips curled into a grin. They'd been friends for more than four years now; the lover thing was both sporadic and temporary. They agreed to a no-strings-attached, friends-with-benefits relationship until one of them found "the one." Egan knew Macy would be the first to go; he had no intention of ever loving again. No way. His heart would never be whole enough to love again after the devastation his family had been through.

Egan snatched the pillow back down, wishing it would all just go away. The stress. The pain. His heart physically ached most days; he imagined it all hollowed out and barren, like a cold, empty cave. It was all he could do to get through another mind-numbing workday without losing it. Egan glanced over at Macy with her tousled blond hair and fresh morning face. She was a pretty girl, and they certainly had fun together. It would just never be more than that, for either of them. But in the meantime . . . he cast his pillow to the floor and wiggled his eyebrows in her direction.

Macy shrieked and grabbed her pillow for cover. "Uh-uh, mister. We've both got to get moving this morning, and I know what that look means." She playfully swatted him with her pillow when he rolled on top of her, but it quickly fell aside as his mouth crashed down and consumed hers. Her lips were warm and soft, inviting. His hands found her hair, and he moaned when she reached around and grabbed a handful of his naked butt, digging in her fingers as the kiss deepened.

Yeah, this is way better than getting to work on time. Egan closed his eyes and blocked his heart, letting only his body give way to the heat of Macy's familiar touch.

EGAN STROLLED INTO his office an hour late. Even though it was a friendly good-morning tumble, he still took his time and made Macy feel appreciated. She was a gorgeous woman, after all. He raised his espresso shot to his lips, the corner of his mouth lifting in a half-smirk as he remembered the satisfied look on Macy's face when she'd hugged him goodbye and headed two doors down to her own brownstone earlier that morning.

Dropping his laptop bag onto his desk and setting his coffee aside, Egan picked up his work phone and dialed in to listen to his messages. The first was from his mother, frantic because she couldn't find the dog again and Egan hadn't answered his cell phone earlier. Egan sighed, his brows furrowing as he listened to her ramble on about where on earth Ozzie could have gone. By the end of the call, she was crying, begging for him to come to the house to look for the little terrier, and Egan's head pounded with the start of a tension headache.

He hung up before listening to the other messages, calling his mother from the landline.

"Hello?" she answered tentatively.

"Hey, Mom, it's Egan." He smacked his forehead with the palm of his hand. Of course it was Egan. He was her only son left. *Stupid, stupid.* "Sorry . . ." he trailed off, knowing there was nothing else to say to cover for his slipup. He could hear the soft sobs coming from the other end of the line. "Mom, I'm at work, but I got your message about Ozzie. Are you okay? Have you been taking your medication?"

"Of course I have, dear. I just went for a little walk this morning and accidentally left the back door open while I was gone. It could have happened to anyone."

Egan groaned, running his hand through his short brown hair. She was getting worse; that much was clear. "Mom, where are you now? Are you at home?"

"Of course I am. Where else would I be?" she snapped, his sweet mother gone for the moment.

"Mom, you don't have to worry about Ozzie anymore, okay? She's gone, remember?" His voice caught on the word *gone*. He stared out his office window, tears threatening to muddle his million-dollar view of the Hudson. His mind was no longer on Ozzie but on his little brother, Declan. He remembered him not how he last saw him—rigid, pale, empty—but from the last day they spent together, listening to music on the lawn at Central Park. He could still recall the moment of peace on his brother's teenage face as he smiled up at the sun, his feet bopping along to his favorite Flogging Molly song playing on his phone. It was the first time he'd seen Declan smile in a long time. It was also the last. That was two years ago, but it still felt like yesterday. The coffee in Egan's stomach churned, and he felt like he was going to be sick.

"MacGuire!" A voice boomed from down the hallway, pulling Egan from his memories as a thin veil of pain settled back over his heart. "MacGuire, where the hell are you?"

Egan glanced down at his watch, his mother still talking to him through the receiver, though he hadn't even noticed. "Uh, Mom, I really have to go. Can I call you back after work?" He didn't wait for an answer but slammed the receiver down and turned to face his office door just as his boss's thick frame crossed the threshold.

Egan knew it spelled trouble when Reid Patterson came all the way in and closed the door behind him. *Oh, shit!* Egan vaguely remembered the meeting he was supposed to be at this morning. The one Macy had reminded him of in bed. He groaned. Reid would be royally pissed if he messed up this deal for the firm. Macy had a strong reputation of working with celebrities and public relations involving charitable work. She was the perfect answer to their current public image nightmare.

"Before you say anything, Reid, I know I messed up. This is totally my fault. I fucked up," Egan began.

"You bet your ass you did, MacGuire. I have legal in there, the marketing team, that PR maven we've been wooing, Human Resources, everyone—except you. This is the third meeting this month that you've blown off. But this was the big one. You know how much we need a new level of PR for this campaign. Our image has been backsliding ever since the merger, and we need to get some good news out there fast. And I have you strolling in here late most days, missing meetings, holding your dick in your hands when it comes to your job—"

"Whoa, hold on now, *boss*." Egan held up his hands to his friend and senior executive. "You know damn well I've been doing the best I can, giving as much as I can to this job. It hasn't exactly been the easiest few years for me, Reid."

Reid shook his head slowly. "I know, but it's not enough, Egan. Not anymore. I have corporate breathing down my neck, demanding a home run with some new PR to cover all these merger-related fuckups. I have overlapping personnel. I have budgets for programs that you are supposed to be managing with funds still waiting to be dispersed through the grant programs. Your head's not in the game anymore, Egan. You're like a walking zombie these days, man. You come in, do what you can to scrape by, and leave. Where's your fire gone?"

They stared each other down, silent. Egan's mind raced. *This cannot be happening.* Reid knew damn well what happened to the passion that used to fuel Egan. It died along with two of the most important people in his life.

Egan crossed his arms over his chest, his fingers twitching. He could not screw up this job any further. He'd started at

LivTech Financial right after graduating with his MBA from Wharton. His father had been a corporate investment banker with the number one bank in the US at the time. He'd pulled some serious strings to get Egan a VIP pass through the front door of one of his company's top clients and straight into his dream job in corporate philanthropy. He'd been managing multimillion-dollar campaigns for the past six years and had earned many awards for his ingenuity in creative partnerships with charitable organizations across the globe.

Egan swallowed hard. None of that mattered if he couldn't do some of his own damage control. He scratched the back of his neck as he spoke. "Look, Reid, I know I messed up. Big time." Egan paced his spacious office, nerves jumping across his skin. "I'm sorry. You know what I've been dealing with since Dad and Declan died. I'm trying . . . I really am. It won't happen again."

He hated the look of pity that flashed across his friend's face. But there it was. Reid put one of his meaty hands on Egan's shoulders, squaring his body so they now faced each other eye to eye. "You have to take a break, man. You can't keep going like this. I've protected you as much as I can. I don't want to let you go, but it's the next step. You know it is."

The shock and pain couldn't have hurt more than if Reid had just gone ahead and kicked him straight in the balls. The air in the office felt thin, as if it were evaporating. He struggled to get his breathing under control so that he seemed calmer than the insane panic that was rising inside of him. "Look, it won't happen again."

"Egan—" Reid lowered his normally loud voice to a whisper, aware of the people glancing in at them through the interior glass windows framing Egan's thirtieth-floor office space. "Take a short-term leave of absence, please, for your sake. I won't fire you—yet. Just take a personal leave and get your shit together. On a personal level, I know these past few years have been hell on you. Fuck, I couldn't have gone through the losses you have and still be standing either. It only makes sense. You never took the time you needed to grieve. You are running on fumes, and your heart hasn't been here in a long time." Reid dropped his hand, shoving it into the pocket of his crisp navy suit pants. "Take six weeks. I can't promise this exact job will be waiting for you when you get back, but it's better than me letting you go for good right now. It's the best I can do, my friend. I'm sorry."

Egan stood in stunned silence as Reid dropped some paperwork onto his desk and headed toward the door. He turned around and said, "Have these filled out by noon and your workload handed off to Estella by four. Your leave starts today."

Egan sank into his leather chair and spun around to face the Hudson. Thousands of people as small as ants rushed through the network of streets below him. *I just lost my motherfucking job.* No, not lost it. A leave. Egan grabbed his espresso and chugged the last bit before throwing his Styrofoam cup across the room and missing his intended shot into the trash can. He looked around the room that had been like a second home for the past six years, especially during those darkest first days after Declan's death when he buried himself in his work to escape. His heart seemed to close the last inch he had left open as he picked up his LivTech pen, signed the forms, and kissed his dream job goodbye.

You can find Faith in Love eBooks and paperbacks on all retail platforms and begin reading today!

AFTERWORD

Dear Readers,

Where do I even begin? If it makes you feel better, my editor still doesn't forgive me for the ending of the book (said mostly in jest)—but like most readers, she understands why it needed to end this way. It may take you longer to get there, or you may never get there, and that's okay. This duet is definitely *not* for the faint of heart. Since the first page of *The Truth Pact*, these characters have asked you to go on an unbelievably painful journey with them that stretched their ideas about love, grief, and healing. It changed them, and I'm sure it's made you do a lot of reflection as well. Whether you hate them, love them, want to scream, cry, rejoice, or feel bittersweet about where their journey took you and ended for them, one thing is for sure—hopefully, it's one you'll never forget.

Even as the writer, these characters challenged everything I thought I knew about where this story was going. It didn't end at all like I'd plotted it out at the beginning. I had hard boundaries about intimacy, love, and the final outcome. But no matter how hard I tried, I knew I needed to lean into the characters and write their story the way *they* wanted it told. And that's what I did. Don't get me wrong. I spent many days crying over certain scenes and the overall intensity of this duet, too. These were, hands down, the hardest two books I've ever written—but also the ones that will never leave me.

Because I was right there with them in all the feels of their love just as strongly as their grief. And nothing made me happier than the chemistry that flowed between them when they were together and happy. And that bright love with no boundaries or limitations is what I will carry in my heart forever when I think about Liv, Ryan, and Brighton.

There are two quotes from Disney's WandaVision that speak to me so much about the intention behind *The Truth About Love* duet, and I hope they speak to your heart, too.

"But what is *grief*, if not *love* persevering?"

"*True love* does not

have a happy ending,

because true love *never ends.*"

All I know for sure is that Liv and Ryan may not have meant for their life to change the way it did after meeting Brighton and letting him in, but I believe they changed and grew for the better as a result. Even until his last breath, Ryan felt nothing but the strongest love for the two people closest to him. Not everyone will understand their love or accept how unconventional it was. But it was *their* love.

And true love never dies.

For those who want to take a deeper dive, I have The Truth About Love Duet Book Club Q&A on my Web site at www.colleenalbert.com. It holds some additional answers and deeper discussion that you may be looking for after this raw and emotional journey. And if that's not your thing, but you still want to vent, decompress, or have a place to process all the big feels with other readers, we also have the

TBE Spoiler Group on Facebook waiting for you. And we gotchu, Boo. I promise!

Thank you for all the amazing reviews, private feedback, personal stories, social media shares, and recommendations for this duet. I have learned so much about my readers and cherish each one of you who has reached out to me with your heart and feelings on your sleeve to share them with me. I will hold the space for you, just as I asked you to hold it for Liv, Ryan, and Brighton.

Thank you so much for going on this crazy, emotional journey with me.

Until next time, carpe diem!
Xoxo, Colleen

ACKNOWLEDGMENTS

I stink at keeping these short, but it's because I'm just so damn lucky to have the most amazing people in my life. That, and my team keeps growing with each new release, much to my amazement and endless gratitude.

Much appreciation goes to my entire "team" that I couldn't live without—Erin Servais of Dot & Dash, LLC is hands down the best editor ever and I'll fight ya over it. Denise McGhee and Lynn Mullan, thank you for being the last eyes on my duet and catching all my silly slip throughs. I had fun laughing at a few of the things you caught this time around. Readers—anything left that I've missed is on me and not a reflection of Erin, Denise, or Lynn's tireless work. Mad love also goes to Regina Wamba for the stunning photography on the covers, and for capturing the images that spoke to my heart for these books. I knew as soon as I saw them that they were perfect! Marisa Wesley of Cover Me Darling, LLC – you outdid yourself. *insert round of applause here* Thank you for your patience and vision as we pushed our creativity until we got them exactly right. Thank you to Stephanie Anderson of Alt 19 Creative for the most beautiful paperback interiors ever!

I literally wept when the whole, visually stunning creation came together. And to Kate Farlow of Y'all. That Graphic. for the perfect graphics that continue to tell their story, as well as my purdy new bookmark for this duet! And last, but not least, the newest addition to the team—Becca Manuel. She created the most gorgeous visual representations of these books with cinematic trailers that take the wind out of me every time I watch them. You are a mad genius, and I am so happy to work with you!

I'd also like to thank Grey's Promotion for all their hard work on the entire duet from start to finish. They were amazing to work with and provided such professional support and coordination for both releases. I could not have done this without you.

And the biggest part of my team—Carolina León. It would be embarrassing if I listed all she does to support me. All I have to say is you're an angel on earth and I am blessed to have you in my corner. Thank you for your hard work, humor, uplifting spirits, amazing attitude, and driven personality. I feel like with you we can tackle and handle just about anything that comes our way!

Constant and immeasurable gratitude goes to my early alpha readers, my Colleen's ARC Angels team, my Colleen's Angel Squad Street Team, new ARC readers who signed up through Grey's Promotions, my Colleen's Angels VIP Readers' Circle, and all the bookstagrammers and bloggers who support me day in and day out—and especially pumped up the jam to help me get the word out about this duet. You are *everything* to me. Your support, hard work, kindness, and creativity mean more to me than you can ever imagine. *I see you* and

I appreciate every single share, comment, recommendation, kind word, encouragement, and most of all, your friendship.

Thank you to the alpha readers on this duet who braved early copies and gave me their honest feedback to make it better—Erin, Jackie, Heather, and Rorie. Thank you for not throwing your kindles across the miles at me! And Heather, what can I say but, tulips?

I couldn't make it a day without the strong women in my life who help me through each day—Deena, Erin, Heather, Jacque, Jen, and Sheila. Y'all are the ohana I chose, and you're stuck with me. "A family is forever. We could never truly leave each other even if we tried."—WandaVision.

And to my kids—thanks for believing in Mommy and being my biggest cheerleaders. I will always have your backs and thank you for having mine. (But no. You're still not old enough to read my books yet.)

D—I feel like people are starting to get uncomfortable with my mushy dedications and acknowledgments, but here's what I have to say about that: SCREW THAT SHIT. Thank you for being the inspiration behind all the best parts of the men in my books. Ryan would do anything to make Olivia happy, and that is something y'all have in common. As Tony Stark once said, "I have to protect the one thing I can't live without. That's you." You are the only true hero of my heart—my Cap. Thanks for loving me the way you do and giving me fuel to help others believe in the magic of unconditional love, too. (Okay, so maybe it was a *little* mushy.)

BOOKS BY C.M. ALBERT

ARDEN'S GLEN ROMANCE SERIES
Faith in Love
Proof of Love
Visions of Love

LOVE IN LA QUARTET
Book 1: *The Stars in Her Eyes*

CONSUMED SERIES
Book 1: *Consumed by Love*

STAND-ALONE BOOKS
Last Night in Laguna
The White Room

COCKY HERO CLUB
Mister Stand-In

THE TRUTH ABOUT LOVE DUET
The Truth Pact
The Brighton Effect

ABOUT THE AUTHOR

USA Today bestselling author C.M. Albert writes heartwarming romances that are "sexy and flirty, sweet and dirty!" Her writing infuses a healthy blend of humor, high-heat romance, and most of all—hope. When not writing, or kid-wrangling with her handsome hubby, she's either meditating, kayaking, reading, hugging a tree, or asleep. But first, coffee. #TonyStarkForever

JOIN C.M. ALBERT ONLINE AT:

WEBSITE: colleenalbert.com
FACEBOOK: facebook.com/cmalbertwrites
READER GROUP: facebook.com/groups/ColleensAngels
INSTAGRAM: instagram.com/cmalbertwrites
TWITTER: twitter.com/colleenmalbert
TIKTOK: vm.tiktok.com/ZMJpyfT6C
GOODREADS: goodreads.com/cmalbert
BOOKBUB: bookbub.com/profile/c-m-albert
PINTEREST: pinterest.com/cmalbertwrites
NEWSLETTER: subscribepage.com/w5x4p1

CPSIA information can be obtained
at www.ICGtesting.com
Printed in the USA
JSHW030821190521
14908JS00001B/4